Señor Vivo
and the Coca Lord

Louis de Bernières' novels are *The War of Don Emmanuel's Nether Parts* (Commonwealth Writers Prize, Best First Book Eurasia Region, 1991), *Señor Vivo and the Coca Lord* (Commonwealth Writers Prize, Best Book Eurasia Region, 1992), *The Troublesome Offspring of Cardinal Guzman* and, most recently, *Captain Corelli's Mandolin*. The author, who lives in London, was selected as one of the twenty Best of Young British Novelists 1993.

LOUIS DE BERNIÈRES

Señor Vivo and the Coca Lord

Minerva

A Minerva Paperback
SEÑOR VIVO & THE COCA LORD

20 19 18 17 16 15 14 13 12 11 10

First published in Great Britain 1991
by Martin Secker & Warburg Limited
This Minerva edition published 1992

Random House UK Limited
20 Vauxhall Bridge Road, London SW1V 2SA

Random House Australia (Pty) Limited
20 Alfred Street, Milsons Point, Sydney,
New South Wales 2061, Australia

Random House New Zealand Limited
18 Poland Road, Glenfield, Auckland 10, New Zealand

Random House South Africa (Pty) Limited
Endulini, 5a Jubilee Road, Parktown 2193, South Africa

Random House UK Limited Reg. No. 954009

Reprinted 1992, 1993, 1994
Reissued 1995
Reprinted 1995 (three times), 1996 (three times), 1997 (three times)

Copyright © Louis de Bernières 1991

A CIP catalogue record for this title
is available from the British Library
ISBN 0 7493 9962 7

Printed and bound in Great Britain
by Cox & Wyman Ltd, Reading, Berkshire

Papers used by Random House UK Limited
are natural, recyclable products made from wood grown in
sustainable forests. The manufacturing processes conform to
the environmental regulations of the country of origin

To the Honoured and Respected Memory of

Judge Mariela Espinosa Arango

Assassinated by Machine-Gun Fire in Medellin,

on Wednesday 1 November 1989

Contents

Part One

For lo, the winter is past, the rain is over and
gone;
   The flowers appear on the earth; the time
of the singing of birds is come, and the voice
of the turtle is heard in our land;
   The fig tree putteth forth her green figs,
and the vines with the tender grape give a
good smell. Arise, my love, my fair one, and
come away.

The Song of Solomon

Part One

1 *President Veracruz Summons The Minister of Finance*

Ever since his young wife had given birth to a cat as an unexpected consequence of his experiments in sexual alchemy, and ever since his accidental invention of a novel explosive that confounded Newtonian physics by losing its force at the precise distance of two metres from the source of its blast, President Veracruz had thought of himself not only as an adept but also as an intellectual. His speeches became peppered with obscure and recondite quotations from Paracelsus and Basil Valentine; he joined the Rosicrucians, considering himself to be a worthy successor to Doctor John Dee, Hermes Trismegistus, Sir Francis Bacon, Christian Rosencreuz, and Eliphas Levi. He gave up reading his wife's women's magazines, from which he had previously derived most of his opinions, and took up reading *La Prensa*. He usually ignored the domestic news, since he knew that most of it was supplied by his own Ministry of Information, and was therefore probably fiction, turning instead to the foreign news, and then to the letters page. This latter was the forum in which the nation's intellectual elite and its coterie of the powerful and the wealthy expressed their opinions, and just recently His Excellency had become an avid reader of the frequent letters from Dionisio Vivo, which were always about the coca trade. He read the latest of the coca letters and made a note on his pad that Señor Vivo should be awarded the Gold Condor Medal for Gallantry, and then crossed it out, remembering that it could only be awarded to military personnel. He substituted a memorandum that a new order of chivalry should be created for civilians, and decided to call it The Order of Hermetic Knights. His secretary was later to misconstrue this instruction owing to his lack of faith in the President's ability to spell and his own

3

inability to read the latter's handwriting, and this explains why there is now an Order of Knights Hermit with its own coat of arms, which has never had any members except President Veracruz himself, who had automatic membership of all orders of chivalry, a privilege voted him by a grateful congress after the Los Puercos war.

His Excellency became irritated by constant interruptions from the telephone, his personal secretary, his wheedling wife, and the large black cat that he had never become used to thinking of as his daughter, and retired with *La Prensa* to the presidential lavatory. He turned off the loudspeaker in there which played Beethoven in order to drown out the rumblings and explosions of the foremost intestines of the Nation, and sat down on the pedestal to read the letters page, mentally making a note to get some kind of heating coil installed in the seat.

His Excellency was still, after all these years, obsessed with the problem of the budget deficit. It was true that at last the insatiable greed of the military for stupendous and apocalyptic weapons had been curbed; it was also true that prices for coffee and tin were not too bad these days, and, best of all, the emerald mines were producing well. But it was also a fact that the country had never recovered from the backfiring of the 'Economic Miracle' which had demolished the industrial base in the time when Dr Badajoz was Minister of Finance. Nor had the capital ever regained solvency after the pharaonic construction spree of its former Mayor, Raoul Buenanoce. To make things worse, the government-sponsored expeditions to discover El Dorado had all failed, having consumed perplexing amounts of cash in the process, and the President's alchemical experiments had yielded up only some very interesting paranormal phenomena and a great deal of sexual ecstasy. His Excellency regarded his consequent rejuvenation and spiritualisation as an unmitigated bonus, but he was tormented nonetheless by the intractable manner in which the economy always failed to arrive anywhere near the targets set by even his own most pessimistic projections. He came to the conclusion that none of his lackeys could be trusted, and decided to believe only what he read in the press. Sitting on the lavatory in the presidential suite, he made two decisions. One was to abolish the Ministry of Information, and the other was to summon the Minister of Finance in order to demand from him an explanation about a point that Dionisio Vivo had just made in his most recent coca letter. He flushed the lavatory out of habit, even though he had done nothing to disturb its fragrant waters, and went to his office to make a telephone call.

Emperador Ignacio Coriolano, known (because of rumours about his private life rather than because of its similarity to his name) as 'Emperor Cunnilingus the Insatiable', arrived at five o'clock in the evening. He was a man of fastidious dress but poor hygiene, who had for several years borne upon his shoulders the heavy responsibility of reducing the preposterous burden of the national debt, without ever having been given any means by which to do so. He spent his days with his head in his hands poring over documents which only proved the impossibility of his task, and his evenings obliterating his sense of inadequacy in the arms of certain tractable ladies whose fees he set down to 'personal expenses', thereby adding to the nation's overdraft.

He arrived to find that His Excellency the President of the Republic was attired in a dressing gown of Persian silk, but that this rich garment had slipped a little and was indiscreetly revealing a presidential testicle. In the interview that followed Señor Coriolano found this a severe obstacle to clear thought.

'Good evening, boss,' said the Minister of Finance, extending his hand. His Excellency shook it, frowned, and said, 'How many times do I have to tell you that you must address me as "Your Excellency"? One of these days you will shame us both in public.'

'Sorry, boss, it's difficult to forget the old days. You know, sometimes I still think that you and I are still selling canned beef in Panama. Those were the days, eh, boss?'

His Excellency cast his mind back and repeated, 'Those were the days.' Then he picked up his copy of *La Prensa* and said, 'I want you to listen to the new letter from Dionisio Vivo, and then give me some explanations.' He read:

'"Not so long ago the Colombian Government received the humiliating offer of the paying off of the ten billion dollar national debt in return for total freedom from government intervention in the drug trade. Naturally, and to its credit, it refused . . ." Now what I want to know, Emperador, is why they have never made a similar offer to us.'

'Our debt is too big even for them, boss, and I guess they couldn't afford to pay off two debts at once, so they chose the smaller.'

President Veracruz made a rueful expression, and then said, 'Now listen to this: "I oppose those who claim that the coca trade is indispensable to our national budget. It is estimated that the coca mafia earns some ten billion dollars per annum. Of this, nine billion apparently finds its way via Switzerland and other countries into investment in legitimate European and United States industries. The one billion that finds its way back again leaves the country immediately because it is spent on luxury foreign goods destined to embellish the palaces of the caudillos. It is very clear, then, that the destruction of the coca trade would be positively beneficial to our balance of payments." Now tell me, Emperador, why is it that this philosophy professor knows more about all this than you do? You have always told me that without a blind eye to the coca trade this country would go to the wall. What is the truth of the matter?'

The Finance Minister glanced again at the disconcerting testicle, and shuffled his feet. 'Those statistics were published only last month, and I had omitted to inform you of them. They derive from a source in the United States, were reported in the *New York Herald Tribune*, and then were repeated in our own press, I believe.'

'But are they true, Emperador, are they true?'

Señor Coriolano flushed, and said, 'I believe they probably

are, I am afraid, boss. We have been operating on a false assumption for a very long time.' He looked at the President's face, and then back at the floor. 'I meant to tell you, but circumstances made it difficult, you know there is a lot at stake, and . . .'

His Excellency folded up the newspaper and slapped it down on the table with a disgusted expression. 'Listen, Emperador, I am not naive, and I know very well that practically everyone is getting a cut, especially if they are a Minister of State. I will tell you something unofficially, OK? You can take as much from them as you like, but don't ever give them what they want in return, and always tell me everything you know, OK? From now on we don't turn a blind eye, because the solvency of the Republic is at stake and it is driving me crazy trying to run a bankrupt country, you understand? When I leave office I intend to go down in the history books not only as the man who won the Los Puercos War, but also as the man who put this place in the black for the first time in forty years.'

The Minister of Finance looked back wryly. 'That would be a greater miracle than the parting of the Red Sea, boss, but I too would like to see it.'

His Excellency raised his eyebrows and remarked, 'And if I catch you out withholding information or giving me lies, I will have you investigated, and that could mean a firing squad, my friend, if it turns out to be treachery.'

'Yes, boss.'

President Veracruz dismissed his Minister and rang up the offices of *La Prensa* to ask for all back copies which contained Dionisio Vivo's coca letters, and went to call in on his wife's chamber.

She was in a negligée, sprawled across her bed, feeding Turkish Delight to the huge black cat. His Excellency took in the touching scene and said, 'The naughty little schoolgirl is feeding my bonbons to the cat again: I think she wants a spanking.'

7

'Oh Daddikins,' she pouted, 'be sweet, and let me off this time.'

'Just a little spanking, then.'

Later on, in bed, His Excellency furrowed his brow and said resentfully. 'Why do you suppose that the coca people have never offered me any money? How come they bribe everyone else?'

'Oh Daddikins, don't worry about it,' she replied, kissing him on the forehead, and thinking about her bank account in Panama.

2 The Cravate

Dionisio arose reluctantly from his bed, went to the window to see what kind of day it was, and went to the telephone to ring the police.

After two wrong numbers a voice full of disenchantment on the other end of the line said, 'Police.'

'Ramon, is that you? This is Dionisio from the Calle de la Constitucion. Listen Ramon, I have another Colombian cravate in my front garden. Can you come and take it away? It is my third one this year.'

'Okay, Dionisio. Can you keep the vultures off it until we get there? It will make identification easier for us.'

'If I shoot them will you take their bodies away as well?'

'You know it is bad luck to shoot vultures,' said the policeman. 'Just scare them off.'

Dionisio laughed. 'You know I do not believe in stuff like that. If I were superstitious I would lose my job and my credibility.'

'You once said to me, Dionisio, that today's science is tomorrow's superstition. Maybe also today's superstition is tomorrow's science. Think about it.'

Dionisio snorted and said, 'God save us from philosophical policemen. You are supposed to be brutal and stupid.'

'You do not believe in God, either,' retorted the policeman, 'so he cannot save you from me. Escuchame, I will come up and take away your cravate. Keep the vultures off.'

'Claro,' said Dionisio. 'Goodbye, and see you in a while.'

Dionisio rummaged through his washing basket and dug out the cleanest of his dirty clothes. He got dressed and went downstairs to look at the corpse. It was a crumpled young man in a blue but now bloodstained shirt. He had no shoes, fashionable trousers, a cowhide belt, and a face of such mixed

9

ancestry as to be unclassifiable. His black hair was thick with cheap shiny gel, and his tongue protruded grotesquely through the slit in his throat. Dionisio remembered how he had vomited and retched the first time he had seen this, and reflected that it was frightening to become inured to it so quickly. He bent down and brushed away some of the ants that were crawling over the man's face and going in and out of his mouth, and then he threw a stone at the vulture that landed noisily and clumsily in the pine tree. 'Hijo de puta,' he shouted at it in a sudden fury, and then realised that he must be more upset than he had thought. He looked at his watch and saw with resignation that he was going to be late for his lecture again, and wondered whether the principal would believe again the same bizarre excuse of a body in the garden. He sat with his back to the trunk of the tree and irritated the vulture by tossing stones at it until Ramon arrived with another officer. They put on yellow kitchen gloves as they came through the gate.

'Hola,' said Ramon, 'another fine start to a perfect day.'

Dionisio smiled at this old classmate who had made the incomprehensible choice of becoming a policeman despite the horror of his friends. They all called him 'cochinillo' to his face, but he took the tease in the spirit in which it was meant, and usually gave as good as he got. 'How is my little Socrates?' he asked.

'I am a little tired of all these Colombian cravates,' replied Dionisio, smiling weakly. 'Why do they always dump them in my garden, and not someone else's?'

'Either,' said Ramon, 'they think that you need a little excitement, and are very charitably providing it, or else they are giving you a little warning. I favour the latter hypothesis myself.'

'A warning?' echoed Dionisio.

'Don't be disingenuous, Dionisio. You know I am talking about the letters.'

'The letters are hardly a big thing,' said Dionisio. 'Anyway, how do you know about them?'

'Everybody does, including me, because despite being a cochinillo I read an intelligent newspaper like *La Prensa*. Believe me, there are narcoticos who read it as well. Your letters have made you a local celebrity, because no one else from around here gets letters published regularly in important newspapers. There are plenty of people who want you to shut up and mind your own business.' The policeman raised one eyebrow and tapped one side of his nose. 'That is my advice as well, cabron, or you will end up like our little amigo here, with your tongue pulled through a pretty little hole in your neck.'

'Do you know who he is?' asked Dionisio.

'Yes I do, and I can assure you that there will be no mourners at his funeral. As far as I am concerned, these canallas can kill each other as much as they like. To lock them up would be a criminal misappropriation of public funds.'

Ramon stroked his stubble thoughtfully, tipped back his cap to a jaunty angle, and spat onto the ground next to the body. 'Come on,' he said to his companion, 'let us do our duty.' They slung the body into the back of the van, and Dionisio came around to the driver's door to shake the hand of his friend. 'I will buy you a drink,' he said. 'Thanks.'

The policeman winked. 'Let us waste no time,' he said, 'in bringing perfection to this world.' He drove away leaving Dionisio wondering whether that was a learned quotation or whether he had just made it up.

3 *Ramon's Letter*

Dear Sirs,

I write as a police officer of Ipasueño, and as a lifelong acquaintance and friend of Dionisio Vivo. I wish to make a public reply to his comments upon the unreliability of the law-enforcement agencies.

As he rightly states, the choice presented to us is 'plata o plomo'. Either we participate in the profits or be tortured to death. However, we would have little fear of the latter fate if there were more of us, better trained, and better armed. We are pitifully few; the country is vast, with great tracts of it unexplored, let alone mapped. In fact there is even doubt as to where the borders lie, especially in the Amazonas region, and this has caused a great many pointless and disreputable wars with our neighbours in the past. It is physically impossible to police such a country as ours, and regrettably many of our police are so demoralised by the perpetual struggle to perform the impossible that they have given up altogether.

Secondly, it is a well-known psychological fact (at least Dionisio Vivo tells me that it is) that anyone can be bribed by being offered a sum amounting to ten times their annual salary. The annual income of a policeman is considerably less than that received by an unemployed single person on social security in the United States. Is anyone really surprised then that the police seem to be so corruptible? I do not know any policemen who do not have to take second jobs in off-duty hours merely to stay alive. I myself have a herd of goats.

Lastly, I would like to say to Dionisio Vivo that in my professional opinion his life is endangered, and I also want to ask him a question. Does he know that in this country crimes of passion outnumber coca killings by three to one? Is he contemplating an epistolary crusade against that too?

Ramon 'Cochinillo' Dario,
Police Officer,
Ipasueño.

4 Dionisio Renounces Whores Out of Love For Anica

Ipasueño lay across a plain and mountainside on the western reaches of the Sierra Nevada de Santa Margarita. The whitewashed houses rose up above each other glistening in the sun like the snows high above them, and the inclined streets were raucous with the sound of mule-trains, the crashing of the gears of ancient lorries, and the cries of streethawkers selling arepas and pineapple juice. The streets were narrow and the light restricted because of the overhanging balconies draped with washing. It was a small town, which made it easy to call in on one's friends and to spread rumours, and it was very self-contained. Food was mostly bought from the Acahuatec Indians who farmed on terraces in the Sierra, and from the inhabitants of Cochadebajo de los Gatos in the east. The town was famous for producing the finest Supremo coffee-beans, and for the quality of its cocaine, manufactured by the sulphuric acid and petroleum process. The town was not, however, so famous that outsiders ever wanted to go there, nor so dull that the inhabitants ever wanted to leave. This meant that the population had not changed in its basic nature since the sixteenth century, when it was founded by the Conde Pompeyo Xavier de Estremadura, who was later to perish with eight hundred and fifty souls in an avalanche of snow during an expedition of 1533 to locate the legendary Inca city of Vilcabamba. This is the same aristocrat who was eventually brought back to life by Aurelio the Sorcerer, and who became resident in Cochadebajo de los Gatos, where he met and cohabited with Remedios, the communist guerrilla leader.

Seven years, six months and thirty-three days after the illusory war of La Isla de los Puercos (after which President Veracruz was re-elected on the 'victory vote') Dionisio Vivo, professor of philosophy, was twenty-eight years old, and was celebrating his birthday in the serpentine embrace of Velvet Luisa in Madame Rosa's Famous Casa de Putas in the Calle Santa Maria Virgen. Downstairs Jerez was being sick into the lap of the whore known as The Biggest Boa in the World, and Juanito was using his good looks and his powers of persuasion to induce Rosalita to do it for nothing. The Biggest Boa in the World was shrieking with dismay and was about to waste a bottle of Aguila by breaking it over Jerez' head, and Rosalita was being coy because she was in love with Juanito and was hoping to leave whoring in order to marry him. Jerez and Juanito shared a house with Dionisio and were helping him to enjoy his birthday in the brothel, by enjoying themselves, and thus affirming their solidarity and their brotherhood.

Madame Rosa's whorehouse was remarkable not only for the fact that the girls were pretty and clean, but for its genial atmosphere. Madame Rosa got the girls checked every week at the clinic, and was always genuinely happy when one of the girls married one of the clients, drifting away to a new life of children and domesticity. She was already resigned to the fact that in a little while she would lose the most popular whore she had ever had.

Velvet Luisa had a twin sister who was at university. At the age of seventeen they had tossed a coin as to which of them would go to university first while the other supported them both, and Luisa had lost. She had taken to whoring with verve and vivacity, knowing that she was condemned to it for only three years, and positive that in retrospect it would prove to have been a character-forming and constructive experience. She slept only with clients that she genuinely had an eye for, and brooked no nonsense or violence from anyone, which was why she had a pistol under her pillow and an electric bell for summoning Madame Rosa's husband in the event of a contingency.

Madame Rosa's husband was a formidably huge negro of gentle disposition, who was as fond of the whores as he was

15

of his own daughters and his horse. He had met Madame Rosa in Venezuela, whither she had fled from her previous husband in Costa Rica. This gentleman had himself been an insatiable whoremaster with a vile temper and a habit of drunkenness. Madame Rosa was in truth a bigamist, but she considered that if the Holy Father had known that her first husband used to fire his revolver at huge imaginary spiders at all hours of the day and night, he would undoubtedly have annulled that marriage without hesitation. She had great faith in the Holy Father, and considered that she ran a truly Catholic brothel, with a crucifix on the wall of every room, and days off for the girls on their Saint's day.

Dionisio was stroking Velvet Luisa's perfect black thighs, and was teasing her by just drawing back with his ticklings when he reached the portals of the Gates of Heavenly Bliss. He was saying, 'This has got to be something for me to be nostalgic about, because after today I don't think I will be coming back. I've fallen in love, Luisa, and I think it's going to be a big one, and when I am like this I don't want to make love to anyone else.'

Luisa sat up, looking a little alarmed, and said, 'Don't do that; all the girls here will commit suicide. We all think that with you it is more like making love.'

Dionisio thought about it, and replied, 'That's because I love women more than anything else in the world. I have the suspicion that most men hate them, and that is why they treat them so badly. I think there are a lot of macho types out there who probably would really rather do it with a donkey or a little boy.'

In appearance Dionisio Vivo was stocky enough to reveal some of the Indian blood in his veins, but he had startlingly blue eyes. This was, curiously enough, the direct result of one of the Conde Pompeyo Xavier de Estremadura's exploits in the sixteenth century. Dionisio had a full and sensuous mouth, olive skin, a black moustache, and the kind of luxuriant sideburns that are still common in that country. He was in general quite hairy about the body, and was still well-muscled as a consequence of a narcissistic obsession with his torso during his teenage years. Characteristically he would dress in blue, and it was true that all the girls in the whorehouse thought that he was wonderful both in and out of bed. Velvet Luisa was both jealous and curious. 'Is it true that it is Anica Moreno that you have fallen in love with? Everyone is saying that.' She gave him a searching look and toyed with one of his nipples so that he took in his breath sharply. 'Yes, it is Anica,' he said, 'and tomorrow we are going to sleep together for the first time. It is all agreed between us.'

Anica Moreno was at that time only just twenty years old, and was governed chiefly by her sense of beauty. She had had very few experiences of a romantic nature, the first being at the age of thirteen, when she had masturbated a young man in the front of a Russian-made jeep while on the way to Cochadebajo de los Gatos to see the temple and the statues of the cats. At eighteen she had given her virginity to a married man who had pretended to be in love with her. This man worked for the Catholic Mission to Single-Parent Families, and he disowned her completely when she fell pregnant. She miscarried at three months, leaving no one any the wiser, and became a little inhibited sexually. Thus one could say that she had had her share of sorrows, especially as at the same time her beloved mother had died at an early age of an intractable cancer. This had affected her extraordinarily deeply, as indeed it had affected her father, a very mild and reticent man, conspicuously religious and humane, who had made a fortune in arms dealing.

Anica had some artistic talent which she expressed with refreshing naivety and simplicity in her drawings, preferring zig-zag patterns in bold colours. She was possessed with the absolute conviction that one day she would become renowned as a great artist, and although she was a soft and sentimental person who would not wish harm to her worst enemy, there was a determined portion at the core of her which got her into trouble as a child, and which was a mixed blessing in the time of her adulthood.

These two first met when artistic ambitions induced an interest in photography in Anica. She was slightly acquainted with one of the men with whom Dionisio shared his house. This man was Jerez, a character so worthless and irredeemable that no one ever thought of trying to reform him; they just accepted him as he was (with the exception of the Biggest Boa in the World, who hated to be puked up on). Consequently he had always led an equable and happy life, a fact which intimates how little justice there is in the world. He divided his time and his somewhat minimal energy between a very great many lonely and (to other men) undesirable women of indeterminate age and worn-out appearance. He scratched a living by taking photographs for the two local newspapers, and fancied himself as an artist in his craft. One of his less attractive foibles was to gatecrash private fiestas, and it was at one of these that he had met Anica and impressed her with the fact that he was a photographer. He had invited her to come and see him if her artistic interests should lead her in the direction of photography, though there is no doubt whatsoever as to his real hopes and intentions.

It so happened that she lived almost directly opposite to Dionisio and Jerez, and it was miraculous that hitherto none of them had met before. One day the thought came into her head that she might as well drop in on Jerez so that he could explain the more subtle mysteries of her new camera, which was the gift of her father on her twentieth birthday.

Dionisio was still in his work-clothes, and had his feet up on Jerez' home-made coffee-table, whose top was attached to its base by no other force than gravity, when Anica knocked at the outer shutters of the hallway. Jerez answered the door and let her in.

When she came into the living-room Dionisio thought that she was the most striking woman he had ever seen. Some of the verses of the Song of Solomon sprang unbidden into his mind. She brought with her such an air of humour, self-confidence and gentleness that the house was lit up with her presence as though with a lamp. She put Dionisio instantaneously into such a fine mood that she was given a first impression of him that he was both handsome and jovial, when in fact he was very ordinary-looking and distinctly prone to periods of moroseness.

Anica Moreno was one hundred and eighty-four centimetres tall, and this alone would have made her striking. On this day she was dressed in dungarees of that emerald green which, curiously enough, astrologers associate with Venus. She wore a green and white striped tee-shirt, and old lilac espadrilles, with a spot of green sock showing through where the toes were worn away. This waifish touch alone would have melted the heart of any man. Her hair was strawberry blonde, a rare thing in those parts; it was short and spiky, an effect designed to reveal her artistic nature, and she had a high forehead above grey eyes the colour of a winter sea. Dionisio noticed that she had a very small mouth, but that when she grinned she revealed marvellous shiny white teeth that looked as though they would have spoiled her face if they had been only a fraction bigger. She wore a very large green plastic earring in one ear in the shape of an isosceles triangle.

He could tell that she was quite thin by her arms, whose forearm seemed thicker than the upper part, but he was struck by her gracefulness as she stood with her shoulders back, standing with all her weight on one leg, with the other bent at the knee in such a way that her toe was posed casually on the ground. He was reminded of a little girl at a confirmation. She was big-breasted, but she gave the impression of being embarrassed about this fact, since her breasts were always concealed beneath the shapelessness of her clothing. In fact it was true that she was embarrassed about them, not because of their volume, but because one of them was very slightly larger than the other, a fact indiscernable without close inspection.

Dionisio having been captivated by her charm and vivacity to such an extent that he began to ask himself whether he might have any luck with her, and Anica Moreno having had a woman's thoughts about him, she left the house and did not reappear in it for three months.

After she had gone Jerez had said, 'Lovely body,' and Dionisio had grunted. The best thing about Jerez was that everything that he believed or said was either so crass or so gross that it made one feel either intellectual or virtuous by comparison.

'I tried to seduce her once,' said Jerez, 'but she ran kilometres.'

How surprising, Dionisio had thought.

'I am surprised,' said Luisa, when Dionisio had confessed that it was indeed Anica that he was in love with. 'She is so tall, and blonde hair on a mulatta looks strange to me. I am surprised that you have fallen in love with someone so . . . unusual.'

'I would have fallen in love with you, but . . .'

'I am a whore?'

Dionisio was embarrassed, but Luisa just smiled, and said, 'I have no illusions.' She leaned over him so that her pointed breasts that reminded him of missiles (he called them 'Cupid's Warheads') caressed his chest deliciously. She whispered, 'Make love to me for the last time, then, and make it slow, and make it last.'

He looked into her face and saw her expression. He stroked her cheek. 'You are beautiful, Luisa. Please do not cry. Nobody knows the future.'

5 *The General's Letter*

Dear Sirs,

I have in recent months read with great interest the letters from my son, Dionisio Vivo, in your newspaper, concerning the trade in coca and its undesirable effects.

I have in the past often feared that my son would turn out to be the kind of degenerate who not only abuses coca but trades in it; he certainly showed every sign of it in his teenage years. It is therefore a matter of great pride and relief to me that I am able to find myself in complete agreement with the general tenor of his remarks. As most people know, I have in my own department used the armed forces under my command to wipe out this trade almost entirely.

However, I wish to remonstrate with my son over his remarks in his last letter about the armed forces, when, in recommending the use of the armed forces in combating the coca trade, he says '. . . this would give them something to do other than sit around in idleness plotting coups.' As he well knows, no such plots have come to light ever since the time of Fleta, Ramirez, and Sanchis. Since those best-forgotten days the armed forces have been co-operating upon the well-nigh impossible task of wiping out the dozen or so left- and right-wing guerrillero groups which are so seriously impeding the construction of a decent civilisation in our country. Who would have believed that in this day and age there would still be Maoists and Stalinists? But there are, and the armed forces have sustained terrible losses in the struggle against them. My son owes us an apology.

General Hernando Montes Sosa,
Military Governor (elected) of Cesar, Valledupar.

6 *Ramon Leaves A Warning Note*

Diogenes,

Your father has foolishly revealed your true identity in a letter to *La Prensa*. Now that they know that you are not only a pain in the ass, but also the son of the governor of Cesar, they will want to get you even more. Climb out of your barrel, and leave town as soon as possible.

Ramon.

Dionisio read it through twice, and said aloud to himself, 'Very funny, Ramon.'

7 *Dionisio Is Given A Hand*

Dionisio was awoken by a bizarre tumult outside. He lay in bed waking up as slowly as possible, blinking his eyes and fighting off the urgent pressure in his bladder. He speculated drowsily as to what the noise could possibly be; there were furious croaks, screeches, flutterings, and a series of single knocks on the door that sounded like someone tapping very hard with their bunched fingernails.

He pulled the covers over his head to block it all out, but was forced to give up. He threw the cover aside, lay still for a moment, and then got out of bed and went to the window. He leaned out, but the racket was just outside his line of view, concealed by the creepers. He leaned out as far as he could, and saw to his astonishment that just in front of the door were two large vultures who appeared to be jumping up and down and knocking at the door, in between taking jabs at each other. He watched them with puzzlement, and then shouted 'Shut up' at them. They stopped jumping up and down for a minute and looked at him with an expression that looked like contempt, and then recommenced. 'For God's sake,' he thought, and went downstairs.

When he opened the door the two birds were momentarily very surprised, and craned their necks to inspect him. They hopped backwards and croaked in protest, and he waved an arm at them and said, 'Go on, go away. Let's have some peace around here.'

At that point he discovered the cause of the fracas. He glanced sideways and discovered that there was a hand nailed to the door at chest height. At first he thought it was a model hand, because it seemed waxy and the bloodstains on it somehow did not seem to be the correct colour for blood. He was wondering who would play such a bizarre joke on him,

23

and he touched the object. He took his hand away quickly because he immediately realised that it was not a model.

He looked at it closely. It was an olive-complexioned hand, plainly belonging to a man. It had ragged fingernails, and there was a scar, probably from a knife, across the back of it. Dionisio had the inconsequential thought that a man with fingers as long as that would have made a good pianist. The hand was covered with marks where the vultures had succeeded in pecking it, and between the thumb and forefinger a pen was held in place with rubber bands.

He went upstairs to telephone Ramon, and then telephoned the college to say that he would be late again. The Principal said, 'Vale, this makes a change from dead bodies, only to get a bit of one. I will start off your class, and you get here as soon as possible. What are you doing with them?'

'The Principle of Sufficient Reason,' replied Dionisio. 'Tell them to look it up in all the books and work out in what ways Leibniz' version is different from Schopenhauer's, OK?'

He went downstairs again because the vultures were once more leaping up and down and fighting with each other. Ramon shortly arrived in a car with the same young policeman as before. Ramon got out, stroking his stubble as usual, and stopped a moment to give Dionisio an ironic weary look. 'Agustin,' he said to the other policeman, 'since we are likely to come here repeatedly, let me introduce you to Dionisio properly, except that I am going to start calling him Empedocles, who misguidedly threw himself into a volcano in order to prove that he was a god. I find that analogy very apt.'

Dionisio smiled wryly, and shook Agustin's hand. He caught Ramon's eye, and pointed wordlessly at the hand nailed to the door.

'Ay,' exclaimed the policeman, 'so that is where it got to.'

Dionisio said, 'Were you looking for it, then?'

'Not exactly, Empedocles. Its owner turned up without it on the municipal dump this morning. You will be pleased to know that this is the hand of a gentleman who refused to loan his daughter to El Jerarca and his band of upright followers. They took the girl anyway, and both of them are at this very moment being loaded into a van at the dump in order to be restored to a wife who now has only four children to support without a husband.'

Ramon went up to the door and inspected the hand carefully. 'This is a nail of the type that is used on haciendas in order to nail together a corral. The pen is a very ordinary and common one, and the hand was severed with one blow of a machete. Yes, indeed, this an agricultural murder, and we all know who owns a big hacienda outside town.' Ramon paused, and wiggled the nail until it came out of the door. Still holding it, he stuck the hand in front of Dionisio's face, and said, 'You are the semiologist. You tell me what it signifies.'

Dionisio backed away from it and replied, 'It means that they want me to stop writing the letters to *La Prensa*.'

Ramon looked at him for a moment and laughed without humour. 'You attribute too much subtlety to them, Empedocles. It means that before they kill you they will cut off your hands. I suspect that they may deliver them to the police station, which will save me from having to look for them, eh my friend? They will cut off your hands that wrote the letters, and then maybe they will torture you a little bit more than they have already, and then maybe they will make you a little cravate and let you bleed to death in peace.'

The two friends looked at each other in silence, and Ramon raised an eyebrow and smiled. 'Do you see this pen? On it there will be the fingerprints of the man who put it there. That is how much confidence they have, cabron, they don't care that we know who did this.'

'Are you going to arrest him?'

Ramon gave him a glance that would have been patronising if it had not been accompanied by his usual ironic smile. 'Arrest him? No, we will shoot him as soon as possible, without formality.'

Dionisio was shocked, and it showed in his face. Ramon

put his arm around his shoulder and walked a few paces with him. 'Let me tell you, my friend, if we arrest such a man there will be those rich enough to bribe a thousand judges and a thousand policemen to let him go on a technicality. In order to avoid becoming corrupted, we just shoot them.' Dionisio was about to protest when Ramon suddenly became serious. 'This is now officially our unofficial policy, Dionisio. It is a civil war where the rules are different. Don't get caught up in it unless martyrdom particularly appeals to you. I will tell you a secret, OK? The police and the navy are the only relatively uncorrupted forces in the nation. From now on all the battles will be fought not by the army, but by the police. The police are not only the police now, but also the army, so don't give me extra work to do by becoming another pointless victim. Just pack your guitar and a couple of books, and leave.'

'No, Ramon,' replied Dionisio, 'I am obstinate, and I am angry, and I have to do what I can, even if it is only writing letters.'

'Get a gun, then, my friend, and carry it with you all the time.'

Just before the car departed, Ramon wound down the passenger window and pointed at the vultures. 'Tell those two to go and wait down at the dump. Also, do you know the only thing that was left after Empedocles jumped into the volcano?'

Dionisio looked at Ramon spinning the hand on its transfixing nail and said, 'His sandals.'

As the car started to move, Ramon winked and said, 'Goodbye, Empedocles.'

8 *How El Jerarca's Helicopter Turned Into A Deepfreeze*

Spaniards who travel in South America sometimes have difficulty in buying butter. They ask for 'mantequilla', and receive only a puzzled look. When they explain that it is for spreading on bread, the proprietor of the shop says, 'Oh, you want "manteca",' and the Spaniard thinks he is being offered lard and says, 'No, that is not what I want.' The conversation continues and the confusion becomes more confounding until the proprietor produces some butter and says, 'This is manteca, we spread it on bread around here.' The Spaniard looks at it dubiously; it is whitish, and really it looks more like lard than butter, but it has the texture and consistency of butter. It is really very puzzling. He buys it and spreads it tentatively on his bread, to find that it is not too bad, and tastes half-way between lard and butter.

The Spaniard has become a victim of the social history of a word. In past times there were no dairy herds to speak of, and so one spread lard upon one's bread. And then slowly as herds increased and improved it became possible to market butter. But by now two things had happened; firstly, the word 'mantequilla' had been forgotten, and what went upon one's bread would always be 'manteca', and secondly, people had got to like the taste of lard on bread, and so the butter was made in such a way that it tasted somewhat like lard.

Odd things have happened also to the meaning of 'padrino'. To a good Catholic it still means a 'godfather' who swears to bring up a child christianly in the event of the decease or incapacity of the parents. To one who practises santeria it means the man who initiated you into the mysteries of the magical religion that was exported to Latin America in the slave ships, along with leprosy and a thousand equal miseries. In santeria the padrino takes on an importance greater than

27

one's parents; when a santero meets his padrino, he throws himself at his feet. The padrino leans over and blesses him, and the santero arises, crosses his arms over his chest, and kisses his padrino upon both cheeks. The bond is a touching one, full of trust.

But now the word means a coca lord, a cacique like El Jerarca; it means a 'godfather' in the mafia sense. 'Godmother' has not changed its meaning, and neither has 'godchild', because it is only men who aspire to great depths of evil. Sadly, also, 'compadre', which used to mean one's closest, most esteemed and trusted friend, now means just as often a partner in crime – the person one trusts the least.

El Jerarca was a padrino in the new sense – a man no one trusted, liked or respected – and he was thinking of colonising the arcadian city of Cochadebajo de los Gatos. His intention was to shorten his supply routes for the transport of coca, it was to make it difficult for the law-enforcement agencies to pursue him, and it was to move to a place that everybody knew about locally but which was not on any maps in any army or air-force headquarters.

The first one to see the helicopter was Sergio. He was walking home with a burn on his hand because he had tried to lasso his horse up on the pajonale and the rope had somehow caught the running horse's right foreleg. The rope had whistled through his palm and scarred him before he could let go. When he got into the town the helicopter had already landed in the courtyard of the Palace of the Lords, and the two occupants were already walking through the streets softening up the population.

The two men were pressing huge wads of thousand-peso notes into the hands of everybody they met. Very soon there were hordes of folk pouring out of the doorways to take advantage of this unexpected munificence, and people were shoving and pushing, shouting and trampling. The two men were saying, 'There is more of this when El Jerarca arrives, you just wait and see. All of you will be rich, and he gives you this to show how he will be a padrino to you and look after you,' and some people were shouting 'Viva El Jerarca' without even knowing who he was.

Sergio watched as Hectoro sensibly collected his wad of notes and then rode away to regard the mayhem with growing contempt. Hectoro was observing through half-closed eyes because the smoke from his puro was drifting into them, and his hard mouth was set into a frown, turning down at the corners. As he sat there in his saddle he looked more like a conquistador than ever, with his black beard, his face of a Spanish aristocrat, and his black glove on his rein hand. For a few moments he thought of taking his revolver from his holster, taking the money from those two slick-looking types, giving it to the people himself, and ordering them to leave. There was something about the lack of dignity in the stampede that repelled him.

But just then Remedios approached and stood by him. She was still dressed in the khaki of her days as a guerrilla, and she still carried a Kalashnikov wherever she went. 'Hectoro,' she said.

'Si?' replied Hectoro, who never used more words than a man should.

'I have seen this before. This is what the coca people do when they come to take a place over. Go and get Misael and Josef and Pedro; we must do something.'

Hectoro tossed his head and his frown deepened. 'I never take orders from a woman; you know this.'

Remedios sighed exasperatedly, put her hands on her hips, and then smiled. 'Give the order to yourself, then, but do it quickly.'

He looked down at her. He was fond of Remedios, as everyone was, but he would never let it show, and he would never slacken his lifetime's dedication to the cult of machismo, even for her. He called over a child and told it to go and fetch Pedro and Josef and Misael.

When they came Remedios informed them of the situation, and Misael immediately suggested asking Don Emmanuel for advice, but Remedios dismissed the idea. Lately she had got fed up with his relentless jokes about parts of the body, and he had begun to think that she was a prig. And in any case, Misael himself had an idea that would get rid of them for good without anyone knowing who was to blame. It would have been most undesirable had El Jerarca ever found out, and maybe the people would have blamed them if it was revealed that Hectoro had deprived them of riches.

Hectoro was a man with a liver that had been on the point of collapse for several years, but which was to last him a lifetime against all the prognostications of medicine, the laws of probability, and the inscrutable workings of natural justice. He was an indefatigable drinker of fiery liquors whom no one had ever seen drunk.

In the bar of Consuelo's whorehouse he treated the two slickers to drinks. Whenever they showed unwilling or declined another dose of aguardiente, Hectoro would say, 'Are you men? Come, drink now,' and they would look at him with growing desperation, understand that they were scared of him, and agree, 'OK, cabron, just one more, but then we go.' There was a relentless force behind Hectoro's unsmiling eyes, his haze of blue smoke that reminded them of El Jerarca, his tight lips, his sinewy leanness, and the imperiousness of his order to drink up, cabron. They were terrified of the way in which Hectoro became more icily sober as he tossed down one copa after another without flinching and without losing one iota of his cold intensity.

Misael and Pedro came in and clapped them on the back, engaging them in a torrent of conversation which they could not follow and in which it was impossible to participate. Their eyes grew steadily more glazed and unfocused. They slurred pointless responses, saying, 'Si, si, amigo, I agree, just so, that is the way it is,' even when their heads were on the bar and Misael was amusing himself by saying, 'You are an hijo de puta, your mouth is vertical like a woman's chucha, your mother bore you by a pig, your culo has known a thousand pricks, your mother's milk was rat's piss, your cojones are smaller than raisins,' and everyone in the bar was laughing overtly at the humiliation of the slickers, even the whores, who were happy to take a break for a while from all the kissing and cuddling.

And then Misael produced two pitillos. They were no ordinary pitillos, but were thick as a millionaire's Havana, and full of the best smoking marijuana. They were the kind of pitillo that one smokes in bed with one's lover before making love somewhere in the outer spaces of reality, the kind of pitillo that is the ultimate, one true Platonic Idea of a pitillo. Misael gave them to the slickers, and Hectoro made them smoke them down to the stub until the whole brothel smelled aromatic and the victims were giggling every time they fell over, and demanding more drink every time they vomited.

Hectoro and Misael dragged them to their helicopter as night was falling in, and heaved them into it. They slapped their faces and pinched their thighs until the machine was started and warmed up, and then they watched it depart at a crazy speed in the wrong direction.

The machine was discovered a few days later high up in the snows of the sierra. The Indians who found it came from the village of Chachi. The two slickers were frozen solid, and it gave the cholos the idea of keeping meat in it instead of burying it in the snow and marking it with a stake. The two gangsters remained frozen forever to their seats, having been appointed by the cholos to be the perpetual spirit guardians of the metal meatbox that had been vouchsafed to them through the beneficent dispensations of Viracocha.

9 *Knives*

'OK chicos,' said El Jerarca, 'you have the picture? I want it to look like a perfectly ordinary theft that became a little violent, you understand? Make sure you take his money and anything else valuable, OK? And as far as I am concerned, what you take you keep. And when you have done the job you both get your little ganancias, and you both get your new motorcycle, and maybe then I will promote you and you will both be sicarios, OK? And then I will give you both a magnum that can blow the balls from an elephant, OK?'

Dionisio and Anica were walking hand in hand through the streets, taking a little paseo before meeting Ramon for a drink. The two assassins were following ten metres behind, their hands going nervously to the concealed hilts of their knives, and they were talking in subdued tones.

'What if he resists?' said one.

'Mierda,' said the other, 'you can see he is fat, so he is probably slow as well. We just spill his guts and run for it.'

'We will rob the girl as well?'

'Well, why not? Maybe she has her pocket money with her. She has a fine ring.'

'El Jerarca said not to harm her, though.'

'He did not say not to rob her.' He winked, and the other nodded and smiled his assent.

Anica was feeling very relaxed and happy, and she was feeling affectionate. 'I want to kiss you, querido; come up here a second.' She pulled him up into a little alley and in the shadows she pinned him to the wall and closed her eyes to kiss him. They were locked in this embrace when the two assassins seized their chance, darted round the corner, drawing their knives as they did so, and ran towards the couple. As they drew near they suffered a moment's hesitation because Anica was in the way of the knives, and one of them kicked a can by mistake. Dionisio opened his eyes and saw them.

Real bravery is perhaps when one conquers fear and performs what one is afraid to do. Dionisio on the other hand, although he did not know it, was a man to whom heroism came naturally and of itself. This was because he had had bred into him the strongest instincts of moral outrage, and this would instantly overrule any impulses to flight. His fury rose the instant he saw the two scum approaching with their knives, and he assumed that they were about to try to rob him and Anica. He threw Anica to the cobbles to get her out of the line of the knives, and confronted them.

In his anger, his eyes glinting with contempt, his mouth snarling, his feet planted apart and his arms spread, he had all the appearance of a tigre about to spring on a little coypu. The assassins stopped dead and their eyes rolled sideways to look at each other. Their victim suddenly looked twice as big as he had before, and what had seemed to be fat suddenly looked like solid muscle. 'What do you want, assholes?' he said very clearly and very menacingly.

There was a silence as the two assassins hoped that the other would speak first, then one of them said, 'Hand over your wallet.'

'Chinga tu madre, hijo de puta,' spat Dionisio, and even though this was the worst thing one could say, and an insult which only death could avenge, neither of the two men moved. Behind Dionisio, Anica started to stand up, ashen pale and shaking, and the men turned their attention to her with relief. 'And you, flaca, you can take off that ring.'

'Leave it where it is, querida. If one of them touches you I will tear his balls off by God, and ram them down his throat.'

The two men knew that they had to act, that one of them had to move and get the knife into Dionisio's guts, but neither wanted to be the first. Then one of them, who was ashamed to seem a coward, came forward and feinted with his weapon.

33

Dionisio moved with the swiftness of a great caiman, caught the man's arm by the wrist, pulled him forward, and kicked his legs from under him. As he went down Dionisio knelt beneath him and snapped his arm at the elbow when it came against his knee. The man howled, crawled to the wall, and lay whimpering against it.

The other man, his eyes rolling, tried to turn and flee. But Dionisio was now so colossally enraged that he did not let the man run. He threw his whole weight against the assassin like a mountain in avalanche. The man went sprawling, rolled, and to Dionisio's surprise Anica flashed past him uttering a vicious yell, and kicked the assassin in the stomach with enormous force. Then she kicked him in the face and spat on him as he doubled up with his hands over his bloodied mouth. Dionisio yanked his head back by the hair and with one hand picked up the knife that lay beside him.

Dionisio was a gentle man, a man who was besotted with cats, a man who liked to pass his time mulling over incomprehensible philosophical tomes, playing his instruments, and making love. He was a man who had at the age of eighteen scandalised the National Service selection board by announcing that he was a pacifist. But this was a different Dionisio, a Dionisio with all the bloody righteousness of the Old Testament God, and he only did not cut the man's throat because Anica put her hand on his wrist and said desperately, 'No, querido.'

Dionisio changed the angle of the blade and savagely thrust it up beneath the man's jaw so that it went through his tongue and lodged in his palate. 'Eat it, polla de perro,' he said ferociously, and taking Anica's hand he strode off with her without looking back.

They did not say a word to each other until they reached the bar. Dionisio was still so furious that he could hardly breathe, and Anica was holding her lips so tightly together that they whitened. She was beginning to feel sick, but, like Dionisio, she just walked faster. They arrived at the bar and saw Ramon sitting alone at a table. They threw themselves down on the chairs, and Anica buried her face in her hands and began to twitch and shake uncontrollably. Ramon looked at her in bewilderment, and then at Dionisio. Dionisio's right eye was twitching, he had a wild staring look, and he was breathing as though he had just been pulling a bull on a rope. 'What – ' Ramon began to say, but Dionisio waved his hand at him for him to shut up. Ramon stood up, knowing clearly that something terrible had happened, and, knowing from his experience that he would have to wait to hear what it was, he hastened to the bar and came back with double doses of aguardiente. Anica did not look up to see hers, but Dionisio tried to take his, and found that his hand was shaking too much. He looked at Ramon, and managed to say, 'Thieves.'

'Oh?' said Ramon. 'What happened?'

'Knives.'

'Are you hurt? Is Anica all right? What did they take?'

'They took nothing,' said Dionisio, managing to sip some alcohol, but spilling more of it. 'It was them who got hurt.' Then he blurted out 'Ramon, you should have seen Bugsita kick that bastard.'

He put his arm around Anica and she leaned towards him and laid her head on his shoulder. With her left hand she clutched onto his shirt, and tears began to pour down her cheeks onto his clothes. Dionisio held her tightly and they sat clutching each other as they shook and trembled. He kissed the top of her head and breathed in the smell of her hair. Ramon looked at them like that, and found that the scene made him feel sentimental, so that he felt like crying as well.

It took Ramon all evening to get the full story out of them. As their shaking wore off, it was replaced with a kind of exultation over their exploit. Ramon felt that it was like trying to talk to people who were drunk at a fiesta. When Anica went to the excusado, Ramon leaned forward and said urgently, 'Listen friend, I told you you were in danger. Now take my word for it, will you?'

'Ay, Ramon, they were thieves, that is all. They are both

regretting it now. It was nothing to do with that other business.' Ramon began to shake his head pityingly, so Dionisio continued, 'They did not try to kill me at first. They demanded money.'

Ramon began to lose his temper. 'Look, listen to me for once. Madre de Dios, you are so naive. You know nothing but what you read in books and what you do with your polla. I do not warn you for nothing, idiot, but because I have information that I cannot tell you because it is confidential, and to do with things that you only write letters about. Leave this town, or I will concoct a charge and lock you up for your own safety.'

Disquieted by this outburst, Dionisio insisted weakly, 'They were thieves.'

Anica started to return, her steps careful but unsteady, and Ramon threw his hands up in a gesture of despair and hissed, 'You stupid son of a bitch.'

Back in the alley where the couple had merely gone to kiss, the assassins had been hiding in a doorway and waiting for the night. When it came they dragged themselves agonisingly away. The one with the ruined arm was repeating senselessly, 'He was just a professor, a stupid son-of-a-bitch professor,' and the other was holding his bandana against his wound and letting the blood roll out of his mouth to leave a trail along the dust which was soon busy with ants. They never returned to report to El Jerarca.

That night Anica and Dionisio made love three times with ferocious abandon, their bodies incandescent with lust, as though their brush with death had revealed to them the tenuousness of their hold on life and on each other. From that day forward Anica, who was intuitive about such things, began to think of her lover as a man of preternatural force; but she was also a little afraid, as if she knew that he had a destiny.

10 *The Justice Minister Resigns*

Your Excellency,

This week the former mayor of Cordoba was assassinated in front of his wife and children. Explosive bullets shredded him so completely that his corpse had to be gathered in plastic sacks, and a police guard had to be placed around the spot to prevent the dogs from licking up the blood and the vultures from collecting the little pieces that had not yet been picked out of the trees.

In our national constitution, widely regarded as the most enlightened in the world, it is stated that 'justice is a public service to be rendered by the nation.' The reform of 1945 states that 'property is a social function that implies obligations' and that the state may interfere in the execution of private and public business and industry for the purpose of rationalising production, distribution and consumption of goods, and to give labour the protection which is its right. Also stated is that 'the State protects the lives, honour and possessions of all its citizens.'

Your Excellency, we have had ten Justice Ministers in the last two years. In the last year five alcaldes, ten intendentes, and fifty judges have been assassinated by the coca caciques, and in addition thousands of ordinary citizens have been killed, tortured, and intimidated.

I cannot remain as Justice Minister as long as Your Excellency resolutely declines to make available to me the means to uphold the constitution. The coca-rich acknowledge no responsibility accruing from the monopoly of property and power, and the state has failed to protect the lives, honour, or property of its citizens. The state has failed above all to uphold its own honour, and we are now lower in

37

international estimation than we were even in the time of La Violencia.

I have repeatedly requested Your Excellency to declare a state of National Emergency and to mobilise the armed forces, but Your Excellency has persistently refused. As long as Your Excellency continues in this policy there is no point at all in having a Minister of Justice, and there is no point in having a constitution. For the sake of my family, I regret that it will now be necessary for me to take up residence in the United States, and it is with a heavy heart that I take leave of my Office and my benighted country.

Dr Maria Paz Bernardez,
Minister of Justice,
The Ministry of Justice.

11 *The Disappearance*

'OK, chicos,' said El Jerarca, 'the plan is simplicity itself. This Vivo is becoming too well known just to blow him away just like that, OK?' He took a deep drag on his puro and disappeared behind a cloud of gun-metal smoke. 'The road south out of town has no turn-offs for twelve kilometres, OK? And it is full of dangerous downhill bends, yes? All you have to do is watch until he leaves his house and heads out of town that way. Then you use the walkie-talkie, and after a few minutes you set up your roadblock, and you let everyone through except for him. Claro? Then he goes over the edge in his car, and he has unfortunately suffered a fatal accident.'

El Jerarca smiled at his own ingenuity; he always liked to make the plans himself, just so that he stayed in touch with how it was all done. But one of the boys said, 'Listen boss, what if the chica is with him, what do we do then?'

'Then you take her out of the car, and he goes over by himself. I have certain guarantees from Señor Moreno that his daughter will not say a word except that she managed to jump clear before the car went over. He is a very understanding man, boys.'

They all laughed in their throats, a laugh of complicity such as conspirators always laugh; it was the laugh of men who have been guilty for so long that the only choice is to give up hope of remission and sink further into guilt. It was the laugh of men who have been conditioned not even to trust their blood brothers, and feel so uneasy in the world that they continually avenge themselves further upon it.

Dionisio told Anica that he had a secret place where he used to go in order to think, or to wallow in his depressions so thoroughly that they were over with more quickly. 'It is just south of town,' he said, 'I think you will like it, and we can be alone there.'

Anica was in her tempting shorts again, and Dionisio had put on his swimming shorts under his baggy trousers to save having to change into them when they arrived. Anica hated his baggy trousers because they were not fashionable, but Dionisio refused to wear the skintight ones that she advocated. 'I am not going to squash my cojones even for you, querida, and furthermore they make one too hot, so that rashes develop, and they restrict one's movement too much.' Anica would shrug and make faces that were supposed to indicate how horrible his trousers were, and then launch into a tirade against his belt, which Dionisio also refused to abandon because his mother had bought it for him in Bucaramanga, when she had visited a cousin in Colombia. He would also decline to stop wearing the badges that she referred to as his 'hippy badges'. One of them had a dove on it with an olive branch in its beak, and the other bore a garish representation of the rising sun. He wore them because he wanted to brighten up his appearance and because he approved of the sentiments that they seemed to imply.

Dressed, then, in a manner thoroughly distasteful to Anica, and with her shifting the gears to provoke him, Dionisio drove his ancient car out of town towards the roadblock set up by the gangsters, who had been duly alerted by a man who had appeared to be sweeping the street. About half-way there, he suddenly turned on the lights and swung the car dramatically into the cliff-face. Anica yelled, tried to grab the wheel, and hid her face in her hands.

When she peered through her fingers at last, she saw that they were in a cave. With incredulity on her face she turned sharply in her seat and looked behind her to try to understand how they had driven through solid rock. Dionisio smiled smugly at her. 'See, the creepers completely disguise the opening.'

Anica threw back her head and breathed deeply with one

hand on her heart. 'O bastardo,' she said at last, 'you nearly gave me a heart attack. Truly, I shit myself.'

'Not truly, I hope,' he said. 'Did you bring spare underwear?'

She pretended to hit him, and said, 'Pedant.'

He left the lights of the car on while they got out and looked around. It was a very large cave with a wet floor, and everything seemed to be furry with some kind of lichen. 'Look,' he said, 'stalagmites and stalactites. I can never remember which is which.'

To their surprise they found a brand-new shoe abandoned; they swapped idiotic theories as to how it might have got there, and then they decided to leave it there in case its owner returned for it, perhaps dishevelled from her frolics. 'I hope it is not there for something sinister,' said Anica. 'It seems very odd that something as new and expensive as this should have been left.'

Dionisio went and turned off his car lights, and Anica found that it was still quite light. She looked up and there was a hole on the roof of the cave. 'I reckon it fell through there,' she said. 'Is there a flat patch up there?'

'Yes, querida, and we are going to go up there. There is an easy climb to it through another hole. Up there is a little piece of paradise, like the garden of Eden.'

They went a little further into the cave towards the second patch of light, and scrambled up the rocks. Anica poked her head out and was amazed. 'Dio', you would have no idea this was here, looking up from the road.'

It was a large flat space with a pond in the middle, surrounded by trees stunted into extraordinary and evocative shapes. 'Those trees look like little old men,' she exclaimed.

Anica laid the rug down and took all her clothes off in order to bask contentedly in the sunshine, and Dionisio did likewise in order to experience the sensation of freedom. The couple caressed and made love, and then Dionisio went to the edge of the water to look for crustaceans, because he had the idea of making a paella. But the water had a slimy appearance, and when he put his hand in to take a drink it felt greasy and thick. He bent down to smell it, and it stank of deliquescence. 'I think there is a dead animal in here,' he called to Anica. 'The water is foul. I am not going to swim.'

He found a few crustaceans and gathered them, but his feet became covered with the stinking mud, so he went and washed them in the little waterfall that fed the pond. 'I think that the water seeps through the rocks into the cave,' he said, 'and that is why it is wet in there.'

'Why does it not flow out over the road, then?'

'Maybe it goes down a crack and comes out somewhere else.'

He went and lay down next to Anica and tickled between her legs with a feather he had picked up. She squealed and sat up, and they had a mock fight. They spent the rest of the daylight basking in the sun, dozing, and walking amongst the trees, until it was time to go home and eat.

The body of the young woman with her feet encased in concrete continued to rot at the bottom of the pond in Dionisio's Garden of Eden, putrefying beneath the spot where it had been thrown casually from the helicopter. Her shoe, thrown out as an afterthought as the aircraft flew away, continued to lie undisturbed in the cave, having fallen through the hole in the roof just as Anica had supposed.

As the two lovers slept, the former lover of the body in the pond was listening to the embarrassed explanations of the men at the roadblock. 'Listen, boss, we had a man at the last house coming out of town, and he saw them go past, and that is the truth, boss. There are no turnings at all along there and there was nowhere they could have gone; nowhere, just like you said.'

'OK chicos, so where did they go?' said El Jerarca. 'Make it a good explanation, OK?'

'We waited an hour, boss, and then we thought maybe he has broken down in that old car of his, so we went and we looked for him. We drove up and down that route a hundred times, but we saw absolutely nothing of him, nothing. Then six hours later he comes driving back into town with a big smile on his face like he has just been made president. It is not good, boss, the man must be a brujo or something to pull a trick like that. I tell you it makes me nervous. Maybe he could turn me into a snake or something.'

El Jerarca put his hands on his hips and went to the window to think. 'You are right, chicos, there is something going on. You know those boys I sent after him?' They nodded. 'Well, they never came back. There was not a trace.' The roadblockers caught each others' glances as if to confirm with each other that truly this failure was no fault of theirs. 'So what do we do, boss?'

'There is one thing that never fails,' said El Jerarca.

12 The Grand Candomble of Cochadebajo de los Gatos (1)

Many people mistakenly believe that Eshu is the Devil, probably because every other Orisha certainly corresponds to a Christian saint. Eshu corresponds to no one but himself, however, and as he is full of pranks and mischief, it is easy to believe that really he is the Lord of Hell.

In fact, of course, Eshu is the only Orisha who knows past present and future without the bother of divination, he knows the cure for everything, and if his deeds sometimes seem malicious and arbitrary, then that is because he knows more than we do, and always delivers his punishments by a theft or an accident. He can be reasonable, however, and is satisfied with gifts of mousetraps, rum, puros, toys, and coconuts, as long as you remember to give him a white candle and three drops of water every Monday.

Eshu exists in twenty-one versions of himself, and so it is perhaps not surprising that there is plenty of scope for thinking that he is the devil. Some misguided souls think that he might be Saint Anthony of Padua, or Saint Benito, or even Saint Martin of Porres, but this is beyond the intellect of mere mortals to establish, and so we leave the question undecided.

Some people thought that it was the work of Eshu when Raquel gave birth to a child who looked like an Indian. Antonio, her husband, killed her in jealousy, and later it turned out that the child was a mongol. Little Rafael grew up to be slow, immensely strong and affectionate, and also incontinent. If it was a trick of Eshu, it was in poor taste.

It was also in poor taste when the coca people took Rafael away and made him carry fifty-pound packs of coca leaves day and night across the forest and the sierra, so that he nearly died a hundred times from heat exhaustion, from hypothermia, from frostbite, from tropical ulcers, and from starvation. When he finally collapsed behind the mule to which he had been roped, they set the gigantic alano dogs on him, and had a vast amount of amusement from watching him being torn to pieces and eaten. Perhaps it was not Eshu who was responsible for this, and perhaps it was Eshu who worked out ways to get a little retribution later.

When Father Garcia had his revelations about the nature of the universe and began to become a heretic, people naturally had to translate his message into terms comprehensible to santeria. So when Father Garcia said that the world was really created by the devil, and that the devil had enticed the divinely created souls into bodies, people began to say, 'Well, maybe it was Eshu who made the world, and that is why there is so much mischief in it,' while others said, 'No, it was Olofi who made all of it.' But the fact is that it does not matter very much, for real intellectuals believe everything at once, because this is the best way of being able to explain anything whatsoever, as the need arises. Father Garcia's Albigensian heresy merely became syncretised into the santeria of the people of Cochadebajo de los Gatos, who believed in it whenever it seemed like a good explanation for something.

Father Garcia, with his lugubrious face, very like a hare, and his tattered ecclesiastical robes, considered that St John's gospel was the only true portion of the bible, and he had gained considerable respect on account of his past as a Christian communist guerrillero and his ability to levitate spectacularly while preaching. When he levitated at exactly the point when he was announcing that a Deliverer would soon appear, and that he had been told this by God's messenger, Gabriel, the people naturally thought that Gabriel must be Eshu, since Eshu is the messenger of the Orishas. And when he said that they must hold a great ceremony to honour Him with gifts, the people rejoiced, because any excuse for a grand candomble was more than welcome. What drunkenness there would be, what golden rivers of piss, what splendid fornication, what a scent of incense and herbs, what a twanging of berimbaos, what a thundering of atabaque drums; and all the Orishas would appear in person and dance amongst them, honouring the Deliverer with gifts.

Amongst the crowd of folk who had gathered to watch Father Garcia levitating and talking mystical gibberish was Hectoro, who was mounted on his horse as usual, wearing his leather bombachos, and smoking a puro which he held clenched between his teeth. He rode up to where Garcia was stationed upon his invisible perch two metres above the ground and looked up into his face. 'Tell me, cabron,' he said, 'who is this Deliverer, and what is he delivering us from?'

An expression of irritation passed over Garcia's hitherto seraphic countenance, and he descended rapidly to the ground. 'How should I know?' he replied. 'You had better go and ask Aurelio.'

The second question was solved when rumours continued to spread from Ipasueño that El Jerarca and his coca gangsters were thinking of moving, lock, stock and barrel, to Cochadebajo de los Gatos, apparently because the government campaign against them was hotting up. The city was not even on the maps yet, since it used to be beneath the waters of a lake, and it was ideally suited as a staging-post for the cocaleros which would cut out Ipasueño from the itinerary.

The first question was solved by Aurelio with the aid of a potion of ayahuasca and a flight over the mountains in his form of an eagle.

13 *Two Cholitas*

Dionisio got out of bed one morning and went to the window as usual to see what kind of day it was. He shook his head and blinked a couple of times to make sure that he could really see two little girls tied back to back, sitting on the grass. He ran downstairs and into the chilly dawn.

The little girls were dressed in sacks with holes cut for the arms, and with string about the waist. They were both about twelve years old, and by their features Dionisio knew that they were mostly of Indian stock, with a little negro added in. They were plainly exhausted and in a state of shock, because they did not even speak to him or whimper as he cut the cords that had left deep weals in their flesh. Their faces were streaked with dirt, with clear tracks where the tears had run down their faces, and one of them had a swollen lip where she had been struck. He lifted her to her feet, but she could barely stand, so he carried her upstairs in his arms, laid her on his bed, and came down for the other. It was very clear to Dionisio what had happened to them.

He took them to the bathroom and undressed them; they did not resist, but let him wash them as all the time he talked to them soothingly. Then he dried them and gave to each of them one of his own shirts. He combed their hair and gave them sweet guava jelly to eat, and pineapple juice to drink, then he sat them on the edge of the bed and cajoled them until they told him what had happened and which place they came from.

He took their hands and led them down the stairs, sat them in his car, and as he drove the fifty kilometres to the little pueblo of Santa Virgen he told them stories about an armadillo called Enrique who wanted to become the president.

Dionisio was appalled by the state of the village. It was filthy and neglected, and some of the barracas were burnt out. Rangy dogs scavenged amongst the heaps of discarded rubbish, and Dionisio was amazed that no one had shot the one that plainly had rabies and was staggering insanely in circles with saliva drooling from its jaws.

The people there were as derelict and bedraggled as their dwellings. Skeletal and apathetic, they lounged in doorways and gazed at him with vacant eyes and drooping jaws. 'Hola,' he said to some of them, but they did not respond at all, even by raising a hand. When he returned the girls to their families they did not even thank him or appear to be distressed that the girls had disappeared. They merely nodded at him, mumbled some incoherent phrases, and sent the girls off immediately on errands. Stupefied with incomprehension and amazement, Dionisio wandered about the pueblo until he spotted a very old man whose eyes were still bright, and who told him through broken teeth exactly what had been happening. Disgusted and enraged, Dionisio went home and wrote another letter to *La Prensa*.

Dear Sirs,

In excusing the illegal and anti-social activities of the coca traders in our country who have so damaged our international standing, very many people have cited the good works accomplished by this degenerate mafia in our towns. There is in my own town a whole district built by them for their workers, which has all the amenities associated with civilised life, and which is locally known as the Barrio Jerarca, after the coca-Lord who built it. All the houses are earthquake-proof, the water is purified and runs both hot and cold, and there is central heating should people feel the need on cold nights to employ it. There are civic amenities, such as a swimming-bath and shops stocked with fancy goods, there are night clubs and strip bars, and there are, of course, the palaces of the coca-rich with their helicopter landing-pads and their rococo porticoes. There is a church there which is inlaid all over with gold-leaf, where the statue of the Virgin is in solid silver, and where the aristocracy of drugs are granted absolution for their innumerable and unpardonable crimes by a docile and hypocritical clergy who themselves live in free houses of palatial splendour.

On the outskirts of this district there is a bridge beneath which no one passes because it is frequented by cocaine addicts driven to the outer limits of ill-health, crime and destitution because of their addiction. The road that leads from this bridge out of town has an average of five dead bodies dumped on it every night, all of them showing signs of having been tortured to death in different ways. What is common to all of these ways is that they are of a sophistication, ingenuity, and brutality not seen in Latin America since La Violencia.

In the centre of the 'Barrio Jerarca' there is an infamous nightclub frequented by the criminals and their lackeys. The drive up to the nightclub is lined with prostitutes of both sexes who are desperate to fund their addiction. From this club every night there issue jeeploads of armed and intoxicated ruffians who scour the countryside, even in the most inaccessible places, for very young girls of peasant stock whom they abduct and bring back either to the club or to the palaces of their feudal lords. There they are raped continuously, sometimes for several days, by these feudal lords and their retainers. When they are tired of their pathetic victims they kill those who are plainly going to die anyway. The others they either release into the night, kilometres from home, or else they dump them, bound and gagged, anywhere in the town that they please, or else they take them back to the places from where they came so that they can return for them another time. It used to be the custom, I am told, to pay the parents large sums of money in return for acquiescence in the abduction of their daughters (and indeed, their small sons). But now instead they give them a derivative of coca called 'basuco'. Basuco is adulterated with lead and sulphuric acid; it is lethally addictive when smoked, and leads to the very early death of all who take it. Rural society and the rural economy all around this town for a radius of one hundred kilometres has now totally collapsed as a consequence of basuco addiction. The pueblos are derelict, nobody works, the livestock have perished, disease and starvation are commonplace, larceny and murder are endemic, and no one lives for any other reason than the hope that soon their daughters will be abducted again so that they will receive their next consignment of basuco.

Our country was one of the first in the world to give women the vote. Our country used to be famous for the sentimental adoration of children. Our country used to have fields and plantations that flourished and fed the entire nation without need of imports. Our country used to be renowned for a worship of women that was considered effeminate by foreigners; indeed it used to seem that the pleasure and indulgence of our women was all that we cared about, and our families were matriarchal to the point of imbalance.

There was a time when all men considered it an honour to be granted a woman's charms, and it was a point of honour for a lover to render his service in such a manner as to ensure that for his mistress no pleasure could be more exquisite, most especially when that pleasure was the first of its kind in the lady's experience.

So let the nation open its eyes and see to what depths we have sunk. Our little virgins are brutally violated and traumatised by men who uncaringly destroy for life any possibility that these innocents will ever be trustful of a man again. What kind of adults could they grow up to become? None of them will ever be able to know the ecstasy of sexual love because too bitter memories will be evoked. What kind of wives and mothers will they be, when they have already born bastards to monsters as soon as their first menstruation? What prospect is there for their physical health when at the age of twelve they are already dripping with venereal disease?

What kind of security or contentment will they ever know, when the mere sound of a vehicle evokes terror in their breasts?

All women of this country who claim the right to love as they choose, and all men who love women, should raise their voices against those who claim in ignorance that the coca trade is excused by its 'good works', and we should ask ourselves what kind of sickness it is that causes these men to hate women so much.

> Dionisio Vivo,
> Professor of Secular Philosophy,
> Ipasueño.

He thought a great deal about those two little Zambita-cholitas over the next few days, and eventually realised that the reason that they had affected him so much was that he had a longing to become a father.

His letter was published a week after its arrival, because *La Prensa* was out of print for a week, because a bomb had destroyed its offices.

14 *The Grand Candomble of Cochadebajo de los Gatos (2)*

The good thing about being broadminded and tolerant is that one can take advantage of whatever is in the offing, and, of course, this works both ways. The santeros amongst the people were quite happy to attend Catholic services, and not just because they needed a piece of the Host or a sprinkle of Holy Water for magic, but also because it was good to hear all that chanting, to join in with the hymns, to see the raiment of the priests and the choir and the sacristan, and to see the clouds of incense and the pagan Orishas around the walls of the churches, disguised as Christian Saints in their niches. It was also good to take time off on the Saints' days.

There were many who were aleyos, people who were not santeros, but who were good Catholics, who were not averse to attending the candombles, and watching the astonishing dances and feats of strength, hearing the veridical prophecies, and seeing at first hand how the yaguos could actually become gods and speak in macabre voices. How good it was to see people foaming at the mouth, convulsing, performing impossible contortions and acrobatics, and how good it was to see the fine raiment of the oluwos and ajigbonas and awaros. It was fine to breathe in the incense and join in the chanting, and only half-deceive oneself into believing that really the Orishas were Santa Barbara and San Lazaro and other saints. And how grand it was to join in with the fiestas of drunkenness and fornication afterwards.

Father Garcia did not join in at all, even though it had been he who had initiated the whole fuss. He had been siezed suddenly by a fierce desire to discover the true identity of St John the Evangelist, and he spent the whole fiesta locked up in his house waiting for the appearance of the Archangel

Sandalphon. This formidable celestial being is the manifestation in microprosopus of the Archangel Metatron, and Father Garcia believed that this angel was party to secret information about the author of the fourth gospel. He spent four days, bleary-eyed and praying, before there appeared before his gaze a tatty specimen. This angel was hook-nosed and senile, with crumpled feathers hopping with fleas. The nimbus about its head was of a greyish pallor, it salivated copiously through its missing teeth, and it could not remember its name when Garcia demanded to know it. In disgust, the latter threw open his door with the intention of wasting no more time upon this pitiful creature and of joining in with the festivities, only to find that they were already all over. He went to take a few copas at Consuelo's whorehouse, and when he came back the angel was still there, sitting quietly in a corner with an air of dejection. Garcia looked at it with a certain sympathy and said, 'You may as well go now.'

'Where to?' demanded the angel, in Hebrew.

'Heaven?' suggested Garcia, in Latin.

The angel sighed and made a rueful face. 'Can't I stay here?' it asked. But Garcia shook his head and it rose not ungracefully to the ceiling, and faded away. Father Garcia shrugged resignedly, and made a note in his book: 'It appears that angels fall into decrepidation when not gainfully employed. I wonder whether all this concentration gives one hallucinations. Or can it be listening to too many Colombian stories?'

Most of the rest of the aleyos found a way to be useful during the celebration. Don Emmanuel, with his rufous beard, his impressive belly, and his flair for ribaldry, made pantagruelian quantities of guarapo, involving hundreds of pineapple skins, which he served with a gourd and his usual good humour. Françoise and Antoine Le Moing, who, along with Dona Constanza, were among the few other white people in the city, grilled fish and served it up on palm leaves with rice. Dona Constanza and Gloria made a vast sancocho with fifty chickens in two cauldrons, and wore themselves out with all the plucking, the drawing of entrails, the cubing of cassava, and the washing of potatoes. Professor Luis and his wife, Farides, ran a hangover rescue service, delivering lemon juice sweetened with chancaca to those who lay moaning in the streets from the effects of chacta, chiche, aguardiente and ron cana. All the time Professor Luis was clucking to himself about all the liver damage that was going on, but on the last day he too became famously drunk, and climbed up onto the roof of the Palace of the Lords. He sang 'El Preso Numero Nueve' at the top of his voice and then collapsed, so that Hectoro and Josef had to climb up there as well and lower him down with a lasso.

Remedios, who used to be a communist guerrilla leader and who had never given up her martial frame of mind, patrolled the city with a Kalashnikov accompanied by her enamorado, the Conde Pompeyo Xavier de Estremadura. This latter had been unfrozen by Aurelio, having been dead beneath an avalanche for four hundred years, and although he no longer wore his armour very often he was still confused by his new lease of life. He followed Remedios about, waving his sword, remonstrating with disorderly characters in his archaic Spanish, and helping her to break up fights. He never was to feel at home in the twentieth century until the day when he was to recognise his own ring upon Dionisio Vivo's finger and discover that he had met one of his own descendants.

Capitan Papagato, who was at that time just beginning his romance with the young and beautiful Francesca, changed the bambuco and vallenato records on the gramophone that Professor Luis had rigged up to his windmill, and managed to kiss Francesca a great many times in between. The last unbeliever, General Fuerte, who was thought to be dead but had in fact deserted the army, decided during the fiesta to collect observations about his countrymen with the same thoroughness and objectivity as he had always displayed in collecting information about his country's butterflies and hummingbirds. He wandered about with a notebook, followed by his huge cat, collecting anthropological data about alcoholic consumption and patterns of promiscuity. He jotted down an exchange that he heard between Don Emmanuel and the voluptuous Felicidad.

Don Emmanuel had said, 'I believe in that proverb that a man cannot make love to every woman in the world, but he ought to try.' Felicidad had laughed her inimitably wanton laugh and replied, 'A woman has more sense; she knows when she has found the best lover in the world, and she stays with him.'

'You have never stayed with anyone.'

Felicidad smiled and said, 'But no one can accuse me of not looking very hard.'

General Fuerte wrote down, 'I have never really noticed before, while I was in the army, but truly this country is one huge bed of love.'

15 A Joke, Another Warning, And An Unexpected Bonus For Jerez

Anica had been plotting to give Dionisio a joke present ever since he had given her a perfume bottle which in fact contained a substance that smelled of dogfart.

She went to a crazy old Indian who earned a living by carving perfect representations of different kinds of turds out of clay, which he then glazed and fired, and sold on a tray not far from Madame Rosa's. Then she went to a shop of medicines and bought a child's fingerstall in transparent rubber. This she rolled up and placed in a tiny little box. On the box she wrote 'Para mi Amigo pequeño', and then she wrapped it carefully in green tissue.

She came round and stood in Dionisio's room, and said, 'Look, I have got you a present.' By the way that she was trying not to smile, he knew that something suspicious was going on, and he said 'OK, this is a joke?' She grinned her huge grin despite trying not to, and said, 'Open and see.'

He tugged at the wrapping, and found the small red box. 'For my little friend,' he read. Then he opened it and found what appeared to be an extraordinarily small condom nestling in the cotton wool. 'Oh, bastarda, really it is not so small as that. You are a rat, and . . .' but he was lost for words, and he pretended to pummel her in the stomach while she put her hands on her hips and laughed.

'I do not mean it,' she said.

'No one has ever complained,' he announced, pretending to be offended, and putting on a childish pout. 'I have not either,' she said, putting her arms around him, 'I am very pleased with it.'

'You should know,' said Dionisio, 'that all over the world every little boy is born with a measure in his sweaty little hand. Now you have destroyed my confidence.'

'Well, now you should stop calling me "Bugsita" just because I have big teeth, OK? Listen, I nearly forgot, my father gave me a little note to give to you.'

He was astonished. 'Your father?' He took the envelope and opened it. It was written in a copperplate hand in brown ink, on very fine quality paper. There was no greeting:

I have heard that you are a very fine young man, albeit with some unusual opinions, and I have noted how much happier my daughter has been since she has known you. Most fathers would have intervened by now to forbid their daughter any further contact, because I am well aware that Anica is keeping unacceptably irregular hours, and is alone with you unchaperoned in a manner that a few years ago would have caused a great scandal.

However, I have tried to be a 'modern' father to my daughters, and I do not interfere with their free-will even though I disapprove of most of what they do and say and believe. I do not interfere because I suffered too greatly with the interference of my own family, who nearly prevented me from marrying Anica's mother. I will not put myself between you, also, because it causes me great delight to see Anica happy for the first time since her mother's death.

But I must warn you that certain people have approached me, and that I am certain that your life is imperilled. I tell you this in the strictest confidence, and you must not tell anyone under any circumstances that I have given you this information, not even Anica. As you are with Anica for much of the time, it goes without saying that I am terrified on her behalf in case she becomes an incidental victim of whatever is going to happen. I beg you for her sake to take care, and to cease to meddle in affairs which are beyond your power to comprehend in their entirety. She has told me about the time that you nearly killed two thieves who threatened you both, but you must know that physical courage will not be enough to save you from these people.'

*

'What does it say?' asked Anica. Dionisio fumbled in his mind for something that would put her off completely: 'He wants to know my opinion as professor of Secular Philosophy on St Anselm's ontological argument for the existence of God.'

'Ay,' she exclaimed. 'That stinks. Please do not explain it to me.'

'Please tell your father that I have noted very carefully what he says, and that I will think about it with the utmost seriousness.'

'Listen, we have to go to Janita's because my Norton is there, and I cannot make it go at all.'

Anica's 'Norton' was a very old two-stroke moped to which some previous owner had fixed an incongruous fuel tank from an old Norton. It looked most bizarre, but it was very practical because the moped used almost no fuel and the tank was enormous, which meant that it hardly ever had to be filled up. Unaware that Jerez was still in the house, Dionisio took some tools, and locked the door as they left.

The two roadblockers were turning housebreaker. Similarly unaware that Jerez was still in the house, fast asleep after a night of heavy marijuana smoking, they broke down the front door with a crash. Jerez awoke with a jump, heard the men careering up the stairs, and with great presence of mind hid himself in his cupboard. The two men seemed to know which room was Dionisio's, for they were in and out of it and back down the stairs in a flash.

When Jerez was sure that they were gone, he crept out of the cupboard and very carefully opened the door of Dionisio's room, because he suspected the possibility of a bomb. There was only a sack on the bed, with a note pinned to it. It was a parody of the warning on the side of cigarette packets: 'Las Autoridades Sanitarias advierten que: PARTICIPAR EN UNA CRUZADA PERJUDICA SERIAMENTE LA SALUD.' In smaller writing it said, 'Dinero, es mejor.' Jerez read this to himself very slowly, out loud: 'The health authorities advise that crusading can seriously damage your health. Money is better.'

Jerez felt the sack, and realised that it contained wads of banknotes. He opened the sack, and found that in it were more pesos than Dionisio could have earned in two entire lifetimes of teaching secular philosophy. He sat on the bed for an hour with his head in his hands, and could not think of a single reason why anyone should ever know that he had taken it. So he took it. He hid it in the same cupboard in which he had hidden himself.

It was Anica who pointed out that the door had been kicked off its lock, and Dionisio ran upstairs, fully expecting to find some kind of catastrophe. But instead he found Jerez with his feet on the table eating his way through a sancocho. 'I am sorry about the door,' he said, 'I forgot my keys and I was desperate to get in for a shit.'

'I always said we should hide a key in the garden,' remarked Dionisio. He went to his room and, while looking for something else, found a few pesos under a book on the table. He came back with them triumphantly, and suggested that they all go and get some fried cassava and some Mexican burritos from the shop down the hill.

Later on, back at the house, Jerez came in and found the lovers wrapped in each other's arms on the couch. 'You two never give up, do you,' he said. 'Do you never stop?' Anica stood up and straightened her clothing, and Jerez said, 'Would it not be funny if you two got married? You could put all your names together: "Montes Sosa Vivo Moreno." It sounds good.'

Anica pulled a face, perhaps of pain, perhaps of pleasure, and said, 'Who said anything about marriage?' Dionisio began to think about it.

Jerez pretended that he had to go away for a long time on an assignment, and he disappeared with some of the bag of money. He went to Rio and Caracas and gambled some of it, and spent the rest on the highest-class and most expensive whores he could find. He returned with the most intractable cocktail of venereal diseases that the doctors at the clinic had ever encountered, and they forbade him to sleep with a

59

woman for six months at the very least. He decided to wait until Dionisio was dead before he spent the rest of it. Like everyone else he believed that this would happen sooner rather than later.

So Dionisio never had the chance to test on himself his psychological theory of bribery, which was that anyone could be corrupted by being offered a sum that exceeded their annual income by a factor of ten, and he carried on writing the coca letters. But that night he noticed a turd on the stairs, and wondered how on earth a cat had got in.

16 Memos

FROM: Headquarters, Central Intelligence Agency.
To: Headquarters, Central Intelligence Agency, Hispano-American Division

Please assess reality of recent threat by coca cartels to blow up all US nuclear installations near to civilian populations, and recent offer of one billion dollars on the head of the president unless the policy of extradition is discontinued.

FROM: The Office of His Excellency, President Veracruz
To: Pablo Ecobandodo, Ipasueño

What contribution to the paying off of the National Debt may be expected in return for concessions on the part of the National Government?

Dear President,
    Are you loco? We do what we want, and this isn't Colombia. Go fuck yourself.
        Pablo Ecobandodo.

From: Club Hojas
To: Pablo Ecobandodo, Ipasueño

We regret that your application for membership of our
prestigious club has been turned down by our admissions
committee. We advise that you read a copy of *La Prensa* from
the fifth of May of this year. There you will find a letter
from Dionisio Vivo, now an honorary member of this club,
in which he states clearly why 'the oligarchy' should not
allow a fifth column to be formed within its ranks.
The committee particularly regrets your threats of violence
in the event of refusal, your offers of financial inducements,
and your suggestion that the club should provide gratis the
use of prostitutes to its members.

(e)

From: PE
To: El Guacamayo and El Chiquitin

(1) Arrange for Club Hojas to be blown up God's own
asshole.
(2) Buy the land and build a new Club Hojas twice as big.
(3) Don't admit any members from the old club.
(4) Get plenty of girls and put them in it.
(5) Do it quick.

(f)

From: The Office of His Excellency, President Veracruz
To: The Ministry of Agriculture

Is it true what Dionisio Vivo says in the letter of the twenty-
sixth of June, that the rural economy has collapsed because
of the coca trade and that we are now net importers of food?
If so, please calculate the financial loss to the state revenue.

(g)

To: Rodrigo
FROM: Me

Please deal with this memo from the president's office. I can't stand his Vivomania anymore.

(h)

FROM: The Office of His Excellency, President Veracruz
To: The Ministry of Justice

Is it true what Dionisio Vivo says, that our murder rate is now almost as bad as Washington DC, and that this is because of the coca trade? Is it true that this is discouraging foreign investment and destroying the tourist industry?

(i)

FROM: The Ministry of Justice
To: The Office of His Excellency, President Veracruz

Regrettably, Your Excellency, the answer to both your questions is 'yes'. We beg you once more to declare a state of emergency.

(j)

FROM: The Office of His Excellency, President Veracruz
To: The Office of The President of the United States of America

Please find enclosed a copy of a letter by the famous Dionisio Vivo, in which he argues that the coca trade in this country is the direct consequence of rural underemployment and general lack of industrialisation, as a result of which people can only achieve a decent standard of living by engaging in dishonest trading in coca. Please note that he conclusively argues that the solution to this problem lies in a massive programme of foreign investment in the creation of new industries that will give full employment at a decent wage. You will note that in his judgement an investment of a minimum of ten billion dollars will be necessary.

(k)

FROM: The Office of His Excellency, President Veracruz
To: Pablo Ecobandodo, Ipasueño

His Excellency cordially invites you to an informal meeting at the Presidential palace at your convenience, in order to discuss matters of mutual interest.

(l)

FROM: Cordoba University, Department of Genetic Research
To: His Excellency, President Veracruz

We wish to confirm with you that it really is your intention to get us to examine tissue from a large black cat, with a view to determining whether or not it really is your daughter.

(m)

FROM: The Office of His Excellency, President Veracruz
To: The Ministry of Information

Please forward all files on Pablo Ecobandodo (El Jerarca) of Ipasueño to this office.

From: The Ministry of Information
To: The Office of His Excellency the President

His Excellency is to be reminded that he abolished this Ministry two months ago.

17 *Mythologising And Making Love*

Dionisio sealed the envelope of his latest coca letter, addressed it, and took it down to the post-office, only to find that he had been pre-empted by the destruction of the latter. In the early morning a bomb had removed its front external wall, and a notice pinned to the broken doorjamb announced that the service would temporarily be relocated in the town hall. When he arrived there he found that the postmaster was going about his business with his usual inflexible sang-froid. 'Hola, Dionisio, and how is the Pythagoras of Ipasueño?'

'He is perturbed,' he replied.

'You should be; they did this to prevent you from posting your celebrated epistles to the intelligentsia and the powerful elite who govern us with so much enlightenment and humanity. I wish to thank you personally. This is far more salubrious and spacious than the old office, and the number of cockroaches is far less.'

Dionisio smiled and handed him the new letter. 'Seriously, Dionisio, you should stop writing these. Local people are taking out bets on the precise date of your assassination, and the stakes are so high that there is a peril of one of them assassinating you himself just in order to win his bet.'

'I think that people are saying these things out of a love for drama.'

'And they say that several attempts have been made already, so you surprise me. They say that you have lived because you are a brujo and can make yourself invisible, amongst other things.'

Dionisio put his hand on the postmaster's shoulder and said, 'Vale, well you tell everyone that I am a brujo indeed, and that anyone attempting to reduce my lifespan will himself die instantaneously, OK? We will amuse ourselves by mythologising Dionisio Vivo, is that a deal?'

'That would amuse me very much,' replied the postmaster. 'You have a deal. And I have a letter for you.'

Outside the town hall Dionisio tore open the envelope and found that it was his very first piece of personal fan-mail. By some extraordinary omission it had occurred to no one in the media either visual or printed to request interviews, and so Dionisio had missed the opportunity to become a media star and appear on quiz shows. But all over the country, and completely without his knowledge, Dionisio Vivo societies had sprung up in which people met to discuss his opinions and fantasise about his appearance.

This is not as surprising as one might otherwise believe, because it was a country where all the television stars were foreigners in imported series, where almost no one could afford to buy books, and consequently one could not become lionised as an author. But it was a literate country, thirsty for knowledge and education, which were perceived by most as the most important rungs on the difficult ladder out of poverty. As a result, the country had what was probably the best collection of newspapers in Latin America, if not the world. There were vast numbers of quality local papers, and several highbrow papers which were read avidly and appreciatively even by those who in other lands would normally read the tabloids. It was one of the few countries in the world where journalists could build up the kind of fanatical following normally associated with rock stars. Dionisio's impassioned letters in the most prestigious newspaper of all had, unbeknown to him, won him the status of a star in a country wearied and disgusted by the anarchy of the coca trade.

But it was also a superstitious country, a country where it was possible to believe every religion all at once, where devout Catholics could pray to Oxala, practise santeria, and attend spiritualist séances with a clear conscience. One simply selected from one's gamut of beliefs whichever one was appropriate for whichever occasion.

And so clairvoyants and mediums were hired to give detailed descriptions of the new journalistic superstar to portrait painters, and some members of the Vivo societies with natural psychic powers and artistic inclinations even painted his portrait themselves. There was a general consensus that he was a white man with a beard and long brown hair with the gentle eyes of a doe and the hint of a nimbus about his head. There developed a fashion for portraying him with a scarlet heart in his breast that bled for his country, and so he became a kind of crossbreed between Jesus Christ and the Blessed Virgin. The proliferation of these societies caused a boom in commissions for the artistic world, and an unprecedented increase in the circulation of *La Prensa*, which helped towards rebuilding its offices in bombproof British granite and bullet-proof glass. There was such a demand that when a society for expatriates in Paris was inaugurated, *La Prensa* even contemplated opening an office there to receive enquiries and requests for back issues.

As was to be entirely expected, a fair number of the members of these societies were the kind of young women who in general find their vocations in cloisters. That is to say, they nourished their powerful but sublimated libidos upon fantasies about a distant, unattainable, and idealised man who would haunt their dreams and give them actual verbal messages during their seraphic raptures. For these women who knew that they were too base to pursue their divinity in the flesh there existed an admirable substitute in the postal service. There were others, however, who like the Mary Magdalen of unbiblical myth yearned for him with such hyperbolical ardour that they reported to their friends that they were able to reach stupendous orgasms without even touching themselves. For these it became their unrelenting intention to offer themselves to him in the flesh and, if possible, to bear his child. The phenomenal efforts of concentrated visualisation that these women performed gave rise to numerous and bizarre psychic effects, such as that reported by a virgin of Antiochia, Leticia Aragon, who had purportedly nearly suffocated in a shower of white feathers.

Dionisio opened his first fan-letter, and found inside it a dog-eared photograph of a plump mulatta who was offering him her favours gratis in return for a lock of his hair and travelling expenses. He read it several times with disbelief, and began to compose in his head a tactful refusal. When he got home he found Anica waiting on the doorstep, and he showed her the letter. She read it, torn between jealousy and amusement, and then told him that she had come round because she had had the idea that it would be good to take a shower together.

They undressed in indecent haste and ran into the bathroom, where Anica removed the gekko from the wall 'so that it does not get soap in its eyes' and put it higher up on the tiles. She turned on the shower and they jostled for space beneath its thin stream of water. The shower was Jerez' single successful improvisation, and was made of two hoses which were stuck respectively onto the hot and cold taps and fed up to a saucepan which had had holes punched in the bottom and was then fixed to the wall with a twisted coathanger. The water supply was subject to sudden variations in both pressure and temperature, so that it was often necessary to leap out of the tub in order not to be either scalded or frozen.

They drew the plastic curtain around the shower, and Dionisio noticed that Anica had forgotten to remove her earring, but he did not inform her of the omission because he was reluctant to delay the proceedings. Voluptuously he soaped her all over until every bit of her was covered with such froth that she took on the appearance of being feathered with down. He took her breasts reverently, one in either hand, and massaged them upwards with conscientious circling motions so that her nipples were teased and began to shrink and harden into buds. He massaged her backside, her stomach, and then her long legs, working upwards with the maximum of tantalisation towards her thighs. He worked the soapsuds salaciously into her fine gingery hairs and rolled his hand with the firmest and gentlest of pressures so that she closed her eyes and moaned and clutched his shoulder as if she were entering a trance.

When he had finished he gave her the soap and she performed the same operations for him, except with greater delicacy and tentativeness. When she had finished they took the hose out of the saucepan and sprayed each other with it so that the suds flew all over the bathroom and gently subsided into puddles. Then Anica grabbed the cold-water hose and sprayed Dionisio on the polla so that he shouted and struggled to get it away from her. Then they held each other tight, and she felt his little bird jumping and twitching against her. She stuck her tongue in his ear and said, 'You wait until I rub you all over with olive oil and cocoa butter.'

In the bedroom he went down on his knees and kissed her where she stood, his tongue working with the rhythm and mischief of a master-dancer of Vallenato. His tongue travelled relentlessly up her body and announced itself to her rosebuds, until once more they were standing locked in a kiss with his polla working back and forth in its true home so that she said, 'Querido, la Cama.'

They sank sideways onto the bed and she drew him in and encompassed him so that he uttered that insuppressible groan of surprise that he always did and always failed to remember that he did.

They made love very slowly at first, but then became carried away until afterwards they lay together slippery with perspiration, and entwined. He said, 'Sometimes it seems as though I lose consciousness, when it is as good as that, and afterwards I feel cheated because I cannot remember it properly.'

She stroked his chest and laughed. 'Did you know,' she said, 'that in the days of the conquistadors they used to call it "the little death"? If that is a little death, just imagine what a big death would be like.'

18 *El Jerarca And His Excellency The President Fail To Arrive At An Historic Compromise*

His Excellency was infuriated right from the start. It was supposed to be an informal meeting in complete secrecy in order to establish what could be achieved in reaching an accommodation between the cartels and the government. His Excellency had in mind a contribution to the treasury of a few billions, in return for a blind eye, and possibly even a change in the law. Perhaps it could be made legal to grow coca, but not to process it, for example, so that that could be done in another country; that would bring down the wrath of the USA on that country and not this one. He thought that Paraguay had a policy a little like that, and of course, if coca cultivation were legal, then it would be possible to tax it. Yes indeed, His Excellency had been looking forward to his fruitful secret negotiations.

But what do I see when I am looking out of my window for Pablo Ecobandodo's discreet limousine? I see a huge horsebox draw up outside the gates of the presidential palace, and I see the tailramp dropped. Then Ecobandodo arrives in a pink Chevrolet, with a huge cigar in his mouth and a campesino sombrero with a hatband full of diamonds and emeralds. Then suddenly there are hundreds of press reporters and photographers, with flashbulbs popping and their frantic jostling, and Ecobandodo tells them that His Not Very Excellency President Craphead Veracruz has invited him, Pablo Ecobandodo, to the palace so that he, Pablo Ecobandodo, can tell the president what's what and who is the bigshot around here.

And then that crowd turn up with placards that say 'Viva El Jerarca' and 'Ecobandodo for President' and 'El Jerarca for

Perpetual Dictator' and 'Ecobandodo El Supremo', and it turns out later that the crowd, every member of it, got given a thousand pesos each for doing it and hadn't got a clue what it was all about, but there were four thousand people out there all clamouring for Pablo Ecobandodo that they had never heard of before.

And it gets on the radio and the TV, and the CIA are so damn quick off the draw that two hours later there is a furious cable with the expletives deleted from the President of the United States demanding an explanation and threatening sanctions and hinting at other 'measures which may seem to us to be necessary', so that I have to send a cable back with an explanation that sounds like something almost daft enough to be a CIA report itself. It is an appalling humiliation.

And that Ecobandodo who is fat enough to weigh as much as eight people jammed into a lift, he gets up in the horsebox, and out he rides on a white horse caparisoned in a bridle and saddle and garra so rich that it could have paid off the national debt in one fell swoop. And the poor horse is staggering beneath the weight and looks like it is going to fall over, and then Ecobandodo actually rides it across the fresh gravel of the palace courtyard with all his tame pressmen in tow taking sycophantic pictures and scribbling down quotes, and the fat shit is actually throwing bundles of thousand-peso notes and sachets of coca amongst the crowd that overwhelms the palace guard who are last seen on their hands and knees in full ceremonial dress cramming the money into their polished helmets with the horsetail plumes just like the ones at Buckingham Palace, and they are even cramming it down their high boots and into the little boxes on the back of their Sam Brownes, and it turns out that one of the soldiers had his little box full of contraceptives which he empties out on the gravel to make space for the money, and the newspapers print a full-page photograph of him doing it and invite the readers to send in the best caption, and the winner gets a free holiday for two in Punta del Este, paid for by Pablo

Ecobandodo who will personally hand over the tickets at a gala presentation.

And the fat exhibitionist, he rides the white horse up the palace steps and into the Great Hall of The Republic, and the horse is so weighed down that it has to shit on the red carpet and leave a great steaming pile right here in the palace; a stain that will be a perpetual reproach to His Excellency every time that I have to step over it.

And he gets off his horse, who visibly sighs with relief, and he puts his cigar out on the bust of Simon Bolivar and throws the stub into the indoor fishpond where some unfortunate carp gulps it down and then reappears on the surface in its death throes two hours later.

And he is surrounded by hoods with weapons plainly bulging out of every cranny of their gaudy clothes, and he comes up and says, 'I suppose that you are His Excellency President Veracretino The Ridiculous, and I have just come to spit on your carpet, see, I have spat on it, and tell you that you don't mess with me, now or ever, or I will see you eat shit, OK?' And all his bodyguards laugh, and there is one there who has gold teeth and the worst taste shoes I have ever seen, and he gets out his penis and pisses in the fishpond in a great golden arc, and says, 'That will cost you two thousand pesos for the privilege.'

The man gets back up on his horse and rides away down the steps into the sunlight, because for once it is not raining, and he waves to the crowd and has his picture taken, and after he has gone my little wife comes up to me and she says, 'Daddikins, you know when I worked in that club in Panama? I recognise that man. He came in once and made me do it with someone on a table right in front of all the customers at gunpoint, and then he makes me put fruit up it and pretend to make love with a bottle, and he passes the bottle round all the customers afterwards and makes each one take a swig and eat the fruit.' And my poor darling she is trembling at the memory, and I put my arm around her and say, 'Don't fret, my little schoolgirl, because Daddikins is going to get that

73

man,' and she gives me some Turkish Delight and says, 'Let's hex him tomorrow,' and I say, 'You are a clever little girl.'

And from now on it's war, and I have already informed the Chief of Police and the Chiefs of Staff that henceforth it's our secret policy to shoot to kill, because we don't want those reprobates and criminals buying their way out of justice any more, and, I am pleased to say, it looks as if the stains of the horseshit will come out quite easily with a bit more work, and the cat that is supposed to be my own daughter ate the fish while no one was looking and has suffered no ill effects, thanks be to God.

19 *Fortuity*

'OK boys, I have had enough. That ungrateful bastard Vivo, he takes all that money, and then he still writes those letters and gets everyone worked up and people start up their Vivo societies and start pressuring the police and the mayors, and they write letters to the president and all that goddamn mierda, and it turns out he is son to that filth Montes Sosa who had my cousin shot in Cesar. We are going to take him out once and for all, chicos, and here is just how, OK? You take this little present, OK, and it is magnetic, and you stick it right under the driving-seat of that car of his, right? This baby is a special baby, chicos, it explodes straight up like that "Boom" and it will blow him apart starting with his asshole and his goddamn cojones, OK? So you stick it under there and you pull out this pin, yes? And quarter of an hour after that car makes its first move when he is out of town it tears a hole in his backside, except his backside is not big enough for the hole this baby blows. And you make damn sure he really is going out of town before you pull that pin, boys, because if that baby goes off in town you are in trouble, and it grieves me only a little if you get that Moreno girl as well this time boys because her daddy must have told him something or we would have got him last time, and we can always get our guns somewhere else, boys, can we not? Now listen, chicos, you follow that Vivo and keep a good distance, because I want a first-hand report about when that baby blows him through the roof of that antique, understand?'

Anica and Dionisio planned to go canoeing. As usual she came round and banged on the shutters, but Dionisio had known she was coming because from his own room he could see when she turned off her lights or closed her windows. So as usual he ran downstairs and told her through the door that he was not going to buy any encyclopaedias, and she said, 'Let me in, shithead.' He opened the door and pounced on her, pinning her against the wall and kissing her, standing on tiptoe because she was taller than he was. As usual she made faces and said, 'I know too many people around here; que diran?' And he said, 'Are you ashamed to be seen with me?'

'There is a man out there, querido, and he wanted to talk with me. I gave good morning, and he said "Have a good weekend, are you doing anything special?"'

'I think he fancies you. What did you say?'

'I said we are going to Iragun to take a boat on the river, and he said, "You had better be quick or you won't get a boat," so I said, "Why?" and he said they often hire them all out first thing. I think we had better hurry, querido.'

When they came out of the house the man was still there. Anica smiled at him, and Dionisio said, 'I hear you have been flirting with my woman,' so he smiled and said, 'Anyone would want to flirt with a girl like that.' Dionisio said 'You are right, hombre,' and Anica looked embarrassed.

They set off out of town, and after a few kilometres she said, 'Querido, I think I left my mochila behind.'

'You nearly did; I put it under my seat.'

She tried to reach round under the seat and check that it was there, but she could not feel it, so she said, 'Are you sure it is there?' This sowed a doubt in his mind, even though he was absolutely sure, so after a while of insisting that it was there he stopped the car and lifted up the front seat. It was difficult to lift because of the pull of the magnet on the metal bars of the seat-frame, but he just made a mental note to oil the swivels. When he drove off the bomb was left lying in the road, and the gangsters in the car behind were absolutely staggered and dismayed. 'Mierda maricon, I told you that man was a brujo. How did he do that?'

'Listen, that thing is going to go off soon. What do we do?' They got out and threw it over the edge of the road so that it bounced down the mountainside and came to rest against a boulder. The only damage it did when it went off was to seal up the burrow of a family of rats, who had to spend the rest of the morning digging themselves out.

'Did you notice,' she said, 'that when we stopped to look for my bag, the car behind us stopped?'

'He had a problem with the engine, I think. He was looking under the bonnet. It is these modern cars, they are all rubbish because they only design them to last three years, so then you have to buy another one. That is big business. Everyone should have an old car like mine, then there would be no problems.'

She laughed at him. 'Even if your car broke down every day you would still think it was the best car in the world.'

'Well, it is, Bugsita, it is.'

That day Dionisio told her about his ambitions in life. 'I want a house, somewhere at the same altitude as Medellin, for example. There must be a huge pond full of fish, and the garden must be overgrown like a jungle so that I always get surprises in it. I will have a room full of recording equipment so that when I compose something I do not forget it straight away, and I would have a workshop with lathes and a hole in the ground so that I can work underneath the car. I would have the biggest double bed in the world, and I want a very old motorcycle, and I want a library where the termites cannot get in. Most of all I want very many cats.'

Anica was puzzled and amused. 'I do not know if that is to want too much or too little.'

'What do you want, querida?'

'I have no idea.' She imitated the simpering whine of Miss Venezuela of the year before, who had uttered the immortal words which she now repeated: 'I want only to be happy and successful.' Then they talked to a horse who had poked his head over a fence, and he said, 'Undoubtedly I will have a beautiful grey horse also.' It occurred to him that this would be a good time to ask her to marry him, because he wanted her more than all those other things put together. But his courage failed him.

77

'Look at that,' said Anica. 'What language is it?'

'English, I think,' said Dionisio, scrutinising the graffito that someone had painted neatly on the wall. 'Earl is a real cool dude,' he read, mispronouncing all the words. When he got home he borrowed a bilingual dictionary from Ramon, and was puzzled to find that it meant something like, 'The English nobleman ranking between a marquis and a viscount is an actually existing townsman of a moderate temperature.' He was tormented for days by the question of why anyone should want to inscribe such a gnomic utterance on a wall.

The failed bombers were equally tormented as to why their infallible magnetic bomb had fallen off. The answer was mundane: a few months before, Dionisio had noticed that the floor beneath his seat had rusted through, so he had cut it back to clean metal and replaced it with a sheet of aluminium held in place with pop-rivets, intending to get a piece of steel welded into position when he could persuade someone to do it for a reasonable price. He had forgotten about it altogether, and the magnet had only stayed there at all because it was attracted to the frame of the seat.

But the assassins were now perfectly convinced that he was a brujo, and they were beginning to lose heart so much that one man said, 'I will never shoot a bullet at him in case it comes back, by the Virgin,' and some others agreed, and swore that they too would never fire a bullet at him, even in self-defence.

20 The Grand Candomble of Cochadebajo de los Gatos (3)

In the streets of Cochadebajo de los Gatos an exotic and ethereal perfume was hanging delicately and elegantly in the air. It would have reminded a visitor of the smell of expensive incense in a Catholic cathedral, and they would have been astonished if anyone had told them that it was simply brown sugar and garlic husks ground together and burned on a bed of charcoal. Its function was to drive away evil spirits, such as Iku, Lord of Death, so that they did not turn up and manifest at the guemilere.

For a week everyone had been sleeping with a gourd of water beneath their bed or their hammock, for the same reason, since it is common knowledge that evil spirits dissolve in water as though they were sugar or salt.

But the problem with this was that the water had to be thrown out of one's front door in the morning without anyone observing. But how impossible this was! Felicidad would poke her head around the door at the same time as Consuelo, and they would see each other and duck back in. Sergio would look out, and lo and behold, Dolores the whore was also looking out. Then Tomas would peer round his door-jamb and catch sight of Felicidad peeping around hers once more.

In this way hours were wasted each morning as heads popped in and out of doorways, and tempers became frayed. People began to shout at each other across the street, and one time Francesca became so fed up that she marched out and actually emptied her bowl of evil spirits over Father Garcia's head for having spotted her, so that he had to go into the church to bless himself in order to exorcise the baneful influences.

Eventually Hectoro and Misael went to discuss the problem with Don Emmanuel, and he called a meeting in the plaza. 'Amigos,' he said, 'there is a simple solution to your difficulty, but I will not tell it to you unless . . .' and he arched an eyebrow and winked.

'He is going to ask one of the women to do something embarrassing,' commented Misael.

'No, it will be one of his jokes about testicles,' predicted Josef.

Don Emmanuel was playing the crowd. He raised a finger in the air and waggled it; he grimaced and opened his mouth to speak, only to close it again without saying anything. The crowd were in a fury of suspense, and Consuelo the whore cried 'Ay, ay, ay,' in desperation. She rolled her eyes, and tossed an egg at him.

The egg described a short arc through the air and cracked resoundingly against Don Emmanuel's forehead. 'Whooba,' shouted the crowd in evident delight, and they exclaimed it again when Don Emmanuel scraped the mess off his face with his fingers and ate all of it, including the shell, before their very eyes. Don Emmanuel patted his stomach in mock satisfaction, and belched lengthily, a trick he had learned at a progressive public school in England, before he had disappeared to this country. The advantages of his expensive education having been conclusively confirmed by the rapturous applause of the people, he finished his sentence, '. . . unless Consuelo gives me an egg.'

The people groaned with the bathos, and then heard Don Emmanuel's elegant solution to their conundrum.

Thus it was that early the next morning and on all the following mornings the fat, goat-loving, and squint-eyed man who used to be the policeman and the alcalde in Chiriguana went to each street in turn, closed his eyes, and blew very hard upon his whistle. The blindfolded people who were standing within their doors then simultaneously ejected their containers of dissolved spirits onto the street, to the satisfaction of all but the dogs, the chickens and the giant black jaguars, who very soon learned the Pavlovian art of skipping sharply sideways at the blast of a whistle.

By this expedient Don Emmanuel's reputation for sagacity was once again enhanced. It is also the case that he received anyway the kiss from Felicidad that he had been about to demand as his condition for divulging his plan, and in Consuelo's whorehouse he related to the company the story that he had been about to tell concerning the matador, the bull, and the cardinal's testicles.

21 *Dionisio Gets A Nocturnal Visit*

When all three of them were in the house they never bothered to lock the door at night. It was three o'clock in the morning and Dionisio was already gagged and bound before he had had a chance to wake up.

The two men wore hoods with slits cut for the eyes and mouth, and they did not say a word. They shone a torch in his eyes all the time so that he could not see anything, and he was so outraged that all he could do was kick out at them with his knees and feet.

The struggle lasted only a short time, because one of the men said, 'Oh, shit,' and coshed him across the side of the head with the barrel of a gun.

When he woke up again he was in a bare room, bound to a chair with his hands behind his back. He was thinking, 'So this is it,' when a big man came in still wearing a hood, and bearing a mug of water in one hand and a pistol in the other. Dionisio said, 'I need a piss,' thinking that in this way he might be unbound and be able to take a chance to escape, but the man said, 'Piss yourself then,' and offered the water up to his mouth. Dionisio took a mouthful, swallowed what he wanted, and spat the rest out at his captor. The big man recoiled and said, 'Spitting water will not stop us from cutting you into little pieces and giving you a necktie, my friend, so be polite or we will start on you before we intended, OK?'

Dionisio sat there for two days in the half-light and had to piss himself several times. He got used to the wet feeling and even grew to like the comfort of the warm sensation that the urine gave him when it first came out, but he would not let himself shit. In between getting used to the idea of torture and death he found himself having inconsequential thoughts about how spacemen go to the excusado when they are shut into the same suit for days on end. He thought a great deal about Anica, wondering what she was doing about his disappearance. He imagined Ramon comforting her, and even felt a little jealous of his arm around her shoulder and the way that he was wiping away her tears, but he thought that if he died it would be good if Anica could end up with Ramon. 'Ramon likes children,' he thought. He revolved his memories, thinking of Mama Julia and the General, his childhood in Ipasueno and his adolescence in Valledupar. He thought about the time that he had once climbed a mountain in order to be able to see out over the Caribbean, and how a fog had come down as soon as he had reached the top, thinking that that was a metaphor for life in general. He thought about how hungry he was and yet how he would probably be unable to eat under these circumstances. He remembered every incident of his relationship with Anica, and smiled about it even in his captivity, and he reckoned that his short life had only begun when she had turned up at the door with a camera and a beseeching expression.

On the second day two bodies were thrown into the room with him, and one of the hooded men said to him in a strange accent, 'The contemplation of death has a deeply humanising effect, don't you think?'

One of the bodies was of a black man, and the other was a mulatto. There were dark crimson patches of blood where the bullets had torn out of their backs, and he could see that the exit holes were cavernous. The flies were already busy laying eggs and creating a deafening buzz when the two assassins came in and dragged the bodies out again. One of the assassins was limping.

Having at first been in a state of fear and horrified anticipation, Dionisio later achieved an unexpected calm, and became reconciled to death. He reckoned that it would be like feeling all over what at present he felt in his hands, which was nothing at all because of the effect of being bound by the wrist for so long. He played a game with himself of trying to obliterate by willpower all the itches that normally one would be able to scratch, and sometimes he hung his head on his chest and slept, only to awake with a constricted feeling in his throat and a fierce desire to smoke.

On the third day the two men came in with submachine guns and one of them pointed his at Dionisio and cocked it. He raised it to his shoulder and planted his feet apart, and then pointed it downwards towards his victim's stomach. A cigar fell out of the end of it, and a voice behind the hood said, 'Have a smoke, Zeno.'

Dionisio was astonished and disbelieving. 'Ramon?' he said.

'El mismo,' exclaimed Ramon, whipping off his hood and performing a pirouette. Agustin took off his hood and smiled.

'You bastards,' said Dionisio, 'what is all this about?'

'We thought that we would give you a lesson in real life, Melissus.'

'You can't do that, I could sue you. This is abduction, armed kidnap with the use of violence or something. I swear that when you untie me I am going to rub your faces in dogshit.'

'In that case, Xenophanes,' said Ramon, 'we will not untie you until you have read this little piece of paper.' He drew out of his breast pocket a leaf of paper covered with official stamps and held it in front of Dionisio's face. He read 'Warrant of Protective Custody; Dionisio Vivo, Calle de la Constitucion, Ipasueño. It is hereby ordered that the above be taken into protective custody for a period of three days, the period to begin at the discretion of Officer Ramon Dario, Ipasueño Police. The above Dionisio Vivo may not be detained for any further periods without official renewal of this warrant.'

The warrant was signed by two judges and the Alcalde of Ipasueño, and countersigned by Ramon.

The latter folded the warrant and put it back into his pocket. 'I had this taken out months ago,' he said, 'and I kept it until I needed to use it, so forget about the dogshit,

Anaximander, and thank us for saving your life, and in particular thank Agustin for taking a bullet graze in the leg, and thank me for the bruises I got for these.' He held out two distorted bullets.

Dionisio looked at them and raised his eyebrows, 'Shit Ramon, are you bullet-proof?'

'I am with an armoured jacket on, Thales.'

'Who were the bodies, then?'

'They were the two who came to turn you into a sieve. You are very fortunate, my friend, that there are those in the employ of El Jerarca who understand that one day he will be on the losing side. They get themselves future pardons by supplying us with titbits of useful information. We awaited those two in your staircase, and gave them their last surprise. But I regret that some of your house is now full of bullet-holes, and we didn't get round to clearing up the blood.'

Dionisio turned pale, and all he could think of was, 'But what about my lectures, and Anica, and Jerez and Juanito? What did you do?'

'We cleared your two friends out, and it was very funny you know, because Juanito wanted to stay and join in the fun, and Jerez cleared out so fast that he fell down the stairs. We told Anica in advance, and your college Principal said something like "Oh well, it makes a change from bodies and hands in the garden," so as you see, everything was allowed for. And something else. OK, we shouldn't have tied you up and starved you, and we shouldn't have let you piss yourself, and we shouldn't have used force in the night, but,' and suddenly Ramon was vehement and very serious, 'you damn well needed a lesson in real life. This is the land of grown-ups, now, and if you have any sense you will move out, marry Anica, and go away and live in fairyland where you belong.'

When he was washed and fed, wearing borrowed clothes, smoking the cigar from Ramon's gun-barrel, and was being driven home in the police van, Dionisio said, 'Why have you never married, Ramon? Have you never wanted to? I see you everywhere being followed by children, and you should be a father.'

'These are bad times, Archelaus, and I see too many widows and orphans. Maybe in better times. There is nothing I would like more, my friend, but it is a mistake to marry in times of war. Everyone knows that.'

That evening when Dionisio had just finished counting thirty-four bullet-holes in his walls and was wondering what to do about them, Ramon arrived wearing old baggy trousers and carrying a bag full of materials. 'You wash the blood and I will do the walls,' he said.

Dionisio embraced him and said, 'I still think that you're a bastard.'

22 His Excellency Is Saved By The Intercession of The Archangel Gabriel

Foreign Secretary Lopez Garcilaso Vallejo burst into the presidential office in a high state of excitement. His tie was askew and his flabby forehead was dripping with perspiration. He waved his arms in a hyperbolical gesture, and then placed his hands upon the desk, exclaiming, 'Your Excellency, Your Excellency.'

President Veracruz looked up from the latest Rosicrucian monograph, in which he was being advised to change the colour of a candle flame by mere effort of will, and contemplated his dishevelled protégé. 'Lopez,' he said, 'why don't you ever knock? I am reading a confidential document that not even you can see.'

Lopez Garcilaso Vallejo and the President went back a long way. They had met during one of His Excellency's political exiles in the time of General Panela, when Señor Veracruz had been a frequent visitor to the 'stripclub' in Panama City. This was the same 'stripclub' where His Excellency had come to be acquainted with his young wife, who had been working there as an 'actress'. It may seem improbable that a young 'actress' and a distinguished middle-aged politician should have found true love in a brothel; some may contend that he married her for her youth and somewhat unprepossessing beauty, and that she had married him for his wealth and his political prospects. But the fact was that the two of them found in one another whatever was lacking in either of them alone, and very soon the future Señora Veracruz was refusing to charge him for her Panamanian expertise and declining to accept his presents, saying that she accepted him into her bed out of love alone. She cut back on her regular clientele whenever he was in town, and he in turn lost his taste for the variety offered by her colleagues.

Señor Vallejo had at that time been a manager at the club. He was well-adapted to this metier by virtue of his colossal size, intimidating aspect, and his encyclopaedic knowledge of the occult. This latter was an asset insofar as those who thought of giving him trouble did not do so for fear of falling impotent, losing their hair, or developing ulcers on their nether parts, all of which feats he was reputed to be able to perform with astonishing ease and rapidity. Naturally, he and Señor Veracruz had come to know each other quite well, and the former had ended up as Foreign Secretary through the natural operations of elective democracy and political patronage. His Excellency owed him the colossal debt of having been instructed by him in the hermetic arcana of sexual alchemy, and Señor Vallejo owed His Excellency the debt of having been allowed to publish at public expense all those weighty occult tomes that had been dictated to him personally by the Archangel Gabriel.

'OK, Lopez, what do you want?' asked the President. 'I hope it is important.'

Señor Vallejo sat down heavily and wiped his brow with a silk handkerchief. 'Listen,' he said, 'don't go to the Club Hojas tonight.'

'But I always go on Thursdays.'

'You can't, Your Excellency, I have had a message that it must be avoided.'

'And who did this message come from, Lopez?'

Señor Vallejo, slightly bashfully, pointed to the ceiling.

His Excellency looked up at the ceiling with a puzzled expression, and furrowed his brow. 'You mean you have a message from God? Are you serious?'

'Of course not, Your Excellency, I would not tell you anything so stupid.'

'I am glad to hear it, Lopez, I was fearing for your sanity. Who is it from, then?'

'Gabriel.'

The President ran through his memory to try to think who Gabriel was, gave up, and asked, 'Gabriel who?'

'The Archangel Gabriel, your Excellency. He came from the Tenth Heaven specifically to warn me to warn you not to go to the Club Hojas.'

'This Gabriel, why did he not tell me personally, and what did he look like? You know he could have been anybody, masquerading as an Archangel. I suspect you of credulity. Did you have him followed?'

'Your Excellency, I know it was the Archangel: he had one hundred and forty pairs of wings, and he was clothed in linen. He had an illuminated feminine silver head, a purple slender neck, golden yellow radiant arms with huge biceps, a delicate slate-grey torso, epicene legs in sky-blue, sort of whirling and scintillating, and he had women's blue feet. He was unmistakable, Your Excellency, and he distinctly told me – he has a lisp, you know – that you should not go to the Club Hojas.'

President Veracruz furrowed his brow ever more deeply, wondering, not for the first time, about the intellectual integrity of his Foreign Secretary. 'Did you count all the wings, to know that he had one hundred and forty pairs?'

'I knew that already, Your Excellency,' confessed Señor Vallejo. 'What clinched it was that he had a pair of scales in his hand and a horn slung across his shoulders. Also he always has clouds flowing across his face, with lots of flashes, like sheet lightning, and so I knew it was him.'

'I see,' said the President. 'Well, I don't know whether to believe you, but as I am a cautious man, and, as you know, not entirely narrow-minded about such things, I shall not go to the club. I shall also telephone the club and tell them to close tonight, just in case.'

The Foreign Secretary sighed and said, 'I can't tell you how pleased I am. If one ignores Gabriel's messages, he becomes extremely unpleasant. I once did that, and for six months he gave messages consisting entirely of the most revolting obscenities.'

That night, El Jerarca had the Club Hojas blown into fragments, and sent a telegram to *La Prensa* to claim the

89

credit. No one was killed, and one person was injured. This was Don Hugh Evans of Chiriguana, who had arrived very late, not having known that the club was closed for the evening. When he was twenty metres from the door the blast had sent him flying backwards, causing him to rick his neck upon colliding with a horse, which was itself miraculously unhurt by the huge Welshman's unprecedented impact.

His Excellency sent for the Foreign Secretary's security file, having concluded that he might have been warned not by Gabriel, but by someone inside the cartel who owed him a favour. But just in case, he burned four beeswax candles in honour of the Archangel, and, having lit them, he went to look up the word 'epicene' in the dictionary.

23 The Grand Candomble of Cochadebajo de los Gatos (4)

There were none of the dark gods invited; neither Iku, who is death, nor Ofo, who is loss; not Egba who is paralysis, nor Arun, who is disease; not Ewon, who is incarceration, and not Epe, who is malediction. These were frightened away by the incense, by the feverish making of talismans, and by the fact that everyone had been obeying Olofi's eleven commandments for an entire week.

It was evening in the city of Cochadebajo de los Gatos. Its ancient stones, stained by centuries of inundation, took on a gentle grey shade as the sun began its vertiginous descent behind the mountain, and people were taking gentle paseos and calling in on friends before the guemilere began. The enormous black jaguars, for which the city is famous, patrolled the streets and greeted each other nose to nose. Some of them were playfighting together in tangled heaps, knocking people over and terrifying the dogs and chickens. Others slept in odd places, as cats do; here was one stretched out on Pedro's roof, and here was another, draped along a wall with all its feet in the air in a most undignified fashion. There was one at the foot of one of the jaguar obelisks that lined the ingress to the city, sharpening its claws on the carved stone and seeming to be wrestling with it. Some were calling in on their favourite humans, rubbing their musky cheeks on people's thighs and cadging morsels to eat, and others were just sitting contemplatively, looking like Bast or Sekhmet, staring absently into the distance and occasionally blinking their eyes and yawning. These monarchic animals were completely tame, and were regarded by the inhabitants with a kind of friendly awe. Visitors to the city, however, were generally terrified of them, especially as the cats had an unerring intuition about who was scared of them, and used to go and try to sit on them and lick their faces with tongues like engineers' files. This would lead to comical scenes of panic in such people, and Misael and many others were of the opinion that the animals did it solely for amusement. The people were justly proud of their felines, and believed that this was a city set apart on their account.

When the first playing of the bata drums began, the cats became restless, as though sensing the presence of the gods. They went towards the sound and ringed the courtyard of what had once been the palace of the lords, which today was to be the ileocha of the ceremony.

The three drums of differing sizes spoke to each other in their reverberating voices, and suddenly the world grew dark. The torches flared and guttered. The great Okonkolo drum spoke unvaryingly, and the Iya and Itotele drums questioned and answered, commented and invoked over the top of its relentless tempo. The whole night seemed to be full of no other sound beneath the constellations.

Summoned by the oratory of the drums, the people began to converge upon the ileocha. They made the genuflection before the drums and the altar, they listened to Sergio, who today was the invoker of the deities, and they began to dance. This dance is the bambula. It is a wild dance, the dance in which the Orishas descend into the bodies of their devotees, and one always knows when that has happened, because remarkable phenomena occur. People hate it when a god takes them over; it is not for nothing that they call it the 'asiento' when they are initiated, because it feels like being hagridden. One loses control and one's soul flees the body to make space for the saint, so that afterwards people have to tell you what you did and what you said.

Sergio had before him on the table the skull of his twin brother Juanito; it had been well-cleaned by the termites in its grave before Sergio had dug it up, and one could clearly see the place on the temple where the fragment of army grenade had punched its way through to the brain all that time ago. Sergio hired out the head for sorcery, and he brought it along today because Juanito had always enjoyed a good candomble.

Sergio was invoking Eshu, because Eshu is the messenger of the Orishas; he fetches the Orishas, and without him no work can prosper. Before the altar was a head of Eshu, made of cowrie shells, and before the head was an offering of coconuts, a twisted forked branch, some scraps of smoked possum, and a whistle made of cana brava. There was also a large pot filled with black and red stones. Over the stones had been poured a brew of thirteen herbs, which included abre camino, pata de gallino, and itamo real. There was also goat blood, the blood of a mouse, and the blood of a black chicken. Some of this delicious and health-giving brew had been drunk in advance by those believing in the power of such omieros. For each of the Orishas who had been invited there was such a tureen filled with the correct stones and omiero, prepared especially by the initiates of each one, the sacrifices having been performed only by those who had received the initiation of the knife. The animals were slaughtered in the name of Oggun according to the ritual formula, 'Oggun choro choro,' for Oggun is the god of violence and of steel, and it is he who kills and not the wielder of the knife.

Sergio called upon Eshu in the language handed down by the slaves: 'Ibarakou mollumba Elegua . . .' His voice trembled and wavered against the night, rising into a wail. But nothing happened. Everyone knows, however, that Eshu is the Orisha of mischief, and no one doubted that he was present; he was merely pretending not to be. Sergio repeated the invocation '. . . Elegua kulona. Ibarakou Mollumba . . .' And then Eshu arrived in style.

There was a very old man named Gomez who had only barely managed to survive the migration. He walked with a stick and talked with a wheezy whistle through the teeth. Yet here he was, foaming at the mouth and convulsing upon the packed earth, and here he was, leaping amongst the dancers and performing flamboyant handsprings, pinching backsides, tweaking noses, and jumping on the tables backwards.

93

'Ache,' cried the people in greeting, and Sergio also cried 'Ache, Eshu, Ache. Tell the Orishas that we are prepared, and tell us, Eshu, what it is that you would give to the Deliverer.'

The body of Gomez arched and backflipped, and Eshu grinned his sly grin which always strikes the stranger as malicious. In a voice as deep as the rumbling of an avalanche he gave the reply, '*I will steal from him what he should not have, I will spare him from the accidents with which I feed Oggun, I will open up the roads for him.*'

'Moddu cue,' said Sergio, which is to say 'thank you', and Eshu disappeared, leaving Gomez in a puzzled heap upon the floor, until Eshu returned once more with the other saints and again made Gomez his horse, returning him to the indefatigable dance.

Felicidad's dance became wild. She was an initiate of Chango, who is also Santa Barbara, and he is famous for his philanderings. Felicidad was beautiful, and today she wore Chango's necklace, having alternately six red and six white beads, which matched her dress in Chango's colours. She was whirling to the bata drums, her black hair whipping about her face, when Chango emerged from his wooden batea bowl full of thunderstones and ram's blood, snail juice and palm oil.

Chango took over Felicidad with a terrible blow that sent her sprawling to the floor before he rose. 'Ache,' the people shouted, 'Kabio, kabio sile,' which is 'Welcome to my house.'

'Ache, Chango,' said Sergio, 'and what do you give to the Deliverer?'

Chango pointed his forefinger to the sky and said in his basso profondo voice, '*I give him my thunder, and I give him my bolt of lightning that is in my fingers.*'

'Moddu cue, Chango,' and he danced on in Felicidad's frame, enjoying the party and eyeing up the women.

*

And now it was Leticia Aragon, who had strayed to Cocha-debajo de los Gatos while following her vague itinerary towards Ipasueno. She had been here for several weeks and everyone already accepted her and her unusual ways. Already they would come to her when anything was lost, so that she could find it, and they would look into her face with puzzlement, trying to name the colour of her eyes, and wondering how it was that her hair was fine as cobweb.

When Oshun arrived and took possession of Leticia, her dance became like the flowing of a stream. The people crossed themselves because Oshun is not only Orisha of love, but is also Nuestra Señora de La Caridad del Cobre, decked out in copper and gold. Leticia was robed in yellow because Oshun is so particular about cleanliness that her clothes turn that colour from being washed every day in the river. Oshun is in love with Chango, and so she went to dance with him as he leapt in Felicidad's body, offering him her honey, and showing him the red beads in her gold necklace that she wears for him. Oshun would not address the guemilere until she had tasted of the ochinchin which was prepared for her, the dense omelette made of cress and shrimps that had been skimmed from the streams of the cordillera.

'Ache, Cachita,' the people called, using her pet name, and Sergio asked his question, to which she replied, '*I give him the love of many of my sex, so that he will be consoled for she who shall be taken off, and I give him pleasures to redeem his sorrows.*' And Oshun, being vain and proud of her beauty, threw off her clothes and danced naked amongst the crowd, sinuous and fluid, while the drums renewed the discourse of their conversation.

Sergio summoned her sister Yemaya. 'Ache, Yemaya,' and she too danced over to Chango in Francesca's body, for although she was his mother she had had an affair with him without knowing who he was, and so their greeting was only a little like the embrace of a mother and a son. She also greeted her sister, whose children were in her care, swaying

95

and circling like the waves of the sea. Her necklace was seven crystals and seven blue beads, and on her belt Francesca wore a representation of the crescent moon. *Yemaya gave the Deliverer many children who would always bear the mark of his paternity*.

There was an earthenware vessel which contained turtle blood, glass balls, deer horns, rainwater of the month of May, peppers, Holy Water, river and sea water. It had been buried for six days beneath a palm and six days beneath a ceiba, and had been blessed by Eshu at a crossroad. From this vessel Osain came forth.

Pedro the Hunter was dressed in nothing but blood plastered with chicken feathers, and Osain knocked his legs from under him because Osain has only one leg and walks with a crutch. Misael gave a twisted forked branch to Pedro, and he danced with it upon one leg. *He gave the Deliverer the art of cures*.

Who else appeared at the tambor? Eshu came in five of his paths, Eshu Alabwanna, Eshu Aye, Eshu Barakeno, who turned an old man into a child, Eshu Anagui, who turned a child into an old man, and Eshu Laroye, who hid behind a door. Obatala came dressed in white, *giving incorruptibility and the gift of creativity*, as befits his identity as the Virgin Mary and Jesus of Nazareth. He was cold and trembling because he lives in the sierra, and he danced shuffling while the people called 'Hekua, baba, hekua,' which is 'Blessings, Father, blessings.'

Osun came, promising *to be a guardian angel*, and Yegua, saying that she would control *the transition of death*, and Inle, who is the Archangel Raphael, giving *healing when the Deliverer would be wounded*. Obba said that *the family of the Deliverer would be faithful to him*, and the Jimaguas who are Saint Cosme and Saint Damian came, but *they gave no gift*, since prosperity is all that they have to offer. Orisha-Oko, decked in pink and blue beads, who is Saint Isidro Labrador, gave *stability that would overcome madness*, and there was also Oya. She was pleased with the hens and goats that she had been offered, and she swore that *the Deliverer should not be destroyed by the fire* that she shared with Chango, her estranged husband. She is Saint Teresa and Nuestra Señora de la Candelaria, and she always wears robes as red as wine. She is so fond of flowers that she does not allow her initiates to wear them, keeping them all to herself. Her necklace is brown and red and white, and as soon as she saw Yemaya they began to fight, because Yemaya swindled her out of the sea and gave her a cemetery instead. The assembly was therefore treated to the spectacle of Francesca and Dolores the whore engaged in vicious combat, overturning each other's tureens, rolling up the straw petate mats and coshing each other over the head. It took Chango to break up the fight, because he was Oya's first husband, and he knew that to frighten her off, all he had to do was to show her a ram's skull. Later in the fiesta Oya took revenge by stealing Juanito's skull, and dangling it before Chango's eyes, whereupon he fled, screaming, because what he fears the most is a human skull.

There came all at once the three Orishas with whom Oshun had had love affairs before she fell in love with Chango: Oggun, Ochosi, and Orunla. Oggun is Eshu's best friend, and Eshu arranges car crashes for his friend so that he can consume the blood. He is the Orisha of slaying and bloodshed, and therefore he never rests, walking the earth vigilantly by day and night, and he is the Orisha of metals and the weapons made of them. As soon as he arrived he made a beeline for Oshun, with whom he is still desperately in love even though nowadays she loves only Chango, preferring passion to violence. His colours used to be sanguine, but he lost his reds to Chango, just as he lost his love, so that now he has black and green. Oggun is Saint Peter, who once cut off a man's ear with a sword; for this reason Oggun wears a machete and his straw sombrero in addition to his skirt made of mariwo. He is a lover of dogs, and when he came the first thing he did, after flirting with Oshun and spitting at Chango, was to pick up a prodigious mastiff in his arms and cuddle it. To the Deliverer he gave *mastery of fatal force*.

Ochosi, lover of deer and master of the crossbow, also took possession of Pedro, so that Osain rode Misael instead. He is the patron of hunters, Saint Norbert, and he has learned medicine from his constant friend, Osain, which is also the reason why the latter allowed him to ride Pedro. He drank his offering of milk, honey and maize meal, and he thanked the people for the sacrifice of pigeons. What he gave to the Deliverer was *justice as the reward for his endeavour*.

Orunla was once the Orisha of dance, but he swapped the gift with Chango, in exchange for divination. He is a misogynist; he manifests in the intellect only and never makes his horse do crazy things. He is Saint Francis of Assisi, and once upon a time he tricked Death into avoiding anyone who wears his green and yellow beads. On this day he gave the Deliverer *prescience, to make him strong against the future, and the ability to trick Iku, Lord of death*. Before he left he had an altercation with Yemaya, who was once his wife, and who had humiliated him by divining with the cowrie shells better than he.

Most terrible, Aganyu made a rare appearance. He kissed his son, Chango, with whom he had once quarrelled but become reconciled. He is Saint Christopher, and despite his ferocious temper he gave the Deliverer his *relentless anger of a volcano, and its power of destruction*.

Saint Lazarus came, leaning decrepitly upon a staff. He is Babalu-Aye, and he is a beggar struck with every contagious disease; because he is so poor he dresses in sackcloth and eats only toasted corn. He also loves dogs, and he shares confidences with Eshu and Orunla. Now that Olofi has cured him with purifying rain, he has become a great lover, and as he knows the cure of diseases he is able to heal syphilis with sarsaparilla and cleanse a house with albahaca and apasote. His colour is the violet of diseased flesh, and he is not without a sense of humour, which is why he took over Hectoro, who counted himself an unbeliever and who, even if he had believed, would not have allowed his dignity to be diminished even by being mounted by a god. The reason for this mischievous choice eventually became clear. He not only promised that *the Deliverer's enemies should succumb to terrible disease*, but also said that *the Deliverer would be given the sexual prowess of a horse*. Everyone laughed, especially Eshu and the libidinous Chango, because everyone knew that Hectoro kept three wives at a safe distance from each other, and serviced all of them regularly.

And so the candomble raged for three days. The people danced to the bata drums without resting and without tiring, they drank prodigiously, love affairs flowered in the darkness and in the corners of the courtyards, and they ate the offerings with indecent greed once the Orishas had extracted their essence. The black jaguars of the city lounged amongst the dancers, chewed upon abandoned bones, and got in the way of the gods.

The world is well-stocked with legends of the times when deities walked the earth and when saints performed miracles in Jesus' name. For the most part these legends are a quaint echo of nostalgia for times which now seem naive. But for the population of Cochadebajo de los Gatos and for millions of santeros of all races and colours all over the Hispanic Western hemisphere they walk the earth in broad daylight, still performing miracles, still discoursing with ordinary folk, still arguing, fighting, having love affairs, dispensing favours and punishments, still being greeted by cries of 'Ache.'

They still indulge their tastes too; just look at Francesca, who today is Yemaya, on her hands and knees looking everywhere for cockroaches to cram into her mouth. She is eating them with a delight that is almost too sensual, and it is making Chango feel aroused. The other Orishas are trying to prevent her, because, as everyone knows, they employ cockroaches as their messengers.

24 *Anica's Journal* (1)

Dionisio's fan letters are increasing at a surprising rate as the days go by. They increased from two on the second day to two sackfuls in the second week, so that we cannot really keep up with the work of reading them. We have been classifying them into three piles, one for letters of support, one for declarations of Platonic love, and the other for declarations of carnal intent. These letters are all forwarded through the good offices of *La Prensa*, who have written to D. and told him that they are processing them in their usual way through their X-ray machine. They say they have found fifteen letters packed with plastic explosive, and four gifts of booby-trapped alarm clocks.

We composed a universal letter of tactful rejection for those who desire his child, and a universal letter of sincere appreciation for the others, and had one thousand of each printed at a discount by the printers who normally produce all that propaganda for the four communist parties of differing views who are always attacking each other. It has cost D. so much in postage that in the end I lent him the money to bribe that man at the town hall to process them through the municipal franking machine.

I am beginning to find all this very threatening and uncomfortable, and so is D., I think. Last night in bed he suddenly got frightened and said to me, 'Anica, I sometimes have the terrible sensation that I am merely a part of your history.'

I was startled, and I said to him, 'Oh querido, what does that mean?' even though I sort of knew what he meant already.

He looked at me and I think he did not say what he meant,

because he said, 'All the people that I knew when I was your age are now just a part of my history.'

I think that maybe at last he is taking all these threats seriously, and has some premonitions (too strong a word – 'intimations' is a better word, the kind that he likes to use) of death. I wanted to cry for some reason, and I said, 'Has it ever occurred to you that I might just be a part of your history?' His eyes were glowing in the dark, and I think they would not have glowed like that if he had not been almost crying himself. I was leaning over him and he touched me and said, 'Your breast is like a nocturnal animal, I will always remember the way that it is brushing against my chest.' It was just as if he was about to say goodbye. I have started praying for the first time since Mama died.

Yesterday we had a strange experience. We were just walking along when we saw an Aymara Indian (what is an Aymara doing around here?). He was in full national dress and had trenzas, and he had that proud look about him that makes you feel too unimportant to be worth knowing. He was with a very tall old negro who had more muscles than would seem possible, but he had a nice face and grey hair, and he had one of those campesino machetes with the leather tassels on the sheath. The strange thing was that they both were leading a huge black jaguar on a string.

There were some people there, and they all scattered as if they had seen the devil. But D. is crazy about animals and I swear he is telepathic with them. I have lost count of the times that dogs have just come up to him, and once I met him in the plaza and he was sitting on a wall with a cat on his knee, and two horses and a burro and three dogs all there as well. I keep telling him that he will get fleas and rabies one of these days, but he laughs at me. I think he enjoys getting on with animals because it is one of the things that makes the people around here believe that he is some kind of sorcerer.

As soon as D. saw the jaguars he got terribly excited. I tried to stop him but he just walked up and introduced himself to the Indian and the negro. The negro was someone called Misael, but my heart jumped when I heard that the Indian was Aurelio, who is famous for sorcery around here. They say that he cures even cancers, and they say that the cats of Cochadebajo de los Gatos were a kind of unexpected side-effect of one of his healing sessions. Everyone is terrified of him, including me.

D. asked him if the cats were two of the famous tame black jaguars of Cochadebajo de los Gatos. The negro, Misael, just nodded, but the Indian, Aurelio, sort of narrowed his eyes and took a deep suck on his coca pestle. I am trying to remember exactly what he said. It was something like, 'You are in three kinds of danger.' D. laughed and said, 'Everyone says that, but I believe none of it,' and Aurelio narrowed his eyes again and said, 'One is that you think you know everything, which is what causes the second danger, which is that you will not understand anything, and the third danger is that death will come in the wrong place, and unexpectedly.'

I could see from D's smile that he wanted to ridicule the old man, and I was truly frightened that he would. D. pretends that he only believes in what he can see or touch, but I know that that is a fraud. I know him better than that. Thank God he did not ridicule him, but he started to talk about those cats. He said, 'Why do you lead the cats on a string too weak to hold them?' and Misael explained that it was because when people see the cats walking behind, they think that they are stalking the two of them, and the people shoot at the cats, so they keep the cats on a string to show that they are with them and not hunting them. I didn't put that very well.

D. looked at the cats, and I just knew that he was going to go down on his knees and stroke them. I nearly shit myself. Those cats were so huge, and one of them was licking its lips, and they say that only someone who knows the cats already or is a brujo can safely stroke them. I tried to pull him back, but he did just as I thought he would, and I called him a fool, but he did it anyway.

He put a hand on each of the cats' heads and he talked to them as though they were children, saying 'How are you?' and things like that. One of them licked his hand, and he looked up at me with that triumphant grin of his and he said, 'This cat likes my salt.' He scratched the other one under the chin and round the ears, and then it went up on its back legs and put its feet on his shoulders. D. fell over backwards, and I seriously thought for a second that it was going to rip his throat out. I didn't know what to do, and truly I nearly did shit myself all over again, but the next thing I see D. is rolling around in the road having a wrestling game with that monster, and he is laughing away like he is being tickled. Then he just stands up and nods at the two men, and comes back to me as though nothing had happened, except that all the way home he kept going on about the way the cats smelled fusty and sweet, that it was a beautiful smell, and on and on.

Anyway, before we left I distinctly heard Misael say to Aurelio, 'Is that the man?' and the Indian said, 'Yes, that is the man.' I thought that they wanted me to hear because otherwise they would have waited, wouldn't they?

The news of what D. did certainly spread fast, because today everyone in town was crossing themselves when we walked past, and saying prayers and despachos. D. didn't know anything about Aurelio at all, and when I explained who he was and what he does he just laughed at me and made me feel stupid. I am beginning to think that D. doesn't understand anything about himself. He is like a priest who does not know that he believes in God, or something. He scares me sometimes. I asked him if he had seen the beautiful daughter with the ocelot who often goes around with Aurelio, but who is invisible to ordinary people, and he just made me feel stupid again.

I am very tired and very confused. Sometimes I wonder what I am doing with D. I must be mad. Everyone tells me that it is suicide to go around with him, and yet I stay with him even though I know that they are right. I love him, but

I haven't told him that yet, and yet even though we are sweethearts we never discuss the dangers or even the coca trade when we are together. I think that for him it is a solitary kind of passion, and I don't dare to try to challenge him over it, even though I always get my way in everything else.

People are telling me that D. really is a brujo, and that is why he has me under his spell. I laugh at them and make them feel stupid, just as D. does to me, but there is so much that puzzles me and makes me think. I swear that he really did grow enormous when he nearly killed those thieves, or certainly he looked as though he did, and I can't understand why he gets away with the way he plays with dangerous animals, and the other thing is that whenever he touches me it is like a little electric shock. And why are his hands always so warm?

This is the end of the tenth volume of my diary, and five of them I have written in the time that I have been with D. I haven't written so much since I took the baccalaureat.

25 El Jerarca

El Jerarca was having problems. In the first place, although he was only fifty-two years old he was already beginning to suffer the inevitable doubts and insecurities of old age. He had himself examined by his doctors once upon rising in the mornings and once upon retiring at night, and having learned from a lifetime of double-dealing that no one could be trusted, he never believed what they told him, so that he would imagine symptoms that he did not have, and then look them up in a medical encyclopaedia, so that eventually he exhausted the possibilities and had to start all over again.

His doctors told him that a lifetime of over-eating had corrupted his digestive system to such an extent that it no longer mattered what he ate. They told him that he was so overweight that as a matter of humanity he should give up riding his famous grey stallion, which had taken up a bowed appearance in its back and had become too depressed to be put out to stud. They told him that his heart was so inflated and distorted that its clockwork only continued to function out of being too unimaginative to stop. They told him that he should discontinue his practice of making love at least once a day, but were repeatedly reminded by him that at the age of twenty-one he had made an irrevocable vow that not one day should pass without at least one bout of intercourse, and that it was a matter of personal honour. He was also privately convinced that if he gave up the practice it would diminish the lustre of his personal legend and cause a proportional diminution of his power over his organisation. His doctors told him that his repeated doses of venereal maladies had weakened his immune system to such an extent that the only reason that he was not bedridden was that his body now lacked the mechanisms for manifesting symptoms. His doctors considered that his flesh was so rotten that in private they had organised a betting system amongst themselves as to whether or not he would begin to be consumed by maggots before he had actually died.

Apart from the decrepitude of his body, he was also suffering the anxiety of knowing that despite his incalculable wealth he was marching towards death in the certain knowledge that he would die unloved and unrespected and unlamented; that his death was already being preceded by a gathering of vultures; that finally his life had been more meaningless and less satisfactory than that of a congenital moron without limbs and without reproductive organs.

This unhappiness caused him to become ever crueller, as though cruelty could prove that he had a hold on life, and he began to be caught between a fantasy of immortality and a blossoming love-affair with his own prospective death. But as his cruelty augmented, his grip upon the means of cruelty was faltering.

And this was all because of the accursed and quixotic Dionisio Vivo, who had stirred both the fears and the conscience of the political elite to such an extent that even his most assiduous receivers of gratuities within that elite had begun to become miraculously difficult to contact even when the size of their gratuities was increased. They continued to accept his inducements, but the goods were never delivered. El Jerarca was also aware that all over the country Dionisio Vivo societies were springing up and organising pressure groups which were threatening not to re-elect any officials who did not take concrete action against the cartels in their districts, so that the business of keeping everything ticking over quietly was becoming increasingly problematical. He was completely unaware that Dionisio Vivo had really very little to do with this, because he failed to recognise that in fact an ardent longing for order and peace had already been growing in the country for years, after the bloody exhilarations of civil wars and rampant gangsterism had finally begun to lose their appeal. In other words a certain maturity of civilisation had manifested itself and had hooked onto Dionisio Vivo's letters like a creeper in the jungle which had finally produced white blossoms and havens for tiny hummingbirds and morpho butterflies.

But El Jerarca blamed Dionisio Vivo personally. Nonetheless, for the first time in his life he was powerless, for his men were either refusing outright to do away with him, or were pretending to go after him and then finding excuses for having failed. Those who refused he shot down in his own office, but now it was becoming difficult to summon his lieutenants precisely because of that, and they always sent messengers to say that they were just setting off on a mission that he himself had ordered them to perform but which he could not remember having commanded them to do. He started to wonder whether his own memory was failing or whether he was the victim of a conspiracy to make him think that it was.

The problem was no more nor less than the conviction in the minds of his men that Dionisio Vivo was an invulnerable sorcerer. One of his men had encountered the two thieves by coincidence when visiting Guaraguana and had come back with the story of Dionisio Vivo's fearsome ability to grow gigantic and break people apart like sticks of candy, and it was well known that he was a master of invisibility, could overwhelm magnetic force without thinking about it, and was able to disport himself with the mythological black jaguars of Cochadebajo de los Gatos in front of Aurelio the Brujo himself. It had been greatly put about that anyone attempting to wound him would suffer in his own body the wounds intended for the other.

El Jerarca was himself a superstitious man; he felt the necessity to go to Mass every Sunday and to go to confession, not because he was possessed of a genuine sense of religious awe nor a personal intuition of the parenthood of God, but because he had always done so since a child, and felt that it would be bad luck to stop, especially in a country where the mere fact of going to church was commonly taken to be the outward and visible sign of perfect purity of soul. For the iniquities he had committed either personally or by proxy he rattled off Ave Marias in much the same spirit as an Irishman spits upon seeing a magpie or an Englishman bows three times to the new moon, turns his money over in his pocket, and performs a pirouette. Having confessed his crimes to priests in gilded robes who did not bother even to listen, he always enjoyed the sensation of having had his slate wiped clean so that he could begin to write upon it anew, and this was the nearest he ever came to spiritual refreshment or moral renewal.

El Jerarca was as superstitious as all men are who live in perpetual insecurity and distrust; he always rode only a grey stallion, always drank from the same mug, and always looked under his bed before climbing into it. He had a significant collection of talismans and amulets against every foreseeable eventuality, and had his tame priests bless them every year on the day of the Feast of St Michael and All Angels to insure them against loss of efficacy. Thus the voodoo fetishes, shrunken heads, and morsels of dehydrated animal from Brazil had the nature spirits within them annually subjected to the confusing ordeal of being sanctified by a faith that explicitly excoriated them.

Because he was superstitious and because he had begun to believe the stories told about Dionisio Vivo he became reluctant to carry on ordering him to be killed, mainly on account of the statement of one of his priests that to cause another to commit a crime was the same as committing it oneself. He reasoned therefore that if wounds appeared in the body of the assailant which were intended for Dionisio Vivo, then the same wounds would appear in his own body as would appear in that of the immediate perpetrator of the crime. He therefore caused to be constructed a large bullet-proof steel box, covered it with dedicated altar cloths, and had it censed and then blessed by his priests in the name of the Father, the Son, and the Holy Ghost, and St Barbara for good measure. His intention was to sit inside it during the moments when Dionisio Vivo was to be shot, so that no bullets visible or invisible could harm him at the critical moment. All that remained for him to do was to offer someone so much money to do it that greed would overcome the fear of instantaneous retribution. It turned out to be nearly the biggest hit-money that anyone had ever offered in Hispano-America, because no one would do it for any less. And even despite this, it took the young man several days to bring himself to attempt the assassination.

Anica and Dionisio were due to meet Ramon just before sunset so that they could all have a meal together, but they were very early, so they went on a little paseo just to observe the custom and to see if anything was happening. Anica said that she had just heard that she had been accepted by the university, and he was angry when she said that she would take a room in a student hall, because he knew that they guarded the chastity of the inmates as though they were royal virgins. She said she had already checked it out and that it was very easy to break the rules, especially at weekends. He recovered his temper and told her that it was a good idea to go in a hall because one made a very great many instant friends, and he was happy as long as it did not interfere with their affair. She skipped ahead, pulling him by the hand, and she said, 'And why should it?' He tried to kiss her but she pushed him away, calling him an 'old bastard' and saying that she knew too many people around there, so he said, 'It is not that, it is that you are too shy.' Then he said, 'Would you mind if I applied to do a Master's degree at the university? I was offered a place years ago and I never took it up. Would you think I was chasing after you too hard?' Anica laughed and said, 'No, I would like it very much.' He said, 'This is the first thing I have had for many years that I want to preserve. We should never let this rot away.'

They took a table out in the street, and while they waited for Ramon they watched the old men playing tejo and drinking chicha, even though the latter was illegal on account of its degenerative effects. Anica smoked a cigarette in her elegant manner, and Dionisio fetched the drinks and sat beside her, watching out for Ramon, who was always late because he was conscientious in his job. He strolled over to the old men and told them they had better hide the chicha because his friend who was arriving was a serious lawman, so they thanked him and carried on drinking it anyway.

'Hola, my little Anaxagoras,' said Ramon, raising his hand and then reaching it out to shake Dionisio's. He leaned over to kiss Anica on both cheeks and squeeze her just enough to pretend that he was trying to make Dionisio jealous. He sat down with his eyes sparkling and said, 'Vale, Amigo, what eternal truths have you discovered today while I was going about the humble task of bringing order to society?'

'I have confirmed the truth of a proposition of Diogenes the Cynic, who said that when one's best friend is an intellectual policeman, one will inevitably become the victim of sarcasm.'

'Very true,' replied Ramon. 'Diogenes was wise enough to know that the carrying of a legal firearm on one's hip inclines one to put on airs. Have you thought about what I said to you?'

Dionisio smiled and said, 'I am still obstinate,' so Ramon replied, 'And the evidence is, I suppose, not good enough?'

'In this country, my Cochinillo, everyone knows that the evidence of a policeman is the direct contrary to the truth.'

Ramon stroked his stubble as usual when he was thinking of a riposte. 'Just as everyone knows that the opinion of a philosopher is never remotely connected to the real world, eh cabron?'

They ordered a sancocho to eat between them, and it was just turning dark when the sicario appeared at the far end of the street.

The Alcalde of Ipasueño had recently made it illegal to

wear visors on motorcycles because the assassins of the coca-lords had developed a method of assassination which was almost foolproof, since all one had to do was to ride up to the victim on an unmarked motorcycle wearing a visor, fire one or two bullets, and then disappear at high speed before anybody could react. The incidence of these murders had increased to such an extent that whenever a motorcyclist with a visor appeared in the streets everybody automatically flung themselves to the ground or dived for doorways. The disruption to daily life caused by these dramatic scenes obliged the mayor to pass the law so that people could distinguish between innocent travellers and real murderers.

The man on the motorcycle was wearing a visor. He had followed the couple all day on foot, waiting for a time when they would be sitting targets and chewing his nails down to the cuticles in his nervousness. He was thinking of returning to El Jerarca with the report that he could not find Dionisio, or perhaps bribing him with half of the money to pretend that he was dead, or perhaps going back with the story that the bullets had just bounced off. He had drunk so much beer in order to work up his courage that he desperately needed to piss, but could not relax enough to do it, so that his bladder was aching, his hands were shaking, and he had said fifty-four Ave Marias by the time that he commenced his ride of death.

Ramon had sauntered inside to fetch some chilli to liven up the sancocho, and was just coming out when the street started to clear and even the dogs shot under the tables. From the doorway Ramon saw the sicario coming, and with a deft movement he undid the flap of his holster and drew out his revolver, cocking it at the same time. From the shadow of the door he had already taken up the firing position by the time the sicario had stopped opposite Dionisio and kicked the footgear into neutral. Ramon was just about to fire when the intended victim stood up and faced the sicario for lack of knowing what else to do, and blocked Ramon's line of sight, so that he shouted to him to get down.

The sicario drew out his automatic and levelled it at Dionisio, and the latter noticed with numb astonishment that the hand that held the gun was shaking so violently that the barrel was waving around. Despite his danger he was too paralysed to move, but Anica, seeing at last that the reality that she had striven so hard to exclude from possibility was finally forcing its way into the world, blocked all her fear from her mind and stepped in front of Dionisio. For a moment he was yet paralysed, but then he took her shoulders and threw her sideways, going down after her a split second later.

Ramon and the sicario fired at exactly the same moment. Dionisio as he fell felt a hornet's sting and a mule's kick and a coral snake's bite in the outer flesh of his right arm as the bullet burned a tear in his shirt, creased along the flesh, and thudded into the doorpost behind which Ramon was concealed. Ramon's bullet in its turn took away the outer flesh of the arm of the assassin, and he nearly dropped his motorcycle, only just retrieving it in time to jam it frantically into gear and roar away as Ramon fired two more shots in his wake.

Ramon strolled out into the street to pick up the weapon that the sicario had dropped. He came back with it, and deposited it on the table in front of Dionisio who was just standing up and leaning down to help Anica, who had bruised her head on the table. 'Here is your evidence, Aristotle,' he said.

The sicario went back and reported to El Jerarca that the stories about Dionisio Vivo were true, and that one suffered in one's own flesh the wounds intended for him. He showed his bloodied arm to prove it. Everyone who had been present knew perfectly well that the sicario had been shot by the unseen policeman behind the door, but no one wanted to believe a story of such banality, and anyone who related it was shouted down and ridiculed until even they began to believe the mythologised version. What impressed people even more with Dionisio's invulnerability and preternatural power was that he refused to go to a doctor, and sat down and finished his sancocho with blood running down his arm, boasting to everyone within listening distance of how courageous his woman was. She was still in shock, and she put her arm around him and huddled closely so that his blood soaked into her breast.

Despite his elaborate metaphysical precautions, El Jerarca, upon hearing the outcome of the attempt, felt a sharp pain in his arm that lasted for several days.

26 *Leticia Aragon (1)*

Leticia had been born unusual. To begin with she arrived in the world with the expression of a contented nun, and did not cry when she was inverted and slapped across the buttocks by Mama Florencia the midwife. In the second place, the birth-slime was not bloody and pink and white, but was lime-green and sweet-smelling. Mama Florencia assumed at first that Leticia had been stillborn, and she was wondering how to break the news to the mother when Leticia smiled and blew a large bubble.

Her mother was thrilled with Leticia, with her full head of jet-black hair finer than gossamer and her eyes that seemed to be all colours at once. Never had a child been so amenable and easy. She slept for hours at all the most convenient times, did not make her mother's nipples sore, and did not foul herself unless there were clean nappies in the laundry baskets. When she did fill her nappies, it was with excrement that smelled of mangoes and jackfruit.

Leticia did not talk until she was three years old, and some people were beginning to say that she was mute; but then one day she was sitting under the table while her family ate refritos in the company of friends, and she said something. The story goes that the company was discussing the President's chances at the next election, and her father was saying, 'I think that the conservatives will get in,' when a reedy little voice from down below said, 'I doubt that very much.' Such amazement fell upon them that they searched the room high and low for a ventriloquist, and Leticia's mother said, 'If one did not know better, one would have to assume that the child had spoken,' whereupon she came out from under the table and said very vehemently, 'So what if I did?'

It is well known of course that some children wait until

they have something sensible to say before they utter their first sentence, but Leticia seemed to have been born with her intellectual apparatus already brimming with knowledge. She performed such staggering feats of prowess that it became a common pastime in the pueblo to try to catch her out. People would ask her, 'In what year did General Panela assume the dictatorship? Who was the Commander of the Navy in the first times of the disappearances? What was the name of the padre here in 1941?' and Leticia would furrow her brow, think hard while moving her lips, and come out with the correct answer. So prodigious was her knowledge that she was examined by the cura, Don Tomaso, for the possibility of being possessed by the Devil. But at the conclusion of his investigation he found himself left with no alternative but to state that in his opinion her genius could only be explained either by the hypothesis that the Platonic theory of anamnesis was true, or else by reincarnation. For this opinion he came under the severest strictures from the bishop, who, it is said, passed him over for promotion forever afterwards, and always referred to him as 'that damnable Hindu'.

As she grew older it was with the greatest difficulty that Leticia could be persuaded to remain clothed. She would go out in the morning to play in the platano plantation, and would return in the evening stark naked. Her parents would search desperately for the garments, and Leticia would try to remember what had happened to them, but to no avail, and eventually it became clear by experimentation that she could only remain clothed in raiment that was of a turquoise colour and made of cotton.

Leticia liked to wander around in a dream, and it was this as much as her black hair and her delicate bones that gave her the air of extraordinary beauty. It was not the kind of beauty that makes a man priapic, the beauty of a Bahian mulatta; it was the kind of beauty that is like a blow in the stomach and which physically hurts the eyes. Even when Leticia was very small Mama Florencia was fond of saying, 'There will be men who die out of love for that girl, wait and see.' But no one could have foreseen who would be the first to die.

Leticia Aragon was a being so far from this world that it surprised no one that extraordinary events followed her about like fireflies tied to a Cubana's hat. When she was small her mother never seemed to be able to find anything, even when it had been put down in a clearly-remembered place only minutes before. This drove Señora Aragon perfectly loca with frustration and irritation, and eventually she went to see the babalawo, who cast shells and told her very confidently that no, she was not going prematurely senile, she should look not to herself but to her daughter.

From then on Señora Aragon observed her daughter, and discovered that all her missing possessions were in Leticia's hammock. In a fury, she grabbed her child and beat the living daylights out of it, and this was the first and only time that Leticia ever cried. 'Mama, it's not my fault,' she sobbed as her mother locked her in the chicken house, to be fed upon maize meal and water as her punishment for being a thief and a prankster.

Leticia settled in very well in the chicken house and was soon covered in droppings from when the cockerel stood upon her head in order to crow in a more lordly fashion. But in the three days of her incarceration Señora Aragon's possessions still gravitated towards the little girl's hammock, and at the end of it Señora Aragon finally realised with a feeling akin to revelation that in fact her daughter's gift was a blessing; for, amongst the pans and dishcloths, the humming-bird feathers and the kitchen knives that daily filled up the hammock, was the wedding-ring that had slipped from her finger and been lost when she had been pounding her washing upon the stones in the river. With tears in her eyes and prayers of gratitude to Saint Anthony she released Leticia from the coop, only to find that her daughter and the cockerel had formed a lasting and unbreakable attachment.

It was from this humble beginning that Leticia arose as the finder of all lost things, and she came to earn more for her family than her father, who was the foreman on a not inconsiderable finca. She found Ignacio's prized revolver that he had lost in Paraguay when trying to escape from a policeman, she found Maria's missing cat, she found the gold medal that old Alfonso had won when he was a mercenary in the Chaco War, and she found the key that Don Jesuino had lost when he was tumbling a particularly fine mulatta behind the churchyard wall.

With all this fame and fortune and her ethereal beauty, it cannot be surprising that so many fell in love with Leticia. When she was fourteen it was already impossible for the family to sleep at night for the cacophony of competing serenades outside her window, and by the time that she was fifteen it became necessary to install barbed wire around the walls because so many were trying to part the palm-leaves in the hope of seeing her naked in her room.

If Señora Aragon had been thrilled with her daughter, it is even more true that Señor Aragon was besotted with her. He was a model father; when she was little he dandled her on his knee and told her stories, he played peekaboo and hide-and-seek, he changed her when she messed herself, he bathed her in the tub in the kitchen, and he competed with his wife for the privilege of preparing dainty dishes for her meals.

But as Leticia grew older and flowered into the extreme beauty of early womanhood, Señor Aragon's paternal love grew imperceptibly into something greater and guiltier. He would look at her budding curves and then try to think of something else; he would observe her lips as she spoke, and think about how it would be to have just one kiss. His eyes would be drawn up her slender thighs to that place that so many dreamed of, and he would imagine for a furtive second the absolute pleasure of running his fingers through that paradise. The unfortunate Señor Aragon could obliterate her from his imagination neither in the faithful embrace of his wife nor in the arms of the girls of the whorehouse, and it became a torment.

27 *Medicine*

That evening Anica washed the wound and bound it up, but she made Dionisio swear to go to the clinic in the morning to get injections against it going bad. She knew that he distrusted doctors to such an extent that he claimed that doctors were the greatest single cause of disease and death in the entire world, so she told him that in the morning she was coming around personally to accompany him. She tried to make him promise to be more careful from now on about his movements, but he astonished her by telling her that in his opinion the sicario had really been attempting to assassinate Ramon. She shook her head pityingly and put her hand on his cheek as if to indicate that only a man as indestructibly disconnected from reality as he was could possibly believe anything so stupid, but he said that they had been trying to get Ramon for a long time and that the sicario had not fired until he had started to fall sideways, and had not the bullet gone into the doorpost behind which Ramon was concealed? Anica grasped at what little sense there was in this and almost fooled herself into maybe believing it, but all the same she decided that as soon as the holiday began she would get him away from there no matter what the neighbours would say or how much her father would shout at her. After she had made love to him gently so as not to hurt his wound, she went home and found that Ramon had left her a note asking her to do the very thing that she had just decided.

Dionisio only agreed to go to the clinic because now that he was with Anica he was more in love with life and had developed an idea that he should take care of his health. Nowadays everything that he did was done half for her even when it had nothing to do with her at all.

At the clinic they made him wait for an hour so that he

had to telephone the college and tell them that he would be late because he had been shot. The Principal sighed and said 'Vale, Dionisio, this makes a little change from dead bodies and severed hands in the garden,' and Dionisio went back into the clinic and read all the posters on the walls about poisonous plants and the efficacy of condoms as a prophylactic against venereal disease. He sat down next to Anica and she took his hand because she knew that he was nervous. Then he was called up by the nurse and he had to fill in a form in triplicate and sign a document saying that in the event of death or injury caused by his treatment he would not hold the clinic responsible, and a similar one saying that if he lost any property at the clinic it was his problem and not theirs.

He went into a cubicle and the grim nurse with hairs sprouting out of her moles unwrapped his wound and inspected it. She grunted and poured a helping of antibiotic powder over it before rebinding it. Then she said, 'I am going to give you two shots; one is antibiotic and the other is anti-tetanus. One will be in the thigh and the other will be in the backside, so take off your trousers and underwear.'

Dionisio protested that the tetanus was unnecessary because no tetanus germ could possibly survive a journey down a gunbarrel, but she gave him a look so hostile that he changed his approach and said, 'Why can I not have the injections in my arm?'

'Because,' she said, 'in my experience people tend to struggle and then faint.'

'I do not. I will find it very interesting to watch the needle go in.'

'Take off your trousers,' ordered the nurse with the hairy moles, so that he felt thoroughly frightened and intimidated, and did as she said. He realised to his shame that he was wearing his oldest blue underpants full of holes, and he knew with absolute certainty that the nurse was relishing his humiliation.

The first injection in the thigh was almost perfectly

painless, and he was prematurely revising his low opinion of the medical sciences when the disgruntled nurse stabbed him in the buttock with a needle so long and so thick that it would have astonished even a ceibu bull. As it tore through the muscle a spasm of anguish shot down his leg so quickly that it seemed to arrive before it had even set off. He jerked and shouted, and she stuck it in deeper and said through her teeth, 'Do not clench. It only makes it worse.' But a pain of such exaggerated megalomania would have made even an anaesthetised fakir clench, and Dionisio clenched. As the contents of the veterinary syringe were pumped into him the dolour spread inside him like a burn, so that when he stood up he was engulfed by a cyclone of nausea and he fell flat on the bed. 'There,' said the nurse triumphantly, oozing with satisfaction and lack of sympathy, 'lie down until you feel better, and I will go and tell your wife that you will be out in a minute.'

He tried repeatedly to stand up, but was defeated by the paralysing stiffness in his leg. Eventually he felt so shamed by his weakness that he dragged himself out to Anica by holding onto chairs, fixtures on the wall, and anything else within reach.

She took him by the arm and virtually carried him up the hill. By the time that they arrived he was sweating in waterfalls and feeling utterly sick, so she put him to bed and went to call the college to say that he would be very late because the doctor had made him ill. She sat by him for a long time, and then she asked him, 'How is your culo?' So he said, 'It would have been better to have been shot in the culo and injected in the arm,' not knowing that ever since a survey in 1966 had established beyond reasonable doubt that nine thousand, seven hundred and three registered prostitutes were suffering from fifteen thousand, seven hundred and forty-six cases of venereal diseases, it had been government policy to inject everyone possible with the elephantine concoction that had just assaulted his metabolism and raised its joyous, multicoloured flag of conquest, which took the form of a green, red, yellow and violet bruise that spread all over his buttock, took two weeks to subside, and made some of the natural functions of the body difficult and painful to perform. Anica made him pose for her, and she painted a sensitive portrait of his backside in vivid colours.

During this two weeks Anica thought up various plans to get Dionisio away from Ipasueño.

Anica proposed to Dionisio that they should go to Madrid, where she had friends, and then possibly France, where she had more friends. Dionisio's heart sank, because he was still up to the crown of his head in debt from the last time that he had gone to Spain, even though he had only slept on building-sites. Anica was blessed with a rich and indulgent father, and she had long ago acquired the knowledge that lack of money was not an obstacle to anything, and so had no experience of the kind of desperate straits that leading a civilised life on a professor's salary could bring. He said, 'Oh no, querida, Madrid is so hot at this time of year that even the local people cannot stand it; every day is a perpetual siesta. I thought that you wanted to go to Guyana.'

'No,' she said. 'I have thought about that, but I want to go in the dry season.'

So he said, 'Why do you not go to Madrid? Really I cannot afford it, but I do not want to spoil life for you. When you come back, perhaps we can go to visit my sisters, or perhaps we can go to stay with my parents in Valledupar. I can find some work for a while, and then maybe we can fly to the Caribbean. We can go to Nueva Sevilla. It is very old and beautiful, and it has hundreds of little corners and hiding-places for lovers to court in.'

Anica laughed and exclaimed, 'You think of nothing else,' but privately she thought that Valledupar and Nueva Sevilla were maybe far enough away from Ipasueño. In the mean-time she thought of ways to get him away from his usual haunts.

*

El Jerarca felt none of Dionisio's pain in his distended and steatopygous backside, and this raises the question as to whether or not the pain in his arm was psychosomatic.

28 *Las Locas* (1)

Anica and Dionisio were sitting in the living-room drinking tintos and watching the television. Dionisio was wearing wet trousers because he had a venerable percolator that when it was overexcited shot dramatic spouts of coffee across the kitchen. He had been caught in one of its throbbing ejaculations, and Anica had sponged the grains off him and told him to change his trousers and soak them. He had said, 'Yes, querida, but I will drink my tinto first.' She was leaning against him with her head on his shoulder and her arm linked through his, thinking about nothing at all except how good it was to be sitting like this with her head on his shoulder and her arm through his.

He pulled an Inca out of the packet with his teeth, flicked it straight with his tongue, and took a fosforo from the box. He lit it with one hand by laying the box upon one side, pressing it down with his third finger, and striking it by flicking the match between his thumb and forefinger. 'I love the way you do that,' said Anica, because the deftness of the trick had suddenly increased her happiness.

He tried to show her how it was done, and the first time that she did it the matchbox would not stay upright, and the second time it flew across the room. On the third time the head of the match detached itself and described a flaring arc, arriving with an unerring instinct for destructiveness on a cushion. 'Madre de Dios,' exclaimed Anica, and she leapt up and stamped it out, saying, 'No, I will use only the conventional method in future.'

Just at that moment a woman named Fulgencia Astiz arrived in Ipasueño, attracted by the myth of Dionisio Vivo and vowing to have his child. She had come all the way from Buenaventura carrying only a mochila full of essential supplies and several bottles of infallible love-potions. She had managed to catch lifts on lorries and in jeeps, and had avoided molestation by means of a Corpus Christi blessed as an anti-rape charm and by means of her formidable musculature, which had enabled her to disarm one man with a knife and leave him triumphantly with a broken nose. She took up residence in a cheap guest-house, and every day wandered about the town looking for Dionisio, positive that when she saw him she would recognise him by instinct.

But that evening Fulgencia Astiz discovered that the three women with whom she shared her room in the guest house had all arrived with the same intentions as herself. They had a bitter row about their respective claims to priority in the business of having Dionisio Vivo's child, in which each enumerated her merits and expatiated upon the profundity of her irreversible love, and then they had a fight. As it was all against each, they disappeared into a multi-limbed flailing, spitting, scratching bundle from which there originated language such as to redden the ears of the most phlegmatic lifelong jailbird. When the floor was completely covered with wrenched-off locks of black hair and broken fingernails, and just before Agustin arrived from the police station to quell the brouhaha, they fell into each other's embrace, swearing eternal sisterhood and complicity in their quest, and spent the rest of the evening plotting to achieve it by means of a campaign of Napoleonic severity and grandeur.

Fulgencia Astiz and her accomplices sat on their beds and discussed their intuitions about Dionisio Vivo. Fulgencia believed that she would know him by sight because he was so handsome, but another one said that when she perused his letters in *La Prensa* a faint but unmistakable aroma of carnations pervaded her room, and that she was sure that she would know him by this. Another said that when she dreamed about making love to him she distinctly heard the sound of cyclones tearing corrugated-iron roofs from houses, and the last said that he had come to her as a ghost of the living and spoken with her so that she would know the sound of his voice. They bought a map of the town from the town hall and divided the town into four sections, so that each one of them could scour a section systematically with all her senses on red alert until his whereabouts were revealed. When he had been found they would go to him together and beg him to accept their collective devotion.

The trickle of women into Ipasueño continued. There were women from every region; there were Antioqueñas, with their classical fatalism and dauntless will to struggle even when lacking opposition, with their carefully nurtured neuroticism, their perverse regionalism, and their unconquerable propensity to pronounce their 's' even more thickly than the Castilian. There were industrious Narinenses with their aberrant traditionalism, their passionate political opinions, their extreme sobriety, their embarrassing hospitality, their obstinate opposition to progress until the thing they opposed was already old-fashioned, and their curious vocabulary and manner of speaking in the front of the mouth. There were Cundi-boyacense, with their Indian physiognomy, their elaborate diffidence and their vicuna-like timidity, their thirst for unconnected and useless information, and their impetuous submissiveness. There were conceited Costeñas with their overstated views, their bonhomie, their African blood, their profligate generosity, fatuous sense of humour, lack of anything to conceal, and, in speaking, their suppression of those vital intervocalic consonants which make meaning communicable. And apart from stray women from other countries, such as a Tibetan who believed that the Andes were the true and original Himalayas, there were Santandereanas; these were implacably aggressive types who in more normal times devoted themselves to litigation over boundaries, memorising grievances, worshipping pointless acts of valour, and conducting a diabolical love affair with death in all its more violent manifestations. This was why they outnumbered all the others put together, for they foresaw that Dionisio Vivo was a doomed man; they wanted to be there when he was assassinated, they wanted to witness his heroism, and they wanted their children by him to die with inherited courage against similarly inconceivable odds.

Beyond these generalisations one might add those pertaining to national characteristics, which were shared by all. As we know, the nation is divided not by latitude nor by longitude, but by altitude; for the higher one lives, the less one is extroverted and confiding, and the more one is suspicious and devious. However, the women were at one in resenting comparisons, because of the danger of them being unfavourable, and they were at one in disliking responsibility, because of the danger of losing one's freedom. Slower to anger than the Spanish, they were capable of even greater zealotry and self-sacrifice, stoicism and endurance. Each one of them objectively considered herself to be the very centre of the universe, and consequently they found each other's pride intolerable. They were vehemently impatient of results, and shared a dislike of machinery so great that if the bus on which they were travelling broke down, even in the middle of nowhere, they were always extremely gratified to be so vindicated in their hatred.

They possessed the extraordinary ability to assess a person at a stroke with the objectivity of a behaviourist, the intuition of a Jungian, and the certainty of a scientologist, and esteemed no one more than those who lacked airs and graces. Their wits were sharper than the machetes of campesinos and the spikes of cactus, which compensated for their dislike of work, and which enabled them to amuse each other despite the lack of facilities in their camp.

But more than this they enjoyed in full measure the national gift for friendship and generosity. In their encampment gifts circulated with such rapidity that they could return to their original donors in a matter of hours having passed through the hands of every one of their number, and such vows of eternal friendship were made that the saints became wearied for being so frequently invoked in witness. And, like all their compatriots, they possessed a unique gift for quoting apposite snatches of verse, so that, from having been so much in each other's company, their speech became exquisitely metrical.

At first the women had had the problem of where to live. There were no hotels to speak of, and the pensions were already overcrowded and unpleasant. Some of the women took to living an indigent life in the streets, sleeping in doorways and under arches, and posing a threat to the safety of the pedestrians who stumbled over them in the darkness. Some of the more enterprising amongst them lodged with local inhabitants and worked as servants in return for board and lodging, so that households that had been poorer than beggars suddenly found themselves in the enviable position of being waited upon hand and foot. Eventually the women set up their own camp on the fringes of the town, so that Ipasueno, just like the capital, grew its own little favela, which was constructed out of cardboard, corrugated iron, abandoned pieces of cars, lumps of wood, and the detritus of avalanches, all tied down and together with string and pieces of rags. Ramon had rented out his goat field at a peso per person per day, and found that not only did he have a better income from that, but also the women made pets of his goats and spoiled them, feeding them titbits and pieces of panela, so that their milk and flesh became aromatic and sweet-tasting and fetched a much better price in the market. The patient women put up with the goats eating their habitations from over their heads in return for their wilful but entertaining company.

Less welcome to the women was the persistent company of gangs of wolfish men who gathered at their encampment and pestered and nauseated them with suggestive remarks and salacious invitations. These were treated with the haughty disdain that they deserved, but less easy to deal with were the constant sexual assaults and attempted violations. Matters came to a head when a band of armed thugs from the Club appeared in a jeep and attempted to abduct some women at gunpoint, to save themselves the trouble of raiding the pueblitos.

The crucial mistake that these men made was connected with their ignorance of the ways of Santandereanas, who made up by far the greater proportion of the women's number. As soon as it became evident what was happening, they emerged from their tents and hovels armed with machetes, revolvers, shotguns, and clubs, and overwhelmed the ruffians in a few frenetic seconds. One of the women, without a moment's thought to her own comfort, removed the ropes from her little barraca, which then descended sideways to the ground, and tied them all up in a bundle. They pushed the wild-eyed and protesting parcel straight over the mountainside, without having failed to attach with a pin a lengthy letter stating the reasons for their action to the shirt of every one of them. The warrior-like Santandereanas cheered as the bundle bounced down the rocks, and they repeated the performance with every subsequent invasion of would-be rapists until the gorge was black with vultures, confounding a local saying that the chasm was so deep that no bird would overfly it, and the raids ceased.

More subtle and insidious were the attentions of the dozens of men who travelled in from far and wide claiming to be Dionisio Vivo. To begin with a number of women fell for this ploy, but realised the deception almost immediately afterwards, having found the experience of making love to the impostors insufficiently mystical. One or two of them fell for the charm of the more engaging deceivers and ran off with them, having waived the purpose of their visit, but thereafter the remainder of the women began to operate a simple vetting system, which can be illustrated by what happened to Jerez.

Like most others who arrived claiming to be Dionisio Vivo and hoping for free love, Jerez' appearance immediately aroused suspicion. To begin with he was almost completely bald, had a flabby stomach, a dirty shirt, huge bags under his eyes, a syphilis chancre on his lip, and a ridiculous support bandage around his knee. His face displayed none of the intellectual acuity expected of Dionisio Vivo, and none of the anticipated Christlikeness, not even the nimbus. The redoubtable Fulgencia Astiz demanded to know the exact date when Dionisio's last letter had appeared in *La Prensa*, and the nature of its contents. Jerez divagated unconvincingly and with extreme vagueness upon the supposed contents of the letter, and then Fulgencia demanded to see his cedula.

'My cedula?' echoed Jerez.

'Yes, your Certificado Judicial, which the law requires you to carry. Produce it.'

Another Santandereana with her black hair cascading about her face and a formidable magnum in her hand stepped out and took his cedula from his shirt pocket. She inspected it carefully, noted the ornate renewal stamps and the print of the right index finger, and then she noticed the name. She showed it to Fulgencia, who looked contemptuously at Jerez, who looked very embarrassed, and started to say, 'I am very sorry, ladies, but you are very charming and . . .' But the magnum was jabbed into his back, and he was seen off to jeers, amid a shower of rocks and refuse, and he never came back to repeat the trick. Instead he went to the Casa Rosa, and they would not have him either because of the chancre on his lip.

Living so close to nature and with so few amenities, the women very soon took on a wild and dishevelled appearance, and became an object of curiosity and occasional ridicule to the people of Ipasueño. They were often overheard having fairly raucous celebrations, and all sorts of bizarre rumours started to circulate about them, of which the only ones that bore any semblance to the truth were that they were capable of tearing people to pieces and were followers of Dionisio Vivo.

Curiously enough, the women never took the obvious step of going to Ipasueño College to find him. It was as if they all entertained the suspicion that meeting their hero in the flesh might be a disappointment. There grew up a tacit understanding in their own mythology that one day he would come to them.

Those of a classical disposition immediately saw the parallels, and started to call them 'The Bacchantes', or 'The Maenads', depending upon whether their inclinations were Latin or Hellenic. Ramon, probably the only policeman in the department who knew anything about ancient myth, mischievously took advantage of this and put about a lot of stories about Dionisio which were intended to reach the ears of El Jerarca, but which he had sedulously culled from an encyclopaedia.

He would entertain the credulous habitués of bars with wonderful tales of how Dionisio had once turned into a little goat and been tended by water nymphs, about how he had been seen in a chariot pulled by tigers, about how he had once turned a river into wine so that his pursuers became drunk in it and drowned, about how vines grew up around him and how someone attempting to cut them down with a machete had instead cut off his own foot. He told them that when anyone attempted to bind him the bonds just fell off, that he could change into a lion, and that he had once rescued his mother from the spirit world by swapping her for the one he loved the most. These tales rapidly spread all over town, and Ramon would sometimes be greatly amused to find them retold to himself with even greater exaggeration than that with which he had ornamented them in the first telling.

Anica and Dionisio were aware of the women's presence and their purpose from the very beginning, but it seemed to them that it all had nothing to do with their daily life or their love affair. Dionisio thought of them only with a sense of the quizzicality of the world, and Anica only rarely felt endangered by them, when he made dirty jokes about them or pretended that he was about to go and see them. Like everyone else, other than the classicists, Anica and Dionisio referred to them as 'Las Locas'.

29 *Valledupar*

At last the time came for them to make the arduous journey to Valledupar, a city so frivolous that the natives hang pineapples on lemon trees just to confuse the tourists, and the same place that General Fuerte's donkey had once given birth to kittens. It was also the root and foundation stone of the burgeoning movement towards local democracy in the nation, and had been ever since Dionisio's father, General Hernando Montes Sosa, had called an election and confirmed his position as governor without resort to electoral fraud. From that town had set out the military expeditions to quell the imaginary communist insurgencies in the region of Chiriguana, which itself was inundated in the spectacular flood which resulted in the discovery of the ancient Inca city named by Aurelio as Cochadebajo de los Gatos.

The couple loaded the antique vehicle with their possessions. It was a notably sultry and lugubrious day, and they sweated in rivers on account of their fetching and carrying. They loaded numerous musical instruments so that Dionisio might compose songs and play to himself, and soon found that there was not much room for anything else. Then they decided to take Anica's Norton because Dionisio wanted her to be independent if she wished. This proved to be an impossibility on account of its size and asymmetrical shape, until they had the inspiration of tying it to the roof with ropes that came through the windows. This meant that they could not open the doors any more, and so they had to enter and leave the car by climbing through the windows themselves.

As the couple began the two-day excursion down to the torrid Llanos, Dionisio had the sensation that one of his lives was ending and that nothing would ever be the same again.

For the first time that he could recollect he had been sublimely happy for several months without interruption, he was strong and bulging with health, and he had realised with astonishment that he was young. It had been a very long time since the days when he had woken up each morning unable to decide whether or not he had died during the night. Anica in her turn had forgotten to cry about her mother's death for several months.

The drive to Dionisio's home was largely uneventful except for his car's token protests. It burst a water hose at one point, and at another the distributor worked loose so that the engine backfired abruptly and stopped. The worst thing, however, was that the home-made silencer began to come off after hitting a hump in the road, and the racket made conversation very difficult. Apart from this, the roads were in their usual state of grotesque deformation, full of potholes, ravaged by floods, so that only drunks would keep to one side of the highway, and only optimists such as Dionisio ever expected to arrive anywhere.

Down on the Llanos everything was different. Down here the cattle were not sleek and fat as in the sierra, but were bloated with parasites and afflicted with picturesque despair. The cats were not philosophical and elegant, but scabby and dishonest. The grasses were not lush and generous, but paltry, and seared by a heat that distorted the view in every direction, had such a radical effect upon the metabolism that it was necessary to urinate only once a day, in the evenings, and made it possible to bake cassava bread by simply leaving it on the roof. The humidity was so profound that not even the famous saunas of Finland could rival it for the sensation of being a prisoner in one's own body, which in turn felt as though wrapped in a sodden military blanket. The adobe and palm-thatched huts of the poor pueblitos seemed each one to have a buzzard or a vulture perched upon the roof in the posture of bored sentries from a conscript army. In each doorway there seemed to be the same bundles of ragged clothes surmounted by the inscrutable faces of their occupants, always with a large puro clenched in the teeth, and often with a dirty child hanging on with one hand and eating guava jelly with the other.

They stopped by a lemon grove for the night and slung Dionisio's Acahuatec hammock between two trees. The night had cooled the world to a balmy temperature and there was no sign of rain, so they sat amongst the trees listening to the redskin monkeys and watching the fireflies while they drank coffee and talked about whether or not bats could spread rabies. When they climbed into the hammock there were comical episodes caused by the fact that it is very difficult to get into a hammock two at a time without suddenly being tipped out. Anica lay across the hammock crossways to stabilise it so that he could come up as well, and they discovered empirically a secret known to Indians for centuries, which is that it is easiest to make love in a hammock by lying in it diagonally. They slept a guiltless and profound sleep, and woke up in the morning swollen with bites, but already reaped and harvested by the sun.

They drove at furious speed to keep the air circulating in the car, and also to get to Puesto Grande by four o'clock in order to see the famous mechanical negro in the town clock sally out and strike the bell with a hammer. On the hour the little mechanical negro was propelled unsteadily from out of his alcove and hesitantly banged on the bell four times before retreating backwards again. They felt a sense of anti-climax as one often does with technological wonders, but went into the Miami Motel to celebrate nonetheless. In the bar, which was full of chickens and where there lived a monopolising hog that ate cigarette-ends and cigar butts, Anica said 'Do you think that we are both locos?'

As they neared his parental home he began to feel a warm sensation growing in his body. Even though the family had originated in Ipasueño, the General had been resident in Cesar for so long now that Dionisio regarded Valledupar as his real home, especially as its quirkiness and eccentricity suited his nature almost to perfection, despite the stupefying heat and catastrophic rainstorms, the ravenous and insatiable insects and the intrusively raucous darktime chirring of the crickets.

His parents now lived in a neo-colonial mansion with peeling paint and cool courtyards. There was a reconstruction of the original Aristotelian peripateticon draped with bougainvillea, and a vast garden that his horticultural mother had turned into a beneficent forest by marking every important event with the planting of a tree, which meant that they suffered from a prodigious surfeit of avocados, guavas and citrus. The General was used to organising military fatigue squads to collect these up in baskets; these he would place in front of the guards at the gates with orders to give them away for nothing to poor women and to hungry travellers.

The house itself possessed the air of a place reconciled to time. It spoke of the recollection of glittering celebrations and presidential visits; it was a house that had gone into genteel retirement in order to cultivate roses and relax upon its foundations without any bitterness or regret. In its hallways were family portraits, including one of the Conde Pompeyo Xavier de Estremadura, complete with a hole in his nose which, out of a feeling of vengefulness against the portrait's stern and reproachful expression, the General had put there in his youth with the aid of an air-rifle. On the walls were a collection of swords, pikes and muskets from the colonial age, and there was a clock so old that it dated from the time when no one was so hurried that they felt it necessary to have a minute hand. One of the family cats had once got into the habit of dropping live mice into the mechanism, where there was now a small but thriving colony that had mastered the art of knowing the precise times when it was essential to avoid the various pieces of machinery.

Dionisio's family was an old one with a documented history that gave each member of it the reassuring feeling that they had the right to exist. The General himself was so enmeshed in the family traditions that he sometimes forgot which century he was in and had to be reminded by his wife. He possessed a conciliatory frame of mind and a puzzled expression, and supervised his own emotions with a military sense of order coupled with a discreet humanity.

Dionisio's mother on the other hand showed every sign of once having been a fan of Carmen Miranda, a fact principally betrayed by her coiffure, which she had not changed since her youth and which still became her now as it had then. She was a paradoxical vegetarian who delighted in serving up succulent roast meats, which she would watch her family eat with voracity while she herself toyed with Spartan portions of braised vegetables. She had a gift for embarrassingly acute naivety and always understood other people better than those acquainted with the gloomy metaphysic of psychology or the equally pessimistic one of Christianity. She was a fanatical connoisseur of obscure superstitions, which she practised assiduously as a kind of hobby, without believing in any of them. Her husband was convinced that she had been born a century too early, since she was known throughout the area as a rescuer of wounded animals and birds; he believed that a civilisation can be judged by its treatment of animals, and he calculated that it would be a hundred years before the rest of the nation treated animals as well as she did, an hypothesis he had worked out with the aid of statistics from the Ministry of Agriculture and a large graph which was now framed and hung in a corridor, next to all the pictures of the units with which he had served.

When the couple arrived and passed the inspections of the guards at the gate, they drew up in front of the house and were still climbing stickily out of the windows of the car when they were deluged by a welcoming committee consisting of servants, the General, the family pets, and all the other wounded animals who joined in out of a need not to be excluded. The General kissed his son on both cheeks and enclosed him in a martial hug, and then gallantly kissed Anica upon both cheeks as well, uttering well-chosen compliments and congratulating Dionisio upon having found such a tall lady. Mama Julia appeared from the house and embraced everybody, including her own husband, and summed up Anica's character with one glance. In the evening she informed her son that she loved Anica already, because of her purity of soul. Dionisio explained at enormous length all of her virtues and attractions, and Mama Julia snorted and said, 'That is exactly what I said, except that I needed only one phrase.'

Anica fell immediately into the routine of the house, and Dionisio slipped instantaneously back into the role in the family decreed for him by fate, which was to be the only one out of all the household (including the servants, whom his parents treated like honoured guests) who had the courage and lack of imagination to clean up catshit, get rid of snakes and spiders, despatch maimed birds, and catch rodents that had been let go in the house accidentally.

30 *His Excellency's Alchemical Assault*

Ever since His Excellency and his wife had begun the practice of sexual alchemy, the former had taken great pains to ensure that his performance was underpinned by adequate metabolical foundations.

On this day of his implacable revenge against El Jerarca he had consumed litres of tea made from damiana specially flown in from Mexico. This efficacious herb not only possesses aphrodisiac qualities, but has similar effects to marijuana upon the psyche, which His Excellency also found to be an excellent source of erotic predispositions. On days when he practised his hermetic mysteries he was usually not in a fit state to govern the country, and consequently his office would be closed while he ambled about the palace gesticulating and murmuring to himself, as untoward events perpetrated themselves within the sealed doors of his altered consciousness.

His Excellency also consumed prodigious quantities of guarana and catuaba, which he had brought in from the Amazonas region, where an Indian chief had introduced them to him during one of his rare presidential visits to the interior. This induced an excellent state of affairs in both mind and body which almost rendered the ginseng and the vast doses of vitamin E superfluous.

His Excellency had recently heard that in the United States it was possible to be fitted with a curious device; this device was an hydraulic sac that could be fitted within the erectile tissues of the penis. In the abdomen, at the end of a tube, was a reservoir of inert liquid, and in the scrotum was a pump. All that one had to do was squeeze the scrotum in a discreet but vigorous manner, and the fluid would flow from the reservoir to the penis, erecting it magnificently, and all one had to do to detumesce with the dignity of a king was to palpate the pump in the correct fashion. It occurred to His Excellency that theoretically it should be possible to perform sexual alchemy continuously with this device installed. He had already sent off for the brochures, under an assumed name, and the two reasons that he had never got around to having the miraculous operation were that in the first place the pressure of executive business was too great, and secondly the thought of having an incision made in his penis filled him with irrational horror. The ingenuity and the humanitarian nature of the concept, however, altogether changed his perception of the United States, and he began to regard that enterprising country as a model of civilisation. This predisposed him to a greater sympathy towards the demands of their government that something should be done to crush the coca cartels.

President Veracruz and his amenable wife spent the whole day attempting not to think about sex, in order not to dissipate any psycho-sexual energies that might be useful later during copulation. The attempt not to think about it concentrated their attention upon it in the most paradoxical manner, and this explains why it was that they frequently slapped themselves in the face in order that the pain should prove a distraction. (Rumours and reports that he and his spouse were mad should be confounded by this explanation, and the Mind of the Nation should be set at rest.)

In the early evening when the moon was full, and shining directly into the windows of the highest boudoir in the land, His Excellency and Señora Veracruz took a bath and carefully washed each other all over in order to irrigate away not only the daily grime of high office, but also the invisible spiritual contagions that are a fact of daily life. They dried themselves in towels freshly laundered in Andean spring water, guaranteed to be free of all chemicals and industrial additives, obtainable on the Calle Fernando in bottles from Erasmo Hidalgo's Emporium, Purveyors of Rare Artefacts and Recondite Luxuries.

The ceremony having become refined over the years, the couple then robed themselves in their respective chambers. His Excellency emerged as Osiris, complete with the atef crown, which looked somewhat like a very large white condom with a vast green worm at front and back. Pasted to his chin was a long waxed beard which curled forward at the bottom, and his body was swathed in a white robe that was designed to resemble the bandages of a mummy, Osiris being not only the God of Resurrection but also the God of the Judgement of the Dead. In his hands he bore the crook and flail, and upon his countenance he wore an expression of the most prodigiously earnest loftiness of purpose.

Señora Veracruz emerged as a very fetching likeness of Isis. In her hand she bore a sistrum, and upon her head was an impressive confection consisting of a pair of elegantly curved cow's horns encompassing a burnished solar disk. Upon her forehead was the upper neck and head of a taxidermised cobra, and a lock of hair fell in front of her ears in authentic style. Around her long black wig she wore a gold band, her throat was adorned with an ornamented necklet, and on her upper arms and her wrists she carried triple bracelets. Her slender body was encased in a sheathlike white strapless dress, her feet were bare, and her eyes were made, by means of a black pencil, into superb likenesses of the eyes of Horus.

Their giant black jaguar, being the first of their magical children, was brought into the room with a red collar sparkling with gems, and in this way the atmosphere of authenticity could be augmented by having present a beast that could pass either for the Goddess Sekhmet or the Goddess Bast. This impressive animal curled up on the rug and fell asleep during the ritual that followed.

The couple, having assumed the form and therefore the powers of their respective divinities, stood opposite each other and placed their hands upon each other's shoulders. They then intoned with great conviction and solemnity the entire forty-two verses of the noble Protestation of Innocence,

140

which is to be found in all reputable declensions of the Book of The Dead.

Having recited this with the aid of the entire text pinned up on the wall as an aide-memoire, Señora Veracruz announced to her spouse, 'You are my King, you are the Risen Osiris, you are my priest,' at which point he uncrossed his arms that had been resting upon his chest in the sign of Osiris Dead, and raised them up, palm outwards, in the sign of Osiris Living.

He then declared, 'You are my Queen, you are the Living Isis, you are my priestess.'

They undressed each other where they stood, resisting the temptation to ungodlike haste, and sank down upon the bed. There followed a lengthy period in which they caressed each other in all apposite areas with the utmost languor, occasionally stopping for refreshment in the form of freezing champagne, which the French Ambassador had once recommended as a very potent aid to erotic enterprise. This gentleman maintained that there is at the base of the stomach a flap which closes whenever something very cold enters it. When the temperature is more amenable to digestion the flap opens and dumps all the champagne at once into the gut, which explains its exhilarating effects.

When they could bear the tantalisation no longer and the correct ambience for mystical copulation had been created, Señora Veracruz lowered herself upon the presidential polla with divine aplomb, and employed the most subtle and exquisite Panamanian muscular contractions to keep them both on the brink of explosion for a very lengthy period of time. Whenever His Excellency felt the urge to melt into orgasm he would contemplate his wife's extraordinary headdress, and found that this had the effect of bringing him back from the precipice.

During this sublimest of rituals there were always some interesting paranormal phenomena caused by the intensity of the concentration and the magnificence of the bliss. Upon this occasion the huge black jaguar levitated, and slept on in its curled-up posture fully one metre from the ground, and the hands of the palace clocks bent at right-angles. In addition the room filled with the aroma of asafoetida and toasted cumin, and Señora Veracruz distinctly felt the hands of an angel running up and down her back.

When this happened she could restrain herself no longer and she broke into a climax so shattering that her headdress of cowhorns and solar disk flew from her head, and that of His Excellency fell forward over his eyes. But this did not distract them from their supreme concentration, for at the moment of supernal disintegration they were visualising with all their power their longed-for 'magical child', which was the sudden death of El Jerarca.

Afterwards, when the great cat had crashed suddenly to the floor and all the clocks in the palace had lost ten minutes, Señora Veracruz lay sobbing and panting in her husband's arms. 'Oh Daddikins,' she cried, 'I want more,' at which point an expression of dismay passed over his face and he thought all over again about having the operation.

31 Guacamole Sauce And The Naked Admiral

Mama Julia was scandalised by the creaking of the floorboards at night as the lovers flitted to each other's rooms under the impression that the noise of the excusado flushing and the chirring of crickets would drown out the sound. But the General said, 'Shit, woman, it is perfectly obvious that they have been married longer than we have,' and so she held her peace, and generously colluded in the respectable pretence that all nights in her house were nights of Catholic chastity.

Mama Julia and the General departed on their own holiday, to Costa Rica, and did as custom dictated, which was to summon La Prima Primavera to take charge of the house. No one knew exactly who she was or whether she was in fact a cousin or not, but she had been a member of the family for so long that it no longer mattered if she was an impostor, or even if she was really herself or somebody else. Mama Julia was convinced that even with a squad of servants Dionisio was incapable of taking care of things, and would have been very put out if she had ever discovered that he could. La Prima Primavera was a Zamba woman in her late sixties, who had devoted her youth to outrageous promiscuity and her old age to finding a husband. She suffered from a personality disorder which no doctor would ever have been able to cure, which was that she could not understand jokes, despite having an earthy and risqué sense of humour and a disconcerting habit of uttering obscenities. Less seriously, she always put the wrong answers in Mama Julia's books of crosswords in indelible ink, causing Mama Julia many moments of despairing rage until she got into the habit of remembering to hide the books in a trunk before she arrived. La Prima Primavera was inquisitive about everything, but paradoxically never seemed to know about anything; she took offence when none was intended, and did not take it when it was, but she shared with Mama Julia a gift for caring for wounded animals, and she shared with her a weary sense of the inevitable whenever Dionisio brought a girlfriend home. But she fell instantly under Anica's spell, and forgot to feel bitter whenever they embraced. Dionisio told Anica that La Prima Primavera had had a passion for lamb in guacamole sauce ever since she had worked in Mexico, and that she could expect them to have it served every day, a prophecy which was accurately fulfilled.

After La Prima Primavera had arrived, laden with suitcases that seemed to be filled with lead and compressed igneous rock, and after the General and Mama Julia had departed, there began the time when Dionisio and Anica were at their happiest. Anica suddenly threw away all her inhibitions as if they had been ragged clothes. She held his hand in public, kissed him voraciously before the very eyes of the guardians of public decency, and accepted at last that each of them was better together than either of them could have been apart.

With the parents away and La Prima Primavera at the other end of the house snoring and swearing whilst she dreamed of camels with lions' heads copulating with the President, it was an easy matter to slip into each other's rooms without even having to flush the excusado first. Anica would be waiting under the mosquito net, getting younger by the day, making all those expressions that preceded acts of love. She would bite her lower lip and raise her eyebrows, while her eyes went luminous with the anticipation of pleasure.

They would lie at first side by side, allowing the day to slide away and allowing the interpenetration of their bodies' warmth and mustiness, until it was time for their hands to seek to wander. Then would begin the journeys of the tongue and lips, he over her long limbs, she over his rougher savannahs, until at last they would be fast asleep, exhausted and contented, while the frustrated mosquitoes coated the net with a black vibrating mass that would always unaccountably disappear at dawn.

One evening they went to see the Naked Admiral. He was a friend of the family who was responsible for naval recruitment in the whole department, which was why he found himself hundreds of kilometres from the sea with almost nothing to do except construct follies in his gardens. He was an ardent naturist and had shared with the former Governor, General Fuerte, a patriotic interest in ornithology and lepidoptery. In his youth he had formulated the theory that sperm production is reduced by the wearing of clothes, and he had never since worn any except when off his own property, a fact which meant that his wife never dared to have dinner parties or invite dignitaries to stay. Surprisingly, this lack of hospitality never slowed the Naked Admiral's promotion, as it would have done in the army, or in the armed forces of a country such as Great Britain, for example. When the Naked Admiral eventually became completely senile he went naked the whole time and would drive away from his house as nature had intended him to be, with no idea of where he was going and with no idea of where he had been when he came back. His silver-haired wife died of mortification, and finally he was put into a nursing home where his nakedness was not an embarrassment to anyone. In that benign establishment he would greet people at the door with rapturous politesse and the impression that he was the owner of it and was holding a perpetual party, thus recompensing himself for a lifetime without social gatherings at his home in Valledupar. He was to die with a serene expression and a priapic erection that testified to the validity of his juvenile hypotheses about sperm-production.

The Naked Admiral had summoned Dionisio because he knew that he was always looking for work in the academic holidays, and he was in love with the idea of having his follies constructed by a moderately well-known philosopher. On this occasion his thoughts had turned to death, and he had resolved to have built a pyramidal mausoleum exactly the same as that commissioned by Mad Jack Fuller, the British Member of Parliament for Rose Hill from 1801 to 1812. This famous man was a particular hero of the Naked Admiral, who had already constructed a domed rotunda, an anchoritic tower, an obelisk, and a church spire without a church, in imitation of the volatile Englishman. Dionisio and Anica looked at the plans, with the Naked Admiral pointing out its features with the aid of a thick forefinger that somehow appeared to be even more naked than the rest of him, and Dionisio saw straight away the impossibility of imitating it. He pointed out that there was no local supply of stone, and that it was so tall that he would need to construct scaffolding out of canes and planks, which would add to the cost. The Naked Admiral thought for a moment and agreed that it should be constructed out of tapiales rendered with adobe, and that it needed to be only high enough for him to be able to sit in it naked when he was dead, wearing a top hat and holding a bottle of claret in his right hand.

'Do you know why the Ingles refused to be buried in the normal manner, Dionisio? It was because he said he would be eaten by worms, and the worms would be eaten by ducks, and the ducks would be eaten by his relatives. He was afraid of such incestuous cannibalism, you understand. And another thing, I want the floor to be covered with broken glass so that when the devil comes for me, he will cut his feet.'

The Naked Admiral's wife appeared, bearing cups of guarapo and slices of pineapple. She was a silver-haired lady whose cheeks were permanently flushed with embarrassment on her husband's behalf. She felt the obligation to make up for him by affecting exquisitely old-fashioned manners. She would break into compliments so lyrical and embroidered that some people thought that she was sarcastic, others that she was being ironical, and others were reminded of funeral orations over the catafalques of national heroes. She had been engaged for years in a shadowy academic project that took up nearly all her time, and would speak at length about her archival delvings without ever intimating the subject of her burrowing. When, after her death, her papers were finally sorted, it transpired that she had for twenty years been collecting and collating all references to rabbits in European literature since the time of the Romans. Her executors never found out what she had been on the point of proving when she had died of mortification at her desk with her pen in her hand, and the word 'Conclusion' written at the head of an otherwise blank sheet of paper.

When they left the house, Anica and Dionisio discussed whether or not the old couple were mad and came to the decision that they gave the impression of being two perfectly sane people with a lot of money and very little to do.

As they went home, and Dionisio was already thinking about the details of the construction of the mausoleum, Anica said with wonder in her voice what she had been longing to say ever since she had first clapped furtive eyes on the Naked Admiral. 'Did you notice that his polla has a big kink in it?'

32 *The Firedance (1)*

He was called 'Lazaro', but his real name was Procopio, and in his life he had been known by many other names. Nobody knows precisely how the affliction is transmitted, but it is known that when Lazaro was a little boy living in the Amazonas region he had had a pet armadillo that had sickened and died, and which could have been the carrier.

He came from a caboclo family that lived in the forest in a hut with stilts. In the dry months they hunted jaguar and ocelot for the skins, and in the wet months they lived by taking the dolphins and hunting the parakeets for their feathers. Some people said that Lazaro became the way he did because there is a curse upon those who kill dolphins, and other people said that it was because the jaguar god became angry. It is true that most people avoided Lazaro's family, because the dolphins are capable of becoming human and impregnating girls at fiestas, and the female dolphins make love to a man with such exquisite twitches of the tail that many men have inadvertently drowned whilst overcome with ecstasy. When that happens, the dolphin swims around the body for hours, singing with sorrow, and then nudges it onto a sandbank so that it can be found and buried decently before it is eaten by the caimans. Quite often the dolphins save the lives of those who are drowning, and sometimes the dolphins make a mistake and try to save those who are not drowning at all, but are really diving for turtles. That is something that one just has to put up with from time to time, and it serves to prove how simpatico the animals are. The caboclos allow the dolphins to take fish from their nets, and when the dolphins become human and emerge from the river with their different-coloured eyes and their beautiful muscles, they make love with whomever they choose, because it is bad to refuse a lover who loves so tenderly. Dolphin children always return eventually to the water, and so there are perhaps entire districts where the dolphins are half human, which makes it doubly a crime to kill them. Another reason is that dolphins love each other so romantically, so playfully, so completely, that it is obvious that they are sent by God to teach us by their example to do the same.

Such is the power of love in dolphins that a cream made of the genitals of a female bufeo, rubbed into one's own, can make one perfectly irresistible to members of the opposite sex, and so this cream is eagerly sought not only by canoieras, the prostitutes who make love in canoes while being rowed up and down by their pimps, but also by those who are of a promiscuous disposition and those who need help in pursuit of an amour. Some people know how to counterfeit this cream, with its distinctively pungent aroma and oily texture, but there is also a secret trade in the genuine article. It is bought discreetly from those accursed people who flaunt the will of God and hunt it.

Lazaro's family hunted the dolphins and made a good living from them, but no one wanted to know them, and no one was surprised when Lazaro fell ill so slowly that at first nobody noticed it. Later on people were to mistake it for Leishmaniosis, the disfiguring disease caused by infected sandflies, but later still it became very obvious what it really was, and that was when he finally had to leave.

It began with infectious lesions that were barely noticeable, and Lazaro noticed that by the end of the day his legs were swollen. By morning they would be all right again, and so he shrugged his shoulders and accepted it as a small cross that he would have to bear until it got better. His nose always felt stuffy, and sometimes it would discharge a bloody mucus. When he put a finger up a nostril to clear it, sometimes he would detach a crusty scab and would go and bury it with a muttered despacho against illness.

Someone who lives naked in the forest and spends most of his time in the water is unlikely to get too hot, especially when in the shade of the great trees, but at the times when Lazaro was glistening with perspiration from hunting, his mother would notice that areas of his dark skin had grown coppery, especially upon his legs and his arms, and she believed that it was because the Indian side of him was emerging from living so much like one himself.

Lazaro was already married to Raimunda, and had two little ones, when the nodules started to appear on his face. There came a time when she could not bear to touch his face or to kiss him, and would make love with him reluctantly only in the dark. His little ones, small as they were, would shy away from his caresses, and sometimes he would weep alone in the forest. He went to see the cascabele who dressed entirely in rattlesnake tails, and he went to see the paje who knew secretos, but nobody knew how to get rid of the excrescences on his once-handsome face.

His ears grew thick and lumpy, and the skin of his face grew into dense folds, so that people began to refer to him as 'the elephant'. His legs swelled up and made the name more appropriate. They said that if one gave him an animal name he would sooner or later start to look like that animal, and so they called him other names out of a spirit of malicious experimentation. They called him 'the Lion', and his nose swelled and broadened. His eyelashes and eyebrows thinned and disappeared. At the point when his skin became dry and scaly, they called him 'the Fish', and one morning he woke up and found that Raimunda had left him and taken the children. Unable to bear his sorrow, he took a canoe and rowed upstream towards the mountains, where a man could die at an altitude closer to God and with a greater sense of peace.

33 *The Mausoleum*

In Ipasueño Dionisio's friends had noticed that he had disappeared. He had not bothered to inform anyone of his plans, and they had immediately come to the conclusion that he had been assassinated at last. Some of them called in on his house, but neither Jerez nor Juanito knew where he was, and neither did anyone see his unmistakeable car about the town. The idea that he had driven away in it on holiday seemed preposterous because no one believed that it was capable of going long distances on roads that were a problem even for tractors. His friends took to wearing black armbands and spreading the rumour that he was dead, until the whole town knew about it and El Jerarca found attributed to him the very deed which he had been unable to perform. Jerez had the idea of auctioning off all of Dionisio's possessions to the souvenir-collecting public, but Juanito shamed him out of it, saying that nothing should be touched without the permission of the relatives. Ramon privately believed that Dionisio was perfectly all right, but took the view that rumours of his death would help a great deal in the turning of local public opinion against the coca gangs. Señor Moreno, who knew perfectly well where Dionisio and his daughter were, was on a trip to buy Kalashnikovs from an army officer who had obtained them from a coca capo in exchange for explosives with which he intended to blow up the offices of *La Prensa*. The coca capo had obtained them from The People's Liberation Force as part of a deal where the soi-disant communists provided guards for his supply routes in return for cash. The People's Liberation Force had originally acquired the Kalashnikovs from Señor Moreno himself, who had bought them from the captain of a Panamanian cargo ship in Barranquilla, who had picked them up from an

Arabian arms dealer, who had bought them in from Angola and from the Afghanistani mujaheddin after they had seen long service in Vietnam. Señor Moreno stood to gain a great deal of money in repurchasing these well-worn and itinerant weapons, and he did not discover anything about his daughter's boyfriend's death until it had already become obvious that he was not dead.

Dionisio's head of department was a lady of melodramatic disposition, and she took premature action in notifying *La Prensa* of his death in suspicious circumstances, and providing the newspaper with an emotional tribute in the form of an obituary. The only people who did not believe that he was dead were the women of the camps, who said that he came to them in dreams claiming to be still alive and offering them encouragement. Not one of them had felt any sensation of desolation or loss attendant upon his disappearance, and so they turned out to be the only ones who were right about him, which was because they were the only ones who had not been rational about the whole affair. When Dionisio eventually returned to Ipasueño he found that his job had been re-advertised, the chair of Secular Philosophy had been named after him in perpetuity, and a citizen's subscription fund had been set up for the erection of a statue of commemoration in the plaza, and, should his body ever turn up, for the construction of a rococo mausoleum in execrable taste. Both of these El Jerarca planned to blow up, until he heard from his people in Valledupar that Dionisio was alive and well, and began to work on another idea that was suggested to him by Señor Moreno himself, who had decided that the only way to save Anica's life was to separate her from her lover.

While these events were unfolding in Ipasueño, Anica and Dionisio were happily making wooden frames for the tapiales, constructing another wooden frame to serve as a former for the Naked Admiral's mausoleum, taking immense siestas,

eating prodigious quantities of La Prima Primavera's guacamole sauce, and making love languidly in the stultifying heat
of the late evenings. They spent the days absolutely filthy
from their labours, which scandalised those who had certain
preconceptions of the necessary appearance of a General's
son.

Building the mausoleum was immensely hard work; Dionisio wanted the foundations to be very deep in order to
withstand hurricanes and earthquakes, because he wanted
the structures to be strong long after his death so that there
would remain on earth some evidence of his existence. But
the problem was that he was building on the detritus of
centuries of rural life. The fragile spade he had borrowed
from his mother's collection of implements crashed time and
again against pottery shards, bricks, tree roots, wire mesh,
donkey shoes, adze heads, unrecognisable lumps of cast iron,
and even a musket abandoned by some forgotten conquistador engaged upon a journey into death. In the febrile heat he
lost litres of perspiration which ran down his body and stung
his eyes, so that Anica would take turns with him until she
too could not bear it any longer, and they would go to the
Naked Admiral's kitchen and scrounge fruit juice from the
tractable maids.

Eventually he called in on the Regiment of Engineers and
used his father's name to borrow an earth-mover with which
Anica instantly struck up a rapport, and she deftly dug out
the foundations in a couple of hours while the servants and
the Naked Admiral's lyrical wife set up chairs under a tree in
order to watch. Her venerable gardener from thenceforth
stoutly maintained that Anica was really a man, despite the
fact that the rounding of her breasts was very obvious beneath
her shirt.

The lovers worked only short hours, because that is in fact
how the most work gets done. They worked through the
morning until it was so hot that even the trees sweated, while
the Naked Admiral's wife ensured that they were always full
of fortifying herbal tisanes. They spent a great deal of time

sitting in the shade idly flicking cigarette-ends at the lizards and talking about Ipasueno scandals. Then they would go home and eat La Prima Primavera's guacamole fantasias, and spend the afternoon swinging in hammocks for siesta beneath the reproduction of Aristotle's peripateticon, dozing and watching the little birds in the bougainvillea. At the first cooling of the evening they would return to work and travail with rhythmic bursts of energy, so that every day they saw a beautiful structure emerging from the earth. He would look at Anica's face as she glowed with pride in what they had achieved together, and he in his turn would feel pride in how she had thrown herself into hard physical labour worthy of a convict on a penal colony.

As the dusk rapidly transformed itself into darkness and the bloodsucking bats swarmed out of their hollow trees where the ground beneath their roosts was crimson with droppings of pure blood, the lovers would go home, wash, and retire once more to their hammocks beneath the bougainvillea.

In retrospect Anica greatly enjoyed building the mausoleum, especially the bit when they drank two bottles of Chilean wine and then smashed them on the floor to cut the Devil's feet. She would only accept a third of the goodly pile of pesos that they were paid by the Naked Admiral, so that Dionisio could better afford to go to Nueva Sevilla.

34 *Hope Is When Army Officers Are Democrats*

That morning Dionisio awoke with the taste of raw onions in his mouth and the sensation of having been wrapped in cobwebs. When he had sufficiently awoken he understood that this was because Anica's brother was due to call in that evening after having spent the day at the military barracks in Valledupar attending a course on counter-insurgency. It was not just that Dionisio was violently prejudiced against all military types except for his own father and the ones he knew personally, but that he strongly resented anybody whatsoever who distracted Anica's attention from himself. Anica and Eloisa, her sister, worshipped their brother in the elite Portachuelo Guards, and he was fully anticipating having to pass the evening with an obsessively clean-cut neo-fascist who talked in formulae and was used to being admired.

When the young Captain arrived in a jeep in a fog of dust and had been waved past by the guards at the gate, Dionisio was instantly nauseated by the man's two metres of almost Nordic good looks and the row of medal ribbons on his chest.

Anica, starry-eyed with sibling adoration, suggested that they take him to a bar in town, and Dionisio, irritated as if by fire-ants, agreed with poor grace. But at the bar Dionisio began to find that the brother was after all not so obnoxious, especially when Anica whispered to him that her brother had been frightened to meet him on account of his fame as a letterist and a possible martyr to the drug mafia. 'I arrived,' said the Captain, 'believing that you were already dead. I read your obituary in *La Prensa* this morning, and I was fully prepared to have to spend the evening consoling my sister. You must imagine my confusion when I found you intact.'

Dionisio was impressed that an army officer could read a quality newspaper, and was bemused by the idea that anyone could have reported him dead for no reason. 'Do you have the paper?' he asked.

He read his own obituary and an editorial lamenting his demise and praising his fortitude, and immediately began to think up witty ways of writing to the paper to announce his continued and uninterrupted existence. The other two joined in the game with enthusiasm, and soon all three of them were howling with laughter and emptying bottles at a rate which would have alarmed even a depressed Scandinavian.

Now that all awkwardness had dissipated and Dionisio had forgotten to be froward, the two men found that they had much to discuss. The Captain described how his officer-training had been little better than brainwashing and brutality, about how he had been near to suicide, about how the officers never knew what the non-coms were doing, about what a relief it had been to find himself at last in the Portachuelo Guards up in the sierra. More interestingly, he had, as a young lieutenant, been one of the squad that had liberated the political prisoners from the infamous Colonel Asado's Escuadron de la Muerte. He described how General Fuerte had led them to the Army School of Electrical and Mechanical Engineers at eleven o'clock in the morning, how they had simply walked in and found hell on earth. The Captain's lip trembled when he described how everything stank of burned flesh, how everything was covered in blood and excrement, how the prisoners were mutilated beyond possibility, how they had begged him to kill them. 'I cannot go on,' he said, 'but it is my opinion that General Fuerte was a liberator to rank in his own way with Martin and Bolivar. There will never be another man like him.'

Dionisio was excited, and his eyes glowed because they were filled with tears at the man's memory. 'He is a hero of mine as well. But everyone knows he was assassinated by the army. They even blew up his hearse at the funeral. It was my own father who succeeded him who said that in public at a news conference.'

The Captain leaned forward and said very sincerely, 'Do

not make the mistake of believing that a uniform makes one a monster. Remember that it was the army that cleaned the whole mess up as well; it was men like your father.'

'And yourself.'

'I propose a toast,' said the Captain. 'To democracy and to the memory of General Carlo Maria Fuerte.'

'Long live the one and the memory of the other.'

They drank a deep draught and sat in a long silence before the conversation resumed. When they said farewell at the end of the evening Dionisio and the Captain shook hands for a long time and then embraced. 'I hope to see you again, Dionisio. Keep writing the letters.'

'Anica must remind me to tell them that I am not dead, or I will forget and they will believe my next letter to be from an impostor. You are the first person to tell me to keep writing, Felipe; everyone else warns me to stop.'

'General Fuerte did not stop. You are a civilian general in the same fight. But for the love of God, take care of my sister in all this.'

When the Captain had gone Dionisio said, 'He is a fine man. I like him very much, even though he is an army officer.'

'You did not let me say anything all evening,' complained Anica, and then she reflected, 'But I am not surprised that you get on well with him. You two are like enough to be brothers.'

'The day when I am like an army officer is the day when the whole world must have changed.'

'Then obviously it must have changed.'

Dionisio did not see Felipe again until the day in Cochadebajo de los Gatos when to their mutual astonishment they found themselves fighting side by side in the same cause.

Part Two

For the enemy hath persecuted my soul; he
hath smitten my life down to the ground; he
hath made me to dwell in darkness, as those
that have long been dead.

Therefore is my spirit overwhelmed within
me; my heart within me is desolate.

I remember the days of old.

Psalm 143.

Where do I start? At the beginning? It is all too terrible, like something from a yanqui movie. The other evening I got an urgent telegram from Ipasueño supposedly from my father, saying that I had to return instantly. I was very alarmed, because God knows what could have happened, but I could never have suspected that it would be as bad as this. D. offered to drive me back himself, but I said I would go by train and bus. So he offered to pay half my train-fare, but I said no.

When I eventually got here I was exhausted and still very worried because I had been thinking all the way about what could have gone wrong, but when I got to the house there was a car at the front with two men in it reading comics. My heart sank because everyone around here knows them, and knows that they are two killers who work for that fat shit. One of them was El Guacamayo, who is called that because he dresses up like a macaw in bad-taste clothes. He's got gold teeth and he stinks of revolting cheap perfume that he probably puts on to impress whores. The other one was El Chiquitin, who is called that because he is so small.

I was about to run away when El Guacamayo pointed a gun at me and said something like, 'Inside, chica, or you get lead in you right now, OK? I have a little message from someone important.'

My whole mouth went dry and my heart was going so fast that I thought I would faint. I thought that at the very least I was going to be raped and cut up, which is what those bastards always do to women. I couldn't put the key in the lock because I was shaking so much, and El Guacamayo wrenched it out of my hand and opened it himself.

They pulled me by the hair into the living-room and threw

me down on the floor, and then they taunted me. They were saying, 'What do you think we are going to do, flaca? Shall we cut off your breasts to make purses? Shall we enlarge your little honeypot so it gives your famous lover no more pleasure? Shall we see what it is that he likes so much, and then write him a full report on it?'

I was trying to sit up, and they kept kicking me down, and I was just saying, 'Why? Why?' and I was begging them to leave me alone, and El Guacamayo said, 'Who does one love the most?' and the other little shit said, 'One's family, of course,' and then the other bastard said something like, 'Precisely. Now listen to this, guapacita, the message from a very important person is "Leave Dionisio Vivo, or we will kill first your father, then your sister, then your brother, then your stepmother, then your stepmother's dog, and then you, in that order."'

I was still saying, 'Why? Why?' and El Guacamayo said, 'Because we will be well paid to do it,' and they started laughing because that is about their level of wit, the shits. Then they said, 'And if Vivo hears anything of this, or anyone else, you will all die anyway. Painfully and slowly.'

I said, 'Why?' again, and the little one said, 'Because he can't get Vivo directly. Don't you think that this is excellent revenge? We think so, don't we?' And they laughed again at me and dragged me up by my hair, and I was sick on the carpet which made them laugh even more.

I said, 'How long do I have?' and they said, 'One month, which is enough for a few farewell fucks.'

Then they stood up and straightened their clothes in front of the mirror, like they were film stars or something, and El Guacamayo, the shit, he was combing his hair and putting oil on it. Then he came up to me and grabbed me and tried to kiss me, but it made me feel sick, and I clenched my teeth. But he kept pushing in his tongue and it was so revolting that I couldn't think of anything to do except bite it as hard as I could. He threw me off and put his hand to his mouth, and then he started to take off his belt to beat me, but the little shit stopped him and said they'd been told not to harm me yet, and he put big emphasis on the 'yet'.

El Guacamayo pushed me against the wall and then they left, and I ran up to the bathroom and I kept washing my mouth out over and over to get his saliva out, and I was shaking so much that I was sick again, except that nothing came out. I had to change my clothes and I went downstairs and I smoked about ten cigarettes in a row, and I went to see Janita.

She hugged me a lot and made me tell her what happened, and we were both crying and I was still shaking so much that she had to hold both my hands. She said I had to go straight to Ramon at the Police Station, and she said that I had to go back to Valledupar and tell Dionisio because his father is a general in the army and would bring in the soldiers and wipe out the bastards once and for all because he was that kind of general, and I kept saying, 'No, I can't, what will happen?' and she was saying, 'You've got to,' so I said, 'OK, I will,' but somehow I know that I won't. Oh God. I am angry with God. He is a bastard as well. I believe that he is some kind of devil with the sense of humour of a sadist degenerate. I would like to kill God for what he allows to happen when we are all only trying to be happy. God is a shit.

Now I am going back to Valledupar, and I don't know what to do.

36 *Nueva Sevilla*

Dionisio had given one hundred pesos to the stationmaster to telephone him when the train was coming in, and because there had been no floods, no avalanches, no accidents, and no one had stolen any rails to build bridges with, the train was only seven hours late.

He flung himself into her arms as she stepped out of the carriage, but she only managed to smile wanly and stiffen in his embrace. His heart sank, because he knew that there was something wrong, but thought that it was a recurrence of her physical shyness. He began to feel the familiar niggle of resentment.

The General and Mama Julia had returned from holiday bearing gifts, and La Prima Primavera had decided to stay on so that she could regale them with guacamole sauce. The General rumbled about this, saying that he had always known that it was a mistake on Mama Julia's part to plant so many avocados in the grounds, and he began to find excuses to eat in the officers' mess at the barracks.

Anica, embroiled in her own tragedy and unable to share it, became pale and withdrawn. She was so tense that she could not make love any more, and she told Dionisio that she could not do it with his parents in the house in case they were overheard. He pointed out that they had done it every night before his parents had gone on holiday. He felt that he ought to respect her feelings, but he also thought that he knew that there was nothing to worry about. He thought that she was being wilful and obstinate, he felt irritated, and he felt insulted that she would not believe what he said. He wondered whether she might not be having one of her periodic relapses into virginity. He became moody and detached, like a dog that someone has forgotten to feed. He expressed his irritation by ignoring her, hiding his head in the pages of *La Prensa*, and by becoming sarcastic. He could not resist the powerful impression that he was being stalled for something other than her stated reasons, and so it was that he began to treat her badly at the very time when she needed his love the most and was being consumed with desperation. She fell into a misery so profound that lines appeared around her eyes, her hands began to shake, and she hovered always on the edge of tears. She felt his distance almost as bitterly as if he was keeping it in the full knowledge of what had happened to her in Ipasueno.

The Aerocondor plane was a relic of the Second World War and was too tired to fly above the mountains. Instead it flew between them and caught every buffet of the winds. The air hostess in her smart red dress with matching hat and lipstick was thrown about unmercifully as she stoically went up and down the aisle apportioning orange juice in foam-plastic cups, before tottering away again on her patent high-heeled shoes. Dionisio proved to Anica that if you left the juice in the cup for long enough, the plastic would start to dissolve. He thought that she would be delighted by it, but she was thinking about losing him, and she offended him by her indifference. She sat with her chin in her hands wondering how it was that even in a Dakota flying amid the sierra she felt harried by the machinations of evil men.

It was depressing to go in the coach through the backstreets of Bastanquilla. Everything seemed to reflect her state of mind. It was all dereliction, there was not a spot of new paint anywhere; the decay had gone far beyond the merely pictur-esque. He looked at her and suddenly felt as though he had come here with a stranger. Her solitary tears had puffed her face, she had withdrawn all her affection and was obviously acting out an imitation of her own habitual jollity. The cord of light that had invisibly connected them seemed to have been broken, and he settled into a prescient depression that was fully congruous to hers. He shot darts of black hatred at the buzzards and vultures atop the houses, because he was reminded everywhere of death.

Hours later, having lost litres in perspiration, having been squashed and battered by people carrying sacks of coconuts and sucking pigs, having got stuck behind God-knows-how-many-campesinos driving ceibu cattle across the road, having caught glimpses many times of the serene Caribbean, having looked at all the palms with their messianic fronds waving like semaphore, they arrived in Nueva Sevilla.

They found easily a room in a little pension off the Calle Santa Marta, right out on the edge of town. It was cool and dark even though there was no fan and little ventilation. They established that there were bedbugs in the beds and cockroaches in the shared kitchen, and that the excusado was blocked and fetid. Dionisio went out and came back with chemical powders and a rubber plunger, while Anica threw open the balcony shutters and moved the two truckle beds together so that there was a greater chance of leaving Dionisio with his child in her womb. As she unpacked their belongings and listened to the sea she started to feel some of her misery fade away, and she resolved that for this holiday, right up to the last day, they would be once again old friends and new lovers. When Dionisio had returned she put her arms around his neck and said, 'Querido, let us go down to the sea.'

They put on their swimming things under their clothes and went down to the sea. The shore was covered in Coca-Cola and Pepsi cans, empty Marlboro and Kent packets, and all the eternally indestructible plastic flotsam of United States economic expansion. Dionisio held up a Coca-Cola can and said, 'It would not be so bad if they still called it Inca-Cola.'

'Is it safe to swim here?' asked Anica. 'Where do they discharge the sewage?'

'I think it all goes along the coast the other way. But they say that the sharks eat one person a year, especially people in yellow swimsuits. Fortunately yours is green and mine is blue.'

'Have they eaten this year's victim yet?'

'Apparently.'

'O bueno.'

It was a deliciously hot and cloudless day that was only bearable in the water; Anica felt sure that at last she would become tanned enough to match the rest of the nation's inhabitants. She went in and out of the water, sunbathing until she got too hot, and then returning to the sea. He watched her swimming breaststroke in small jerky circles and felt his love for her flood back into his solar plexus. She said, 'You are not permitted to horse about, because I do not want to lose my contact lenses. If I lose them I will kick out your teeth.'

A few metres out they stood enclosed in each other's embrace, kissing saltily as the water lapped about their chins. She put her hand down to feel him growing hard, and he slipped his down to feel her growing wet and turgid. She looked at him with her eyes shining and said, 'You are an evil old bastardo.'

Back in the pension Anica said, 'I have a nice surprise for you. You do not have to use rubbers anymore. I have gone on the pill.'

Dionisio was astounded. Such chemical technology was almost unavailable, and he knew no one who used it. 'This is a joke?' he asked.

'No querido, I got them from my father's doctor. He gets them from West Germany for his wealthy clients.'

He remembered something he had read in a magazine. 'But you have to take it for a month before it is effective.'

'I know. I have been taking it for a month,' she lied, avoiding his infallible intuitive lie-detection by pretending to arrange the pillows.

They fell hungrily into each other's embrace and made love on her side of the bed. They had fallen out of practice and out of rhythm, and he came too soon on account of the unfamiliar exquisiteness of contact with real flesh. But all the same, as if by sorcery, they found that they were lovers again, laughing and kissing in the darkness, uttering idiotic endearments, lying entwined with the sensation of homecoming.

37 *The Firedance (2)*

Lazaro passed in his canoe through a shanty town where the destitute migrant workers, the dispossessed, the greedy opportunists, and the romantic optimists were mining for gold. In this tropical inferno there were no trees.

Lazaro missed the trees. He walked with his hideousness in a landscape made hideous by excavation and denudation. In the great pits men were working like termites, carrying their pails of mud up the sliding, glistening faces of these arbitrary holes in the earth. They were burrowing amid the heaps of spoil, slaving by the river, poisoning both it and themselves with the mercury of the separation process.

Downstream, the Indians were dying from eating fish poisoned with the metal, and the fish themselves were dying of it also. The once black waters had turned light brown, and the rains were washing the deforested banks into the riverbed. Nowadays the caboclos further downstream found that when the floods receded they were left not with virgin forest floor, but with an ocean of sucking clay that set hard and then cracked.

In the town at night the skeletal and rachitic workforce took their recreation amongst the corrugated iron and the middens. Indian girls with drooping breasts and mal-nourished stomachs, with dead eyes and the assurance of an early grave, gave away their favours to drunks in return for home-made rum and a few centavos. As they died of syphilis and influenza their little babies were abandoned by the river to what wild animals were left, and new girls arrived who had been rounded up by armed canoes or bribed with promises of beads and powerful husbands wearing cloaks made out of the pelts of pure black jaguars. After many rapes and beatings the girls would learn that they could suffer the present and forget the past with a bottle to their lips and a man with glassy eyes and a tubercular cough heaving between their thighs.

At night the place would reverberate with the gunshots of those who murdered in order to take the few flecks of gold gleaned by a bandeirante in his months of relentless toil. By day the buyers with their armed bodyguards would acquire the gold at rock-bottom prices, and those who refused such deals disappeared without mystery and were instantly forgotten, except perhaps by their trueloves at home, who waited for them to return rich, having known all along that they had in reality lost their loves forever.

The National Army, who had come in the first place to open up the area and build the 'New Frontier' in the name of the Fatherland and Economic Progress, watched in horror as the public disorder grew beyond their power to police it. Officers suffering from jiggers and maggots in their skin would observe helplessly as their men succumbed to unnameable fevers and fits of heat-induced dementia; they would send pathetic pleas for medical supplies and reinforcements, only to receive despatches encouraging them to 'keep up the good work'. Some would send reports back that all was peaceful and that there was no further role for them, in the hope that their unit would be recalled. Many soldiers deserted and were lost to the forest, some joined the gold fever; most of them found a way to die.

Lazaro joined the army of beggars hoping to live off the crumbs that fell from the tables of illusory wealth. Don Ignacio the cura took pity on his ugliness and gave him a monk's cowl that had been his own before he had left the monastery to take up this mission to the lost children of the slimepits and the auriferous mud. Don Ignacio lost his life to a knife in the back and a robber's desire for his bone crucifix, but Lazaro was to wear the cowl for the rest of his life.

The nerves in his legs and arms began to harden, and he lost some of the control in them. They became as hard as wood. His septum collapsed, and in the darkness of his cowl his nose disappeared and his upper teeth loosened and were lost. Lazaro lost the ability to close his eyes properly, and in the shattering sunlight he sought out dark corners, where his begging became a litany of misery addressed to no one because it was in reality a reproach addressed to God.

In this town of misfortunes which would have astounded the imagination of Hieronymus Bosch, Lazaro took advantage of his disease and charged fifty centavos in the taverns to those who wished to stub out their cigarettes upon his extremities. They stubbed them out even in the necrotic and suppurating ulcers, because it made an amusing fizzing noise and the cigarette-end would absorb the pus and blood by capillary action. For five pesos Lazaro would then eat the cigarette-ends amid the howls of mirth and the shouts of encouragement. He would have smiled himself, but the progress of the disease into his cranial nerves had given him the palsy. For five pesos also, Lazaro would allow the bold frontiersmen to cut away the granular nodules that grew upon his hands and feet, and in this way he punished himself for his misfortune and would have earned a living from it too, did not his condition make it impossible for him to resist the attacks of nocturnal robbers and the gangs of mischief-makers.

One day, a month before the rains, Lazaro recollected his desire to die in the sierra, and at night he stole a canoe and paddled upstream to where the waters were black, and the fish unpoisoned. The last thing he heard from the town as he left it was the characteristic keening of an Indian woman.

38 *Rain*

Anica was attempting to put the future aside and live in the present as she always had in the past. But impending disaster was breathing at her back and her moods swung between irrational optimism and disconsolate pessimism. She sometimes snapped at Dionisio, and she sometimes lost her sense of humour. He once pulled off her shorts in the sea, and she was furious with him when normally she would have laughed. She became annoyed when he stroked her thighs as they walked along, because it seemed to her to show a disrespect for her private grief, whereas before it used to send shivers up to her groin. He offended her by refusing to go into a dance-hall on the grounds that the music was so bad that it was a sacrilege against St Cecilia and Euterpe and Terpsichore, when she just wanted to go in and lose her unhappiness in dancing. She was offended by him when he got trouble with amoebas and had stomach cramps and diarrhoea. He felt as though he had swallowed a kilo of shards of glass, and spent hours moaning on the excusado; she felt that his misery was pathetic by comparison with her own, and she offered no sympathy, but left him there and went off to walk in solitude amongst the bazaars and the street-hawkers, cursing him for a weakling, only to return later full of repentant concern in order to wipe the fever from his face and ask him if he was all right.

Even so, the couple developed a routine for their vacation. They would get up late, when it was too hot to lie together any more. They would eat a breakfast of eggs and bread and strong coffee. They would go to the sea to swim and sleep, they would eat arepas and drink freezing beer at midday, and then take siesta back on the seashore amid the shade of the palms. When the sun began its precipitate descent to the horizon they would walk home through the strafing of the mosquitoes to take a shower before going into town for a meal. They tried every restaurant one after the other, and Dionisio said, 'This country runs on sancocho more than it runs on petroleum.' They would drink iced wine, and then they would go home to make love late into the night. He reminded Anica of her stepmother's warning of what could befall innocent virgins when alone with a man in a strange place, saying, 'She thinks you will come back pregnant.' Anica smiled secretly, and fervently wished.

The old couple in the room nextdoor moved out and were replaced by two plump and Rubensian nymphs whose life was a permanent party for all manner of local Romeos. There was much shouting, ribald laughter, slamming of doors, scuffling, rattling of bedheads against walls, and orgasmic wailing, so that one day at four o'clock in the morning Dionisio could not stand it any more and he burst in on them in mid-orgy.

The two naked girls and the four naked men sprawled amid a chaos of bottles and bedclothes stopped dead in mid-frolic and all four men lost their erections simultaneously. They were terrified of this huge man with the wild eyes and disarrayed hair who shouted at them with Hephaestan fury and overturned the beds on top of them, demanding an instant cessation to their interminable racket every night. The next day when they saw Dionisio they did not believe it was the same man because he seemed half the size of the man who had terrorised them, but they conducted their bacchanalia thenceforth in frightened whispers that somehow augmented the pleasure because it was like the teenage thrill of making love with a handkerchief in one's mouth in order to remain inaudible to one's parents.

Anica was deeply dismayed by the arrival of her period because it demonstrated the failure of her intentions to come to fruition, and she became fractious until the time of her fertility recurred.

During this time when Anica was distressed by the normally welcome appearance of her menses and Dionisio was involved in acute self-questioning as to what he could have done to make Anica's mood so changeable, it began to rain. It rained for three days, imprisoning them in their room. They sat on the balcony watching the water rise in the street like a river, and listening to the enervating splash of the incessant torrent of water that rose up again as steam only to fall down again as rain. Dionisio read to Anica the story of the 'Monologo de Isabel Viendo Llover en Macondo', and then she read romantic novelettes whilst he struggled with the inscrutable Portuguese of *Viva o Povo Brasileiro*. On the second day of reading this masterpiece the frustration of the rain and the power-cuts overwhelmed him quite suddenly and he hurled the book at the wall and started shouting, 'Why the fuck cannot Ribeiro write in goddam Spanish? Why do I have to read epics in some godforsaken bastardised language like this? Why do not the fucking Brazilians speak the same as the rest of us?' Anica looked up from her book in which the tall director had just fallen in love with an actress with a hidden past, and held out her hand to him.

When it rains like this, all one can do is read books or make love. But such drastic limitation of choice makes the soul rebel against doing either, and one has to rediscover the meaning of love to make it bearable.

'I am bleeding,' she said, 'but come here, mi amor.' He took her hand and she drew him down, making penance with her actions for the dreadful thing that she would have to do one day soon. She petted him until it was physically painful for him to lie alongside her beautiful, smooth young body. He smiled and kissed her softly. 'Listen,' he said, 'who gives a shit if it is your period? Go and take that cotton cigar out.'

Anica made love to him with her eyes tightly closed because she was analysing and memorising every smallest sensation against her future without him.

39 *Leticia Aragon (2)*

In the pueblo of San Martin the young men formed a club. It was in the nature of a Leticia Aragon Appreciation Society, except that they called it El Club del Dolor. It met informally up to two times a week in their respective homes, and no meeting was declared closed until everyone was too drunk or too lachrymose to continue.

The club listened sympathetically as each member expounded the depth of his passion and the extremity of his despair. They applauded each other's ballads and boleros, discussed sightings and words exchanged, laid wagers upon who would receive the first kiss, the first caress, the first consummation. On this latter subject there was heated debate over whether it was possible to sleep with Leticia and not die of ecstasy, and the more romantic amongst them declared that to sleep with her would in any case be a profanation. This suggestion was always shouted down and ridiculed, but there was not one of them who did not know in his heart that it was perfectly true; Leticia was just not one of those women that one might seriously aspire to bed.

While the young men burned with desire, formed groups for the purpose of performing serenades and retretas, wrote poems on the lids of cigarette packets and burned her name on trees with magnifying glasses, Señor Aragon burnt himself out with his self-imposed restraint.

He had married young, and was only thirty years old when his daughter was fourteen. He was a man in his physical prime, alert and vigorous, handsome and strong, with a perfect black moustache, stubble by noon, and curly black hair that he was only just beginning to lose. He was also a man of the strictest honour who never gave more to whores than he gave to his wife, and who never reached a

natural understanding of his demented passion for his exquisite daughter.

He became morose and quick-tempered, nearly struck his
wife once when she argued with him, and, completely
contrary to the tenor of his nature, he took to disappearing
for days at a time and coming back drunk and reeking of
vomit.

Leticia in the meantime had become a creature even more
detached. Sometimes in the house she reverted to her infantile
habit of nakedness, and on those occasions her father would
gaze upon her hungrily at the very time that he was com-
manding her to dress herself and not to bring shame upon the
house.

She took to voracious reading, living in a world of novellas
inhabited by tycoons and enraptured beauties, handsome
politicians and ladies of dubious intentions. But she was not
so detached that when people began to talk about this
Dionisio Vivo, who was bound to get killed one day, she did
not notice. She asked her mother about it, sensing in her very
marrow that here was someone who was not from a novel
who was a real tragic hero. Leticia confounded her family by
placing a permanent order for *La Prensa* with the tienda, and
read it avidly even though it was always two weeks late by
the time it had travelled by aeroplane, truck, tractor and
mule all the way from the capital to her own little pueblo.

There was something mesmeric about the tone of the coca
letters; she found compassion and anger, taut argument and
breadth of vision, and discovered that there was a world
outside where there really were atrocities, international poli-
tics, and power-hungry villains. She also discovered that in
the world there were genuine Don Quijotes who stand up to
anything regardless of the consequences and who attempt the
impossible and the improbable without the slightest chance
of success.

Leticia became preoccupied with Dionisio Vivo. She
would eagerly turn to the letters page of every edition that
she received, and if there were not a letter from him she

would throw it to the floor in anger, until she would pick it up again to read the news pages. Frequently she would sit perfectly still in the doorway, or outside amongst the platanos, contemplating the thought of Dionisio Vivo as if she were expecting a communication from him upon the airwaves of the ether.

Being what she was, Leticia received her communications. In the candomble she was the child of the Orisha Oshun, goddess of everything that makes life pleasant, who is also the saint Nuestra Señora de la Caridad del Cobre. For this reason Leticia kept her money in the dried shell of a pumpkin, and she wore one red bead to every five yellow beads in her necklace in order to commemorate the love affair of Oshun with Chango. She rubbed her belly with honey and she washed herself in the river at least once every day.

It happened one day that as Leticia was walking to the river to fetch water for her mother, Oshun appeared to her in her disguise as a Catholic Saint, and, shimmering somewhat like a mirage, informed her that she should go to Ipasueño and do what she subsequently did. Oshun told her that in token of her sincerity she was giving her a special gift that no one must ever be allowed to see. Puzzled because Oshun had handed nothing over, Leticia went home with the water, and found in her hammock a bracelet made of five strands of burnished copper. She hid it on a string above her breast, and its presence there, along with the green stain that it made upon her honey-coloured skin, served as a perpetual reminder of her mission.

It was on the day before she planned to depart that her father returned home drunk. He had been absent for two days, sleeping at the finca at night, his dreams boiling over with the bitterness of the unavailability of his daughter. Finally he had decided to go home and confess to her upon his knees, begging her understanding and her forgiveness, in the hope that confession would cleanse his soul.

But it did not work out like that. When he came into her

room she was sleeping in her hammock, looking in the semi-darkness like a sleeping angel. Señor Aragon was overcome with emotion, and tears rolled down his cheeks as he stroked her body through the thinness of her shift. At first this was no more than paternal, but it could not remain so. The thought came to him that he might take her in her sleep, that she might dream it. Gently he attempted to raise her garment, to unlace it at the throat, but the drink made his fingers clumsy, and as he leaned over her his shadow fell across her face.

'I am awake, Papa,' she said. Desperate, he lost control of himself, thinking that now that he had been caught there was nothing to lose by taking as much as he could before the world finally caved in on him and closed him up forever.

He threw himself upon her, clawing at her body, attempting to kiss her lips as he had so often dreamed. But the hammock swayed, and under their combined weight the old fabric split. He had her cornered and was ripping off her shift when Señora Aragon came in and said with soft reproach, 'Alberto.'

The next morning Leticia left a note that said, 'I am going to give away my virginity, suffer much, and bear a child for Oshun,' and after she had gone they discovered the body of Alberto Aragon, who had gone to the river at the place where Leticia used to fetch the water for her mother and sliced his own throat.

40 *Foreboding*

Anica's menstruation began to ease off at the same time as the rain. Equally relieved, she and Dionisio began to go out a little during the respite of periods. The streets ran with brown water which carried with it the usual bizarre fluvial moraine of cat corpses, wardrobes, confused peccaries, and bright blue shirts. At first the air was so freshly washed that the lungs hurt to breathe matter so clean, but then the sun sank its claws into the water and heaved it up and scattered it as steam, so that all cold surfaces were coated with condensation, and elaborate fungi sprouted insolently from every crevice. The hypodermic mosquitoes were replaced by an anaesthetic humidity which caused the steam to seep out of the pores of the skin at the slightest movement, and the only recourse was to immerse oneself in the sea and conduct as normal a life as possible up to one's neck in water.

Anica and Dionisio hired a motorcycle, leaving as surety a gold ring that had originally been given by the King of Portugal to the Conde Pompeyo Xavier de Estremadura in 1530 in gratitude for his mercenary services, and which had been passed down the Sosa family ever since. They thought of going into the great Spanish castle which had been built by African slaves who, upon release, had become the parents of the Nation, but it seemed too huge, too monolithic, and they both were depressed by what must have happened within its walls over the centuries. So they drove on through the dust, speeding past those tinselly little shrines erected every few metres to mark the spots of fatal accidents, in each of which was a daguerreotype of the deceased and some wilting flowers. They flew past old campesino women with dejected mules laden with unidentifiable vegetation and persecuted by flies, past whitewashed barracas with their unsociable cats and incurious children, past Satan-eyed goats and trees laden with dusty grenadillos.

Anica wanted to stop every half-kilometre in order to take photographs, because she had noticed that the sea was shifting from one of her favourite shades of turquoise to another. In these photographs Dionisio posed, in one flexing his biceps, in another crossing his eyes, or standing with a banana in his shorts, a leering grimace on his face, and a pineapple on his head. In later years he would look at these photographs with the incredulous feeling of having survived an age of innocence that was as distant as the Wars of Independence and as impossible to recreate. It was a feeling that was always accompanied by an empty yearning, the feeling of 'saudade' that he had always tried to capture in his music.

Anica took him many times around Nueva Sevilla town, looking for those Indian designs that were easier to find here than they were in the pueblos of the Indians themselves. He bought her some beads because she would not allow him to buy anything expensive; she felt guilty enough as it was, and she did not buy him a present in return because it would have been a farewell present.

Coming out of a tienda they witnessed the progress of a mummified saint through the town, but failed to discover which one it was, owing to the hysterical fervour of those trying to touch its blackened and insanitary-looking feet in order to gain the benefits of one of its infrequent and often humorous miracles, such as that when it had reportedly failed to cure the loss of a leper's hands but had caused him to wake up one morning amongst the garbage where he had been sleeping, to find that there was on his chest a brand-new pair of antique leather gloves. This gruesome cadaver with its demented snarl and yellow teeth, its skin like a dead cow's, and its gingery whisps of hair, was incongruously decked with fresh white carnations flown in every morning from the capital at the expense of the religious orders of its devotees, who bought them from the same company that later gained notoriety by shooting its workers who went on strike rather than continue to die of diseases caused by illegal pesticides imported by unprincipled West German corporations. It is unknown whether or not the saint ever cured any of these workers or ever brought any of them back from the dead, but on this occasion its most resplendent miracle was to cause a traffic-jam unprecedented in N. Sevilla, and to cause Dionisio to catch sight of a little girl with flowers in her hair. He resolved that one day soon he was going to ask Anica to marry him so that they could have little daughters just like that.

They drove endlessly on their motorcycle; it was an ideal way to keep cool in that temperature which made every image waver and caused mirages of N. Sevilla castle to appear in cattle fields. It was ideal for Anica to lay her head on Dionisio's shoulder and kiss his neck, to wind her arms around his waist and memorise his scent and the contours of the muscles of his abdomen. It was ideal for Dionisio to see either side of him her long brown legs, smooth and irresistible, and to take his hands off the grips and stroke them. When he looked behind him he would see her hair whipping in the slipstream, her green shirt knotted carelessly beneath her breasts, her disproportionate earring, her green and white pinstripe shorts. He could see that her eyes were tight closed as if in reverie, and he felt the joy and terror of one whose hopes unfold like a flower as delicate and as easily crushed as white convolvulus.

Late one evening, back at their apartment, they took photographs of each other smiling on the balcony, and afterwards he stood in the doorway and watched her as she lay across the bed. For a few moments their eyes met, and they had the bewildering and disconcerting impression that each of them was wondering who precisely the other one was. It was as though they were strangers appraising each other for a position. She was feeling contemptible, and he was thinking that she was so innocent that without doubt she would be loyal unto death, and was wondering how badly one would have to treat her before she would pack her bags and leave. Suddenly he said, 'I feel very miserable.'

Astonished, and frightened that he might know something, she sat up and said, 'Why?'

'Because I do not want to go back to that syphilitic job in that syphilitic town, and I am afraid that when you go up to the capital you will leave me.' He turned his back to her and leaned against the doorpost so that she would not see that his eyes were watering.

She looked at her feet for a moment, full of the fear that because he was telepathic with animals he might also be able to read her mind, and might know that which she did not even want to admit to herself that she knew also. She was as frightened of him as she was of the threats of the brigands, because she had seen his Old Testament anger and knew that it was more deadly than bullets. She despised herself for feigning innocence. 'Why do you think that I might leave you, querido?'

He put his hands in his pockets, shivered, and hunched his chin down on his chest. Two of his tears ran surreptitiously and precognitively down his cheeks. 'Because I feel so miserable.'

41 *The Firedance (3)*

When Lazaro was defeated by the mighty cataracts and waterfalls of the upper courses he abandoned his canoe and continued by foot. He was in urgent need of a machete in the exuberant growth of the forest, but his hands had turned to claws and the bones in the ends of his fingers had been absorbed back into his body, leaving only fat stumps with the vestiges of nails; he could not have used one. He stumbled and flailed amongst the spikes and lances of the foliage, both blessed and cursed by the anaesthesia of his extremities. He felt none of the stings of the sandflies and the fire-ants, and none of the stabs of the thorns as he travelled always in the direction of the setting sun, which sometimes he could not see through the foliage, and of the cool peaks of the mountains, which occasionally he glimpsed through the onset of his blindness.

The lacerations in his naked feet grew into ulcers weeping with pus and stinking slime whose putrefaction he could not smell, and the bones in the ends of them disappeared. The other bones shrank into spindles and needles and broke repeatedly, unbeknownst to him, and the deformities made it ever harder to lurch onward. When he crossed the patches of naked sunlight the flesh of his hands and feet burst into blisters which he saw but did not feel, and in the evening before sunset he would extract the maggots with a stick held in his mouth or between the remainder of his hands.

By the time that the air had thinned, the nights grown cold, and the luxuriance of the vegetation diminished, Lazaro was already dying. He could hardly breathe on account of the ulcers narrowing his throat, and his breath came in hoarse coughs and strangled whistles. Likewise when he spoke to himself in his prayers and his remembered endearments to

Raimunda and his little ones, his voice was a croak like a vulture, and he lost the ability to articulate because papules had appeared upon his lips, nodules had appeared upon his tongue and uvula, and his palate was perforated where an ulcer had rotted its way through. As he staggered and wheeled in the open spaces of the foothills, blinded by the inescapable light and choked by the coolness of the air, the madness of the nearly dead came upon him, and he sang to himself by a stream in a long dream of beauty as he starved and rotted.

He was back in the forest, and it was the first time that he set eyes upon Raimunda. She was emerging from the water with her fifteen-year-old's breasts round and firm and letting fall the droplets from the dark nipples that had contracted in the coldness. She was smiling because she was holding in her hand a tambaqui fish which she had caught by staying perfectly still beneath the surface, and grabbing it as it went by. From his canoe he saw her, and he exclaimed, 'Hola, muchacha, are you giving that one to me?'

'When the moon eats the sun I will give it to you,' she said, laughing. He saw that her eyes were darkest brown, and that around her neck she wore a necklace of pierced shells. When she laughed her teeth were very white behind her lips, and she licked the water from them in a manner which struck him as mischievous.

She saw that he was strong and handsome and had a canoe full of pirarucu and characin, and she judged him to be a fine fishing man. 'Are you giving that one to me?' she asked, pointing to the largest fish.

'Of course I give it to you,' he replied, 'in return for your kiss.'

Lazaro remembered the first time that he and Raimunda had exchanged the gift of their bodies, on a praia that was flashing with kingfishers. He recalled how they had both gasped with surprise, and how it was that they had fitted so perfectly together in every slow movement. They had slept there afterwards in the dappled light, and then splashed each other in the water until it was nearly night and they realised that they had caught no fish and were surrounded by hummingbirds.

He pictured his delight when little Teresa was born, a perfect miracle of a child who had hardly ever cried and who had learned to swim before she was able to hold herself upright. Sometimes Teresita would mix him up with her mother and attempt to suckle him, so that he would have to stick his finger in her mouth to pacify her.

Lazaro remembered the time when his tiny son had come across a pipa toad and pointed at it as if to say without words 'Papa, why is it so flat?', because even at so young an age, Alfonsito knew that toads were supposed to be big and fat. He had explained to his son that this was a toad as thin as a reed, and 'sapo' was the first word that Alfonsito had ever attempted to say.

'I am uglier than a toad,' thought Lazaro, and in his sleep he wept. 'I am no longer even a man,' he said, 'because I have grown the breasts of a woman and my cojones have shrivelled away. All I have is the hair upon my head to show that I am human. Raimunda, I was as beautiful as you, and once you loved me.' And once more he was with Raimunda making love in the hut on stilts that they had built together and bound to the trees with lianas, and it was raining outside, and the howler monkeys were shrieking, and far off the caimans' eyes were glowing red in the dark with the fire that they had stolen from the gods, and the dolphins were singing to each other as the waters rose.

42 Sacrifice

Dionisio sank a great deal of energy into finding solitary places along the coast. He was adept and energetic in scrambling up and down the scree of slopes, as all people are who have grown up in the sierra and have spent their childhood living in fantasy outdoors. He managed to find two routes down a cliff to a small bay that they had visited originally in a boat.

At the top of the cliff there was an ancient well in the middle of what once must have been a beautiful formal garden, but which was now a neglected wilderness, and heaped up on one side of the wall was a fragile pile of weathered donkey jaw-bones. He scrutinised them with the feeling that they were sinister, and then, months later, when he had learnt about these things from Pedro, he recalled them and realised that they were the remnants of the ceremonies of santeria.

It was a bay of glistening white pebbles that had travelled for centuries from some other place under the placid migrations of longshore drift. There was a cave there that ran four metres under the cliff, and whose mouth was partially concealed by two large rocks with the water lapping at their base. Anica at first complained bitterly about having to climb down the cliff with its precipitous and unnerving face, which was made all the worse by Dionisio's ease in descending it, and the persiflage with which he teased her about her tentative progress. But once they were down she was delighted by the place and by its cave, which was like the womb of Pachamama herself.

They took off all their clothes because it was a place where there could be no sensation more free, more delightful, more sensual, than to swim in nakedness in warm water and then to allow the sun to dry away the water upon the skin. It stirred in them a kind of incredulous, wild bliss.

Once, when he emerged from the sea like Poseidon hung with seaweed and enchanted by the songs of mermaids, gripping the pebbles with his toes for balance, he saw Anica splayed obliviously in her nakedness. Her soft gingery hair refracted the light, her breasts were vulnerably pale, and her lips were moving in her sleep because she was dreaming of all the things that she would never be able to say to him.

Moved by awe he lay down beside her to let the sun evaporate his skin of brine, and as the heat seeped into him and permeated him he felt it simultaneously arouse him. Leaning up on his elbow he bent over her face and kissed her, his hands wandering the gentle slopes and pastures of her body. She lifted a hand in her sleep and gripped his arm tightly, and then they both were shaken with a terrible desire. With one mind, she still half asleep, they picked up their mats and went into the womb of Pachamama.

Gently, intently, they savoured every slip and tug of their engaged flesh until suddenly she opened her eyes and knew that she was bearing his child. She was filled both with exhilaration and grief, the one because now she would always carry a part of him with her, and the other because she knew that now she could not linger over parting.

They lay together in silence in a tight embrace until suddenly Anica realised that they were not alone. Out in the bay there was a rowing-boat laden with lobster-pots, and, just a few yards out, there was a ridiculous-looking little man as bald as a colonial banister standing up to his neck in water watching them.

Dionisio stood up and walked out naked as he was. He waved at the scopophile and shouted, 'Hola, hombre. How does it feel to have seen the greatest of the eight wonders of the world?' Whereupon the bald voyeur with comical panic in his face turned and swam ashamedly back to his boat, and Dionisio turned back to Anica and said, 'I feel sorry for anybody who did not see us just then. He was the only lucky man.'

On the way home Anica felt a sudden desire for chocolate, a desire that she was to experience for all the months of her term. Dionisio stopped the motorcycle outside a tiny tienda with leaning brushwood walls and a sign outside it that proclaimed ironically 'Harrods'. The chocolate was melted to sticky brown liquid inside its wrapper, and she hungrily licked if off the silver paper, which she then folded because she intended to put it in a tiroir de souvenirs that she would keep all her life and fill with memories of Dionisio.

That evening at the restaurant Anica began to try to confide in him her deepest feelings, as if by doing so she could convince him of her philosophy, so that he would not suffer a materialist's desolation in the face of tragedy. She told him that she believed that her mother was presiding over her life and guiding things so that everything would ultimately turn out right. She told him that there was a difference between fate and providence and destiny, and that providence could defeat fate and bring things to their assigned destiny. She paused to await his reaction, but he just wanted to talk about how funny it had been when they had caught the bald man watching them. Anica gave up and sat in silence, wanly thinking about what she would have to say when they got home, and wondering if she would have the strength to endure such time until fate might be overwhelmed by providence.

Because she could not face the task immediately, Anica went out and sketched the bell-tower of a small church, wondering where God was and why He remained silent and impotent and neglectful of the joy of the world. Dionisio went out and found her by instinct and gave her figs to eat. When she had finished her sketch and received no indications of interest nor concern from the morphinomaniac deity, they walked together about the town, up and down the alleys, peering into derelict houses through boarded-up windows, looking at nests of huge hornets, taking a drink in a dirty little bar. They were imbibing for the last time the flavour of that dirty town with its capricious beauties and its inefficient commercialism.

That night he came out of the shower to find her sitting pensively on their improvised double-bed with her head against the headboard. Matter-of-factly she said, 'Querido, I am not happy.'

He stopped with one leg halfway into his trousers. 'I am sorry, what do you mean?'

She bit her lip and began the impossible task of trying to do this business without lying. 'I am just not very happy.'

It dawned upon Dionisio exactly what she meant, because he had had presentiments as clear as mountain water which he had been unable to dismiss. 'You mean, querida, that you are leaving me.' He sat down beside her on the bed and smiled at her, seeing that her eyes were persecuted and troubled.

'I see no alternative. What else can we do?'

His heart lurched, and panic and horror began to insinuate their way into his soul. For a moment he was dumbfounded, and then he hung his head and said very quietly, 'Please, what have I done wrong?'

She put her hand on his neck and said, 'You have done nothing. This is all to do with me.'

Sick paralysis exploded, but in slow motion, out from his diaphragm. Neither of them could ever remember how long they sat there in silence, their minds refusing to focus upon thought, shorting wildly from point to point. Gradually Dionisio began to rock back and forth, clutching his forearm across his belly, recalling with dread and clarity how at times of such infernal grief his muscles would go into spasm, he would not be capable of breath, and he would lie doubled up on the floor choking and gasping, praying the indifferent God in whom he did not believe for a merciful death. A groan sprang from him that surprised him by seeming to have arrived from somewhere else, and at last hot tears began to flow through the fingers that he clutched to his face so tightly that Anica saw that the joints had turned white. She put her arm around him and he began to talk for a very long time. He told her every detail of his woeful history; how it was that everything that he had ever attempted had started out blessed with auspicious augury and had ended in catastrophe, about how he knew deep down that in every way he was a total failure, that all his bravado and machismo and intellectual superiority were a shameful fraud, about how he had discovered this once before and had tried to kill himself, about how he knew that one day this time would come and how there was nothing left any more and how he would never have anything because he could make even gold crumble to dust in his fingers.

'You are not crying about me,' she said softly, 'you are crying about life.'

He looked up at her through his tears and said, 'As you see, Bugsita, I am consumed by self-pity.' Feeling detached, because she had still not come to know the bitter sorrow of what she was being forced to do, she leaned forward and kissed him.

'Judas,' he said.

'You were my lover,' she said. 'You were the best man of my life.'

He looked down upon her with such freezing Olympian anger that she hung her head down and wept, choking, and she said, 'Please, Dio', I am innocent.'

'Those who murder love are worse than the coca bastards,' he said bitterly.

'No, querido,' she murmured. 'They are about the same.'

They remained in cold silence until abruptly they threw themselves upon each other with desperate passion, both consumed with that peculiar poignant lust that inevitably strikes on those occasions when one believes that this will be the very last time with that love, when the contact of flesh with flesh seems to engender an occult white heat. Believing that she was on the pill, Dionisio desperately hoped that nonetheless it would be ineffective, that fate would conspire with him to leave her pregnant, that that would force her to stay with him.

43 *The Firedance (4)*

Lazaro was already ringed by condor vultures when Pedro and Misael found him. They had been trading vegetables from the andenes of Cochadebajo de los Gatos, exchanging them for mountain sheep with the Acahuatecs in the villages of the sierra. They were returning with a train of mules and a young wild bull that they had lassoed amongst the rocks. The bull had fought fiercely, but Pedro had toppled it by getting a rope about its legs, and then he had whispered secretos in its ears until finally it understood that it was in careful hands and would enjoy a life of many spritely heifers in Cochadebajo de los Gatos.

'Ay, and what is this?' exclaimed Misael, when they happened upon what was apparently a dead monk by an arroyo. Pedro bent low and pulled back the cowl. He stepped back sharply and muttered a fierce prayer to Eshu to keep away with his malice and his dirty tricks.

What the two men saw was a copious growth of white hair, beneath which was nothing that resembled a face. There were huge folds of thick skin, ears that were large and of no shape; where there would have been a nose there was a cavity flowing with blood and mucus, swarming with flies and writhing with larvae. The eyes, blocked open, had a film of whiteness about them, and the appearance of death. Most horrific of all, the face was hanging with lumps and growths, many of them rotting and suppurating, and in the gap that was once a mouth could be seen an encrusted tongue that seeped blood from its cracks and craters. The whole face was twitching and jerking in its palsy.

Lazaro awoke from his dream of Raimunda and saw before him Pedro dressed in animal skins, an old man, but a man strong and lithe, with his musket in his hand. Moving his eyes he beheld Misael, another strong old man, with his campesino muscles and his machete in his belt. Lazaro believed that he had died and that standing before him were the choices given to him by the angels as to how he should look in the afterlife. He raised his claw and pointed to Pedro. 'That one,' he said.

Misael turned to Pedro and said, 'He speaks with the voice of a vulture.'

'We should kill the poor wretch,' replied Pedro, 'there can be no life for him. It would be a great mercy.'

Understanding that he was not dead, Lazaro stirred and pleaded, 'Kill me.'

Pedro took a charge from his pouch and rammed it down the barrel of his ancient weapon. He dropped a ball down, and then tamped in a wad. He knelt down before the pitiful specimen and said to him, 'I beg your permission for this, and your forgiveness, cabron, and may Yemaya take you to her arms and Babalu-Aye heal you in heaven.'

Lazaro, unable these days to nod, inclined his head painfully forward to signify assent, and tears of happiness began to flow down his cheeks. Pedro raised the musket and placed the barrel against Lazaro's forehead.

But just then one of Pedro's bitches came forward and sniffed at the crumpled man. She whined, and licked at the sores on his feet. Misael checked Pedro, saying, 'Amigo, if a dog takes pity, how much more should we? Perhaps Aurelio knows how to cure this?'

Pedro lowered the gun and pondered. He asked, 'Can you walk?' and Lazaro whispered, 'No.'

'Vale, then we will take you on a mule. We have a great babalawo, a great brujo who knows more than we, and we will take you to him. De acuerdo?'

Lazaro, too weary to argue or even to long for death enough to insist upon it, inclined his head again, and the two men yoked a pair of mules and suspended a hammock between the animals to take the body. Before they lifted him onto it, Pedro and Misael picked out every parasite and maggot they could find on Lazaro, and they heated up water from the stream to wash him down. Misael took oil from a flask and rubbed it with a cloth all over the cracked scales and sores. He looked at the breasts, the hairless torso and the shrivelled male genitals, and asked, 'Forgive me, friend, but are you man or woman?'

'I was a man, but now I am nothing. I am a beast. I am an elephant and a lion, a fish and a vulture. I am a thing unknown to God.'

'You will be a man again, cabron, with God's help.' Misael burned the cloth, and they dressed Lazaro once more in his cowl before lifting him onto the sling.

In Cochadebajo de los Gatos, Aurelio thought that something was up, and he took ayahuasca in a bitter draught and his spirit became an eagle. Flying in the updraughts ever higher, his eye fell upon alcamarini birds, vizcachas, and cui, but he resisted the side of him that had become a raptor, and he flew on. He passed the place where the ancient mummies of the Indians were crouched in alcoves in the caves, he soared over the place where once Pachacamac had thought of building a palace, and then his eyes rested on the mule train, and he saw Pedro and Misael. The latter was riding upon a mule, and Pedro was walking as he always did. He saw the burden of the mules and inspected the body of Lazaro, so that when the mule train arrived at the city he would be ready to do whatever had to be done. He flew on out over the forest and circled above his other home, the place where he lived with Carmen his wife, whose real name was Matarau, and the place where his daughter Parlanchina was buried. He spied out with his eagle's vision all the places where the right herbs and barks could be found, and then returned to Cochadebajo de los Gatos. He set out at a steady pace on foot, and arrived home in the forest faster even than a marguey could have run it without stopping. He would be back in the city, prepared and ready, when the recua arrived.

Pedro knew the art of covering immense distances on foot in a short time, but without hurrying, but Misael did not know it, and there were other things to consider. Lazaro and the animals would need time to adapt to the ever-increasing altitude.

As they climbed, passing through the pajonales and the quebradas, the punas and the lloclias, they were forced to stop frequently because it became more and more hard for Lazaro to breathe. His gasps came more raspingly and with greater difficulty, and Pedro saw that he was likely to suffocate from the combination of the restricted passage of his windpipe and the rarefied air. One night he gave him so many copas of chicha to drink that he fell unconscious.

Pedro heated up his knife over the fire and walked over to where Lazaro lay in a stupor. He pulled aside the cowl and felt with his fingers for a good place to cut. He pressed the point of the knife into Lazaro's neck, and the stench of charred flesh immediately filled the air. Then, holding the wound open with two fingers, Pedro forced in a wide but short tube of cane. From then on Lazaro breathed more easily and the ulcers in his throat even began to heal a little. Misael had not been able to bear to watch the operation, and he spent that time feeding ichu grass to the mules, preparing beds in the dirty little choza that the Indians allowed them to use for the night, and cooking up cancha to eat.

They spent three days amongst the blue lupinus below the snowline to accustom Lazaro to the worst altitudes, feeding him on a tuber that prevents snowblindness, making him chew wads of coca, and swallow lumps of chancaca to keep up his strength. But despite that, Lazaro suffered from the soroche badly enough for his eyes to bulge and his brains to throb before they passed through the portachuelos and began the descent into the city of Cochadebajo de los Gatos. By the time that they had entered it, some of Lazaro's worst lesions had already begun to heal over on account of the first attempts at care that he had ever received in his life.

44 *University*

Oppressed by the ephemerality of joy, Anica sat beside him on the bus, watching the landscape slip away much as a drowning man is reputed to see his life pass before his eyes. Beside her sat a man whom she had known in the most intimate detail, who had become one half of her body and soul. He had been a bubbling stream in which she had bathed by moonlight, a nocturnal bird singing in the empty spaces of the darkness, an exquisite foil to everything that she had said and done and thought of doing. But now, after all these months, she could feel him becoming alien to her. He was weeping unashamedly in public, and with every tear he was turning into jagged stone.

At the airport with its heat and humidity of the inside of a kettle he refused to sit with her. On the aeroplane, leaping in the windstream like a great pelagic fish carried upon the circular currents of the oceans, he ignored her. At Valledupar he threw himself into the arms of Mama Julia and then into the arms of La Prima Primavera. Mama Julia followed him into the garden, and in the peripateticon she told him, 'Maybe you should have cherished her more.'

He shouted at her, 'Even if I were Jesus Christ himself, you still would think I could do nothing right,' and then he called the dog and took it on the fastest and most exhausting walk it had ever had. When he returned he collared Anica and told her, 'Go and tell my mother that I cherished you,' and Mama Julia told him that she had tried to talk to Anica. With an expression of puzzlement she told him, 'She simply informed me that this is what she always does.'

'What?'

Mama Julia paused and furrowed her brow, 'I told her that one cannot go through life hurting people as and when one

194

feels like it.' She shrugged, 'I think that the girl must have a little bit missing.'

'And that is all that she said?'

'I kept asking her, but she could not think of a reason. Dionisio, I cannot understand her. I thought that she was so good.' Mama Julia was perplexed. She hugged her son. 'I believe that you would be better off with someone else.'

'For the love of God, I want no one else, I have had enough of someone else.'

On the two-day drive back to Ipasueño Anica was subjected to the full weight of his choler; it was a vituperative stream of accusations, reproaches, criticisms, and vindictive observations. She sat stiffly and took it all in, thinking that if this carried on she would genuinely cease to love him, but saying nothing.

They saw each other several times over the next few days; he developed an intuition about when she was coming up the hill of the Calle de la Constitucion, and he would rush out to catch her before she went into her father's house. Twice she agreed to come in for a tinto, and twice they finished in bed making love with all the passion of reunion. Twice she agreed that no, the relationship is not finished, and twice she came around the next day to say that it was. He told her that every time that they were reconciled she wrecked it again deliberately, and she looked at him and said, 'Perhaps you do not understand that I cannot want these reconciliations to succeed. Please, I do not have to listen to all of your insults.' And he grasped her shirt by the collar and held her against the wall and snarled into her face, 'Oh, you do,' and then they were in bed again in the dark and he said, 'Do you want me to fetch you a knife so that you can kill me more quickly and finish your work?' And she sat up suddenly because the thought occurred to her that really whatever she did she might end up responsible for a death.

She found a reason to come round when she had the photographs developed, and they sat upon the floor with the pictures around them in a circle. He looked at them and poured with tears that he could not control, and begged her to make him copies of all of the pictures which featured her, because he did not want to remember any of the others. As she left he saw that she too was crying, and before she went out precipitately, forgetting to close the door, she turned and said in a strangled voice, 'I am sorry I fucked everything up.'

He did his best to win her back. He took her out to a meal, but the food had too much pimento sauce in it, and he spoiled it by crying all the way through. She said, 'This is just like the first meal that we went upon. I did not know what to say then, either.' He wrote her a very long letter in a defiant mood, telling her that she needed a psychiatrist more than a lover and a friend. He told her that he would be frequently in the capital from now on because he was receiving invitations from clubs and academic bodies to go and address them on the subject of the coca trade, but he would make sure that he resisted the temptation to go and see her. The letter horrified her, and she rushed round in a penitent frame of mind that evaporated as soon as she remembered why she had acted as she had. He wrote her another letter imploring her to explain why she had left him, and she came around with a letter half-finished. Dionisio heard her on the stairs with Janita, who was whispering, 'What are you going to say? Tell him the truth, idiota, tell him the truth.'

The letter was so contradictory and confused that Dionisio could make no sense of it, and nor could Anica explain it. But that letter was the nearest that Dionisio ever came to the truth with her. From then on she resigned herself reluctantly to telling outright lies. She told him that she had not been happy with him, that he had been merely an infatuation. She changed the events of their history to forge explanations, and together they steadily and accidentally constructed an unbelievable false mythology. It happened dialectically, because he assumed that it had all been his fault. Casting himself down into a pit wherein he immersed himself in an orgy of self-criticism in the attempt to understand what it was that he had done to drive her away, he would think up reasons of the most arrant implausibility and she would say, 'No, it was not that.' But then in a few weeks she would agree that it was because his breath was bad, it was because he was too old, it was because she felt entrapped, it was because she felt guilt about enjoying the sex so much. In the end he had a pile of long letters from her full of reasons that he had suggested himself, that she had at first denied, that she had then clutched at and come up with herself.

The consequence of this strange process was that slowly his self-esteem crumbled at the foundations below the ground, and his self-confidence melted to water and flowed away down the mountains to soak into the llanos and evaporate into the sky.

But on that evening of Anica's first letter she did not have the courage to continue her pretence, and at the end of it they were officially together again and she was hoping desperately that it might just be possible to get away with it. They made love with such abandon that his clothes were torn in the battle of undressing, and in the morning she put a note through the shutters: 'I am in a hurry, so this is just my quick note to tell you my new address and telephone number in the capital. If you like, and even if you do not, I will telephone you at the house of Rosamunda at a reasonable hour. Have you seen my green triangle? I have mislaid it from last night. My love, Anica.'

He sought it for an hour without success, and then found it in the bed. He went over to her house and put it through the shutters.

Later that day there was another note from Anica:

'Thank you for the earring. Dio', I am afraid that I have to change my mind. You cannot know what sorrow it gives me, but it is definitely over for us. I am so sorry. You must understand that I cannot see you again.'

The strange thing about Dionisio's reaction to this was that he did not really believe that it was over. He continued to behave as if they were still lovers, thinking happily about her, writing her tender letters full of news and saying how much he looked forward to seeing her again. He bought presents to give to her one day, and felt very happy.

But all the time he was flinching inwardly because a part of him knew very well that sooner or later he would have to face up to having lost her, and would have to begin to go mad with grief.

45 *Pedro The Hunter*

On her first night in the capital, Anica dreamed that Dionisio was dreaming of her, which he was. They had dreamed of a mesa that rose high above a jungle that was populated only by scarlet macaws, by capybaras, and by giant otters. From the heights of the mesa there plummeted waterfalls of spoon-bill feathers that fluttered amongst the lianas and turned into hummingbirds and heliconius butterflies. In her dream Anica saw Dionisio naked and alone upon a rock with a staff of judgement in his hand and a crown of gold leaves upon his head. His arms were spread wide and his head was thrown back because he was invoking Viracocha and challenging Him to return. She saw that from head to foot he was covered in gold-dust, and that his lips were red. In his dream Dionisio saw Anica clothed in scales of lapis lazuli, stooping down to run the black soil of the mesa through her fingers, and he saw the plump arm of Pachamama break through the fallen leaves and touch Anica softly on the lips with one finger. Then in both their dreams they looked upon one another and began to walk towards each other with arms outstretched. But with every step forward they receded from each other until each was a tiny speck upon the horizon. And at that point they turned away and walked in opposite directions, so that in a fraction of a second they were face to face and in each other's arms.

Anica awoke with a feeling of exhilaration, and before she even drank her tinto she wrote in her journal: 'I dreamed that D. was El Dorado.'

Dionisio awoke also with a feeling of exhilaration. He felt mysteriously restored to paradise.

Anica wrote in her diary: 'I have been very stupid all this time because it did not occur to me that in the capital it would be impossible that the coca shits could be aware that he was visiting me here. And I have made myself pregnant with his child perhaps for nothing. But I am determined to have this child, and I do not care what my father thinks or what anyone else thinks. I know that D. loves me. This crisis has made it plain to me that he loves more than I suspected. And he is a modern man. He will not make me stay at home and tend babies (I hope) and he is a better cook than I am. I will marry him because I know that he will ask me and because I know that I will always love him and because if that is the case, then why not? And because I want to. Where could we go and live, so that they would never find out?'

Dionisio went to Jerez' room because he wanted to know whether Jerez had returned or not from wherever it was he had gone. The three men in the house never kept track of each other's movements, unlike women who share the same house who always leave each other copious notes even when there is no call for it.

But Jerez never did return. He had found it tedious waiting for Dionisio to be assassinated, and he had taken the sack of pesos and gone to Antiochia, where he had started a successful business hauling the wrecks of lorries out of rivers and refurbishing them. He took to wearing white suits and Panama hats with a blue band round them, he had the nicotine scraped from his teeth, he gave up marijuana and began to smoke Havanas, which made him even more disconnected, and he married a very young girl in white called Consuelo. Her black hair and cherry lips made of him a happy man, and in his old age he wrote a memoir about Dionisio Vivo that for all its omissions became frequently anthologised. He died having become respectable and wise. His daughters married into the oligarchy, and his sons all attended the Harvard Business School and cited frequently their father's example of how honesty and hard work could pay off. They paid their annual subscriptions to the Club Hojas and to the Conservative Party, and began to claim descent from the Spanish nobility.

Dionisio left Jerez' empty room and returned to his own. Even though he had already inspected the weather through Jerez' window he went to his own out of habit to see what kind of day it was. Down below a man with a sack over his shoulder and a large pack of dogs waved at him with a brief movement of the hand and beckoned him to come down.

He went downstairs in a state of puzzlement because he had never seen this man before. He looked like a man from the backwoods, with his sandals made from car tyres, his trousers made of animal skins torn off half-way down the calf, his shirt from which all colour had long ago been washed by frequent beatings in the rivers, his antique Spanish musket held together with wire, and his straw sombrero with jagged edges and circlet of caymans' teeth.

When he emerged from the door Dionisio walked forward and held out his hand, but found himself craning his neck to look into the man's face. He was extraordinarily tall and lean, and had the air of a man who could concentrate for days without sleep and then forget to go to bed afterwards. He was an old man by the standards of his way of life and his origins, but at about fifty-seven years of age he seemed to differ from a thirty-year-old in no other respect than in the metallic blue-grey of his hair. He held out his hand deferentially but without humility, and took Dionisio's. The latter felt his hand tingle afterwards as though recovering from an ant-bite.

'Don Pedro,' he said, surprising Dionisio who had no reason to know that in Cochadebajo de los Gatos Pedro was so widely respected that everyone addressed him as 'Don' Pedro without a thought. 'These,' he said, 'are my dogs.' By way of further explanation he added, 'I am a hunter, but that was mostly in the past.'

Dionisio looked at the milling animals; they were scruffy little mongrels with bright eyes and waving tails. He reached out a hand to pet them and they licked it as if expecting food. He stood up suddenly. 'There is something strange about these dogs. What is it?'

Pedro smiled proudly. 'They have been bred from a dog of Aurelio whom you have met. These are silent dogs. They never speak like other dogs. They are ideal hunting dogs because of that, Señor, but as I seldom have need to hunt these days, it is more of a curiosity than a practicality. I keep them because a man needs to know who he is.'

Dionisio's ears pricked at the name of Aurelio, and he recalled the small old Aymara with the trenzas who had spoken to him in runes and permitted him to play with his cats. 'Aurelio?' he said.

'Aurelio has asked me to give you a gift, to remind you of the three dangers, and to say that he will see you before long. He apologises that he is not here and he tells you that he would have come himself.' He added, 'I wanted to go for a walk, and so I came in his place.'

'A paseo is usually a little shorter than from here to Cochadebajo de los Gatos,' observed Dionisio. 'You must have walked for days.'

'I know how to go quickly without tiring. I was a hunter. I am a hunter.'

'What were the three dangers?' asked Dionisio, who had been too pleased to come across the tigres to remember exactly what Aurelio had said.

Pedro put three fingers to his temple and concentrated in order to remember. 'The first was that you believe that you know everything, and the second danger was that consequently you will not understand anything, and the third danger is that death may come in the wrong place.'

Dionisio wrongly took the first two dangers to be referring to his own worst fault, which he knew to be his intellectual arrogance. He felt a little angry, as one always does when a criticism is too close. The third danger he took to be the kind of superstitious mysticism that is outgrown in mature civilisations. A little contemptuously he remarked, 'And you are a brujo as well, I am to presume?'

With extreme simplicity and sincerity Pedro replied, 'I know how to become the river god at the time of the fishing fiesta, and I know the secretos for curing illnesses. But for the most part in animals.'

They looked at each other with the air of fathers who look at their sons knowing patiently that one day they will grow out of their stupid opinions, and then gently Pedro took the sack from his shoulder and laid it carefully on the ground. 'From Aurelio, who has good reasons for the gift.'

Aware from the movements that in the sack there was something that was alive, Dionisio bent down, opened the neck of the sack, and peered in. His heart melted, because inside there were two very small jaguar kittens with oversized ears and whiskers. One of them was fast asleep, and the other looked up at him and mewed, but without making a sound. 'O los gatitos,' he said, and put in a hand. The kitten reached out a paw and softly let its claws into the skin of his knuckles so that he could not retract his hand without tearing himself. It pulled his hand down and gave it a small nip, licked it, and then let go.

Dionisio was concerned. 'I love these cats, but they are too young to take from their mother. With me they will die.'

'These are different cats, Señor. You will be their mother. You will discover that you do not have even to feed them. They eat only for pleasure, and despite that, they still grow. They will be black and very big, as you will know if you have ever been to my city. These are two cats of Cochadebajo de los Gatos.'

'I have heard of these cats, but I do not believe it. If INDERENA hear that I have two of a protected species I will be in big trouble. Aurelio's gift is a prison sentence and a fine. I cannot keep them.'

Pedro smiled again. 'INDERENA are good people, but these are domestic cats of Cochadebajo de los Gatos. They will not know of you, but if they do, they will have no case against you. They are a species that protects itself, as you will come to know.'

Dionisio lifted the kittens out of the sack and put one upon each shoulder. He felt the warmth of their tight bellies against his bones, and the needle-pricks of their claws as they clung to his shirt for balance. 'Tell Aurelio that I thank him with a full heart, but that I do not understand why it is that he has given me these cats.'

'He wants people to know who you are, and with these cats, everybody will. And now I am leaving.' He held out his hand, and once more Dionisio felt that his hand was tingling as if recovering from ant-bites. Hastily he put it into his pocket, and went back into the house with the cats pulling at his hair and biting his ears. Don Pedro called his dogs together and began to walk home. From his window Dionisio watched Don Pedro go, and then he put the kittens down and tried to coax them with goat's milk. They refused it, and upset the dish. All day he tried them with different foods, and began to fear that they would starve to death, but later on he found that the door of the frigo was open, that there were scraps of silver foil everywhere, and that the cats had eaten all the chocolate that he had been keeping to give to feed Anica's new appetite. He was still counting on being reunited with her.

In the meantime Pedro the Hunter had turned mayombero. He never used evil magic except against evil, and even this caused him some uneasiness from time to time. One had to be very powerful to prevent it from turning against oneself; one could end up like that Congo in Asuncion who had called down evil upon his own father, and had been consumed by ulcers and died.

In his mochila Pedro had a jar which contained the skull-bones of a black dog, the skull-bones of a black cat, sulphur from the volcanic field in the mountains, dust from the grave of a bad priest, salt, a tarantula spider, and guao poison ivy. This powerful bilongo he tossed over the wall of the Hacienda Ecobandoda before he left for Cochadebajo de los Gatos. He was satisfied that El Jerarca would soon be in for all kinds of trouble.

46 *The Womb of Pachamama*

'Everything has changed,' said Velvet Luisa.

Downstairs in Madame Rosa's whorehouse it was just getting to the time when everyone begins to vomit all at once, except for the men who are dancing awkwardly with the whores in the attempt to make their erections less obvious. The record player was playing a sentimental bolero from Cuenca, and Rosario was weeping in a corner because the bolero was too much to take on top of all the chicha and the good company.

Upstairs in Velvet Luisa's arms, Dionisio Vivo was saying, 'Yes, everything has changed, and I think that I am going mad.'

Luisa said, 'Maybe she had good reasons. It often happens that one never knows the true reason for things for years, and sometimes never. Your problem is that you think that just because she has left, then there must be something wrong with you.'

'There must be,' he replied, laying his head upon the voluptuous black skin of her shoulder. 'This always happens to me. I think that everything is perfect and that I have done everything exactly right, and then suddenly the sky falls in on my head and I am left in the dark.' He looked at the crucifix on the wall and continued, 'So there is something wrong with me that is so bad that no one has the heart to tell me. Can you tell me what it is, Luisa?'

She sighed a little impatiently and stroked the hairs of his chest. She made that chirring sound with her teeth and tongue that black people make to express disapproval. 'Everybody loves you,' she said, 'except for you. And that is all the wrong way round.'

'I am just rubbish. I am learning to hate myself, and I

know that I am going loco. You know, I wake up in the morning and my pillow is drenched with tears that I cry in my sleep. I dream terrible dreams where I take revenge upon Anica and cut her to pieces, and I rape her and knock out her teeth, and I wake up sweating like a pack-animal and shaking. And then in the morning before my classes come in I stand at the desk in my classroom and I want to cry all over again. When I come home I go running until I am nearly dead and I drive my car so dangerously that one day I will go over a precipice. What am I supposed to do when I am going mad?'

Luisa saw the fear in his eyes and said, 'Listen, Dio', just come to this whorehouse and talk to me. There is nothing I have never heard.' She told him confidingly, 'Most of the men who come here don't even want to make love. Most of them want to cry and talk. It is OK with me, it is part of the service.'

Dionisio's face took on a perplexed expression. 'I don't want to make love either,' he said, 'but I will pay you anyway. I want to hold you and feel how warm you are. I feel less sick like that.'

Later on, down in the bar, Dionisio was sprawled across the table with several empty glasses. He had taken enough copas to deaden his loss and bring him to the edge of a stupor.

Big Simon Esteso came in looking for trouble. Most people referred to him as Crazyface, because he had a staring look and a cut across his face that had left his lips badly aligned.

Crazyface was dedicated to the cult of his own machismo; he was one of those types who picks upon people bigger than himself and taunts them until they take a swing at him, and he used to boast about winning these fights even when everyone else considered that he had been the loser by a big margin.

Crazyface knew all about Dionisio and the legends of indestructibility, and he did not even bother to taunt him. 'I hear you have been calling me an hijo de puta,' he shouted, picking up a stool.

With absolute lack of interest his intended victim raised his head from his arms and looked at him groggily through an alcoholic haze. Slurring his words he replied, 'Why should I say that? Everyone knows it already.'

Crazyface uttered a demented yell and brought the stool down across Dionisio's shoulders. The whole brothel fell into a shocked and expectant silence, and for a few seconds nothing happened. Dionisio stood up and glared at Crazyface balefully. With all the pent-up anger of the inexplicably betrayed he said vehemently, 'Hijo de puta, your father was a donkey and you are a mule because your mother was a horse who gave rides to everybody.'

Even Crazyface was shocked, and he did not know what to do. Madame Rosa was about to intervene and ask them to sort it out in the street, when Dionisio overthrew the table and advanced upon Crazyface.

What ensued was probably the grandest brawl ever seen in a whorehouse outside of the capital. It appears that some people were trying to pull Dionisio off Crazyface. Dionisio was on top of Crazyface and was so angry that he was punching the floor in the mistaken impression that it was the man's head. There were a lot of people there who wanted to see Crazyface get his just deserts, and they started to pull off the people who were trying to pull Dionisio off. Elbows started to fly, and then fists. Tables were upset and chairs broken over heads. The rooms upstairs emptied and the clients and whores came downstairs in many states of undress to watch, but somehow found themselves involved as well.

Madame Rosa, with great aplomb, was darting about the room breaking bottles over people's heads in order to reduce the number of combatants as quickly as possible. Naked whores and nymphets were pulling hair and kicking out at groins, campesinos were waving guns and shooting them at the ceiling so that the adobe plaster was falling in a rain of dust, and sly old men were taking advantage of the mayhem in order to empty the shelves of bottles and transfer them to their mochillas. Meanwhile Rosalita, having disentangled herself from the embrace of Juanito, who had been trying to make love with her behind the bar, ran off to the Police Station to fetch help.

When Ramon arrived with Agustin the fight was already over. Crazyface was unconscious in the street, having been thrown through the window, and Dionisio was crouching in the middle of the room in an attacking posture demanding at the top of his voice to know whether or not anyone wanted to die, because he, Dionisio Vivo, was ready to oblige. Madame Rosa was waving a bottle and exclaiming, 'Ay, ay, it was magnificent, but who will pay for the damage?' Her fat bosom was heaving, her face was glowing with perspiration and excitement, and one of her circular earrings that she wore for a gitano effect had been distorted into an irregular ellipse.

Ramon took stock of the crushed furniture, the pools of alcohol, the reefs of broken glass, the groaning bodies and cracked lips, and realised that Dionisio was the only one left standing apart from Madame Rosa. He raised an eyebrow after his fashion and called out, 'Hola, Parmenides, a word with you outside.'

Dionisio whirled round as if to attack his friend, but when he saw who it was all the anger and aggression left his face and he threw himself about Ramon's neck. He burst into sobs, and Ramon patted his back and said to Madame Rosa, as if by way of explanation, 'He is often like this these days.'

Ramon led Dionisio out and sent Agustin back to the Police Station. In the van Ramon reminisced: 'Do you remember that time when Jerez called us up to the house because he heard screaming and shouting in your room and thought that you were being murdered, and when we arrived it was you and Anica having a fight with the cushions?'

Dionisio felt a terrible pang in the space that Anica used to fill, and he moaned and doubled over in his seat. Ramon watched with consternation as his friend wept, and he realised that he had said the wrong thing. He tried another story: 'Did you know that we had a policeman here once who could hardly read? We were wondering why it was that all his arrests were in the Calle de Marte, and it turned out that whenever he stopped someone he took them to the Calle de Marte to arrest them, because that is the only street in town that he was sure that he knew how to spell on the reports. And we had been thinking that the Calle de Marte must be a new hotspot for crime or something. And did you know that El Jerarca is so bad at reading that he has to pretend he can do it? He tries to run his rackets as though they are a business, and he has board meetings where people take minutes, did you know that? Vale, one day he is standing up addressing the meeting when someone sends him a note saying "Your flies are undone," and anyway, he looks at the note and says, "Something very important has come up but we don't have time to discuss it at this meeting, so we will discuss it at the next meeting," and he hands the note to the secretary and says, "Put this down for discussion next week," and then goes back to business. That made everyone realise that he couldn't read, and now they hand him notes which say, "Your mother is a whore, your sister is a lesbian, your sons have no balls, you are a fat stupid shit," and he pretends to read the notes and he always says, "Something very important has come up but we don't have time to discuss it this week," and he hands the notes to the secretary who is taking the minutes.'

Dionisio was laughing, but outside his house, when Ramon was virtually carrying him in, he turned around and embraced his friend. 'Ramon,' he said desperately, 'I am going loco, and I can't hold on much longer.'

Ramon sighed and asked, 'Have you tried writing to her?'

'It is that which makes me realise that I am mad.'

Dionisio's letters had started to change in quality; they had begun to be letters full of anger and reproach, heaping her with culpability, accusing her of betrayal, pleading with her that she should change her mind. Each letter contradicted or qualified the previous one. One would be an hysterical outpouring of bitterness and heartbreak; the next would be a cataract of rage and defamation; the next would be a treatise full of reason, resignation, and tenderness. For a while Anica replied, but she could not bear the pain of her lies, and so she stopped. But that made Dionisio believe that she did not care at all, and he grew worse. Anica read his letters and kept them bound in green and lilac ribbons in a trunk.

Almost immediately Anica could discern in his letters what appeared to be the commencement of a slide towards insanity. Dionisio too knew that it was happening because there was always a part of him that stood apart and watched it happen. This part would peer from the wings making ironical asides and wry observations; it was able to chronicle with exactitude the moral and intellectual decline that was like a hand of God pushing his head ever deeper and more firmly below the waters.

It was the most terrifying experience of his entire life, and at its root was his belief that if Anica had rejected him it must have been because he was unworthy of her. He wrote arduous lists of involved and remote possibilities as to what she had found repulsive in him and sent them to Anica, who did not reply. Her silence made him abject. He ran around his house with his face clutched in his hands in a state of desperation and infernal confusion, until he would throw himself upon his bed and the cats would climb up gingerly to lick his face and steady him with their bodies' warmth, until he fell exhausted into a sleep full of panic and nightmares about beating Anica's face to a bloody pulp. He would wake up and strike himself on the temples and bite his knuckles in the hope that the pain would restore his reason and provide him with explanations.

So it was that one empty Sunday, a week after the most memorable brawl in the history of Madame Rosa's whorehouse, he concluded that he was so base that he would have to improve the world by leaving it. He fetched a rope from his car and tied in it a hangman's knot. He drove out into the mountains and found a cliff, walking along it in a fever of delirium until he found a tree on the cliff's edge.

He put the noose about his neck and climbed up into the tree, barely able to see what he was about on account of the mirages in his eyes. He sat on a limb and tied the rope to it as far out as he could reach. He stayed like that for several minutes in order to steady his mind and to ensure that he died thinking of Anica. Then he let himself drop away sideways.

But the bough was thin and flexible and the fall did not break his neck. He hung there with the rope tightening about his throat and he began to feel the fog of obstructed blood clogging up his brain and the unnatural sensation of his tongue swelling in his mouth. His eyes rolled upward and he saw that he was in the womb of Pachamama and that there was a spinning silver light. There was a beautiful young girl with black hair cascading down her back; she was reproaching him and pushing him backwards, and nowhere in the reverberating womb of Pachamama could he find Anica.

47 *The Firedance (5)*

There were three tambos built on the outskirts of the city, installed there by the inhabitants for the benefit of travellers. It was to one of these that Aurelio directed Pedro and Misael when they arrived with the recua of mules.

Normally one slings hammocks in a tambo, but Aurelio made a bed in there and laid Lazaro upon it. By this time, having been carried so far by the mules, having been cared for and fed upon the itinerary, and having descended to a lower altitude, Lazaro was already feeling much better. But he was so bitterly ashamed of his appalling appearance that he had the strength to resist his confinement and to insist to Aurelio that he be set free.

'Have you seen the soles of your feet?' asked the Indian, and Lazaro answered in the negative. 'If you saw the soles of your feet,' continued Aurelio, 'you would know that if you walk upon them in these mountains, on these rocks, then they will be destroyed utterly, and if they do not rot off you, then they would have to be cut off, and you would walk nowhere ever again.' Aurelio showed Lazaro his hands. 'These hands are cut and scarred from a life of climbing and walking in the sierra. Your hands likewise would have to be cut off if you travel in these parts and bring them to further ruin. You will stay here and I will end your disease.' Aurelio looked at Lazaro with such certainty and authority that the latter sank back upon the bed. 'Will I be restored?' he croaked.

Aurelio shook his head. 'I will rid you of these sores, and I will arrest your disease entirely, but I cannot restore what has been lost. Neither will the sensation return where it has gone. I will meditate upon these things later, and perhaps I will think of something. Perhaps a god will come in the form of a bird and whisper to me, but now the important thing is to kill the evil.'

'What will you do?'

'I will build your strength. I will take away the cause in your spirit, and then I will make you very ill. I shall make you so ill that you are nearly dead for a long time, but this illness will kill the cause in your body. After that I will do practical things to prevent you from destroying yourself for the lack of pain.'

For two months Aurelio fed Lazaro on a mush that could pass down his shrunken gullet. It contained ground meat, potatoes, maize, cassava, garlic, and herbs. He made Lazaro drink the juices of mango and guava, lime and lemon, and he made him drink litres of the freezing water that ran down from the mountains and fed the river.

Every day Aurelio rubbed the body with the oil of avocados until the fishscales softened and began to look like skin. He squeezed citrus juice into the sores and lacerations, killing the infections so that new flesh grew over them, and, when the throat was healed by the paste of honey and vinegar, he removed the tube of cane, and Lazaro found that he could breathe without rasping.

In the town there was anxiety, and many people said that Lazaro should be driven out before the infection spread. But Aurelio said that only children should keep away from the tambo, because the illness was caught solely by the young. Such was the awe in which he was held that nobody dared to argue, and there were grumblings only behind his back, and that not very often. Don Emmanuel, he of the big belly and the ginger beard, acted with compassion according to his humour by putting it about that Lazaro really had a severe case of syphilis that was past the infectious stage, and some people believed him.

When Lazaro was cured of the ulcerous obscenities that had blighted his appearance more than anything else, Aurelio summoned Pedro and Misael to the hut for the killing of the cause in the spirit.

They kindled a fire that filled the place with aromatic smoke, and, when it was very hot, they stripped naked and sat down around it. Lazaro was bidden to sit down with them, and he left his bed to join them. Aurelio passed around a large gourd filled with a bitter tea, and they drank from it in turn until each one of them had drunk a gourdful. The three men began to sing in a low monotonous chant, and Lazaro heard Indian drums even though there was no drummer present. He looked up and found that there was someone else with them whom he could not properly see through his semi-blindness, but it was Aurelio's daughter, Parlanchina, who always came back from the spirit world at these times and stood behind her father with her long black hair about her waist and her mischievous smile that would have reminded him of Raimunda.

The world distorted suddenly, and Lazaro was watching from the moon through his belly. Everything turned green, and he felt nauseous because he was being tossed about by a whirlwind full of faces and scarlet macaws. He saw a piranha eaten by a capybara, and a dolphin with reproachful eyes gave him an armadillo with a rotted face and an emerald set in its shell. He screamed when the armadillo turned into a human skeleton that raked at his face with a jaguar's jaw, and then suddenly he came down from the moon and was lying on his back in the hut.

The three healers each lit a puro and blew smoke over him. Aurelio put a hand against Lazaro's stomach and turned it in a corkscrew motion, so that it seemed to disappear inside his belly. He drew it out holding a vampire bat flapping in his grasp, and he cast it into the fire. He repeated the operation and drew out a huge earthworm that he treated likewise. It was still sizzling and shrivelling in the flames when he cast beside it a cipo snake and a huge handful of the parasitic espiga de sangre fungus. Aurelio reached up behind him and the girl gave him the orchid known as 'The Flower of the Holy Spirit', which he placed upon Lazaro's stomach, where it seemed to sink slowly and disappear. They gave Lazaro more ayahuasca and some yague, and he fell into a long dream in which he discovered that his own animal was the hawkhead parrot, and he travelled amid the canopy of the forest observing it through his new eyes.

On the next day Aurelio demanded of Lazaro whether or not he felt strong enough to see death face to face, and still return alive. Lazaro, not knowing what was in store, said that he was. Aurelio explained to him that his disease preferred to be cool, which was why it always attacks the extremities and keeps away from the scalp, which is the hottest part of the body. 'I am going to give you a great and terrible fever,' he told him, 'and I will make it worse with fire.'

The old Aymara moved Lazaro to the centre of the room and built up a fire upon either side of him until he felt that he would burn alive and choke in the smoke all at once. Then he made him drink the poison that he had prepared with the barks and herbs that he had gathered in the forest. It tasted oily and sour, and it burned in Lazaro's stomach as he swallowed it.

One of the effects of Lazaro's malady is that one cannot sweat from the affected parts, and one therefore loses some of one's capacity for cooling down. The combined force of the fever and the fire soon brought him to a state of delirium in which he writhed and twisted, cried out, and trembled, for an entire week. Aurelio placed his hand frequently upon his patient's brow, and sometimes cooled it with water when it became too heated. In his nightmares Lazaro saw before him a human skull, gigantic in size, with open jaws that snapped at his face and threatened to engulf him. One time he found himself rising up out of his body, and was able to drift through the smoke and away from the tambo, over the mountain. He knelt by the side of a lake and looked at his reflection in the water, seeing himself whole and handsome once more, but then it was as if he had received a message of great urgency, and he went back to the hut and gazed upon the atrocity that was his body, and lay down in it to return to his dreams and his terrible fevers.

When he awoke at last to see the Indian still beside him and the great fire merely cinders, he felt so ill that he wished that he had died. 'This always happens,' said Aurelio, 'there is nothing to be done. I am afraid that you will find that your cojones have swollen to a terrible size, and will give you agonies, but that will pass. The disease is dead.' He gave Lazaro water to drink and said, 'You must sleep a long time.'

During the days that Lazaro slept, Aurelio himself slept, recovering from the debilitation of staying awake in that inferno for so many days, feeding the fire and keeping death at the distance of a hand's breadth. At the end of this time, while Lazaro slept still, he made a cast in clay of the soles of each of his patient's feet. Very carefully he used the casts to fashion shoes.

The soles were made of car tyres, like anyone else's, but on those soles he laid a felt made of the wool of a vicuna, compressed into shape with the aid of the casts. He made the uppers of the softest leather from a wild goat.

When Lazaro was well, Aurelio allowed him to walk for only two hours a day, wearing the shoes. After two weeks he allowed him to walk for only four hours a day wearing them. After a month he allowed him to walk as much as he liked, but he made him show his feet every evening.

Lazaro had been naked beneath his heavy blankets for all the time that he had been ill, and when he received back his cowl he found that it had been washed, and embroidered with pictures of jaguars and piassaba palms. It was the compassionate labour of Felicidad, the most beautiful and contrary whore in the whole sierra.

He became a familiar figure in the city, even though no one ever saw his face. He lived alone in his own choza, visited by those who brought him food, and sometimes surrounded by the huge black cats that seemed to sense his loneliness, and did not care about his appearance. The fact was that, however arrested his disease, he still lacked a face, still lacked his fingers and his toes, still lacked the use of his testicles and his manhood, and still carried on his chest his hermaphroditic breasts. He would sit upon the steps of the old palace or at the base of the jaguar obelisks, weeping silently beneath the hood and knowing that he was a freak that no one would ever be able to look at without turning away. Sometimes the little children threw stones at him and shouted out 'vulture' after him as he passed. He would ask Aurelio whenever he returned from the forest about how he might be restored, but the Aymara always only ever replied, 'If there is a way, I do not know it yet.'

This is the reason why Lazaro went once with Pedro and Misael to Ipasueno and never came back, because he was hoping to find there an even greater brujo.

48 *Anica's Last Mistake*

Dionisio Vivo, even though he was not a coward, often felt that he had died many times in his life. On this occasion the goatherd on the crag who had watched his doings with morbid fascination had contemplated his swinging body and the steadily spreading patch of urine for several moments whilst working out what to do. He knew very well that people only do this sort of thing when they choose of their own free will to die, and he felt that it would be a sacrilege against the sacred liberties of man to interfere with a desperate creature's last rational act. He turned and walked away.

But he could not help but return. With a sigh he laid down his staff and his antara side by side on the ground and began to climb the tree. Then he thought better of it and he came down again. He picked up his staff and leaned out to see if he could hook the rope. It was just not long enough, and so he grabbed a branch and leaned out over the abyss to hook it. With all his strength he pulled against Dionisio's weight and the friction of the rope, and hauled the dangling body with its upturned eyes and its protruding blue tongue towards him. With relief he found that there was enough rope to bring the corpse over the edge of the chasm. Hastily he attempted to loosen the rope, but it had pulled too tight. 'Mierda, mierda, mierda,' he intoned as he tugged at the unrelenting hemp, and then he changed his appeals and addressed them to Viracocha. He took out his knife and began to saw at the rope over a place where a quick inspection of his own neck with his fingers revealed that he had no arteries. When the knife finally broke through and the last fibres parted, it left a gash in Dionisio's neck six centimetres long that became a scar almost as livid as the permanent violet and magenta imprint of the rope.

During his National Service years before, the goatherd had reluctantly learned the art of smiting a dummy upon the sternum and giving it artificial respiration. But with a real corpse it was different. He knew that one can stop a heart just as easily as start it, and he put an ear against the cadaver's chest. He detected only the pounding of waterfalls in his own ears. He felt for a pulse, but then could not remember which finger it was that gave one only one's own pulse and not that of the victim. He thumped the corpse's sternum anyway, and then pumped air into the chest cavity by a series of rapid depressions with both hands upon the chest. Then he remembered to clear the body's throat with his fingers, and he began to breathe into its mouth, but at first he forgot to pinch the nostrils, until he felt his own breath coming back at him, and then remembered.

For the goatherd it became a matter of manly defiance of fate to revive this man. He persisted beyond the call of duty, all the time resolving to give up smoking because all this breathing was killing him, and in between his efforts he called the corpse an hijo de puta and an hijo de perra, until in the end he was convinced that the corpse only came back to life because its spirit returned in order to find out who had been insulting it.

The goatherd smoked two cigarettes while he watched Dionisio moaning his way back to consciousness. When Dionisio inhaled the sweet clear air of the sierra he thought that he must be in paradise, and when he opened his eyes and saw the magisterial peaks soaring above him with their points capped with snow and embellished with clouds, he thought that he knew that he was.

The goatherd led him away by draping his arm about his shoulder and giving him simple commands, and as soon as he saw the old car he knew exactly who it was that he had raised from the dead. For the pleasure of driving such an old vehicle he took Dionisio into the town and left him at the police station, where Ramon came in and saw him, and took him straight to the clinic. He was told to wait by the stegosaurian nurse, but he took his gun from his holster and forced her to treat his friend immediately upon pain of instant arrest. Ramon took Dionisio home with him and looked after him himself for two weeks.

The goatherd fully enjoyed the notoriety of having rescued the famous Dionisio Vivo from hanging above the chasm; he did not have to buy himself a drink for months. As the story got around town it became elaborated and embroidered, until finally everybody knew that for the second time Dionisio Vivo had arisen from the dead, and people were saying that he had died publicly and locally simply in order to prove to everyone that he truly was indestructible. And furthermore he now had two jaguars just like those of Aurelio the brujo, and so that confirms all of those stories as well, does it not, cabron? We all know what kind of people have two tame jaguars as black as Cerberus himself, do we not, cabron? And you can see the weals of the rope on his neck and the scar where he cut his own throat without bleeding to death, so that proves it all happened just as they say, amigo.

In the camp the women held bacchantic celebrations, but Janita heard the rumours and wrote to Anica that Dionisio had tried to kill himself, saying, 'Why in the name of God can you not tell him the simple truth? He has enough influence around here to wipe out El Jerarca three times over.' But Anica only went pale and trembled when she read of Dionisio's madness and of his heroic sorrow, and continued to wait for a time when it might be safe to love him.

Dionisio had no more tears. In his spare time he would sit paralysed in bars becoming drunk and lighting one cigarette after another from the stubs, talking with derelicts. He gave up music because he began to hate anything that made him feel sentimental. He gave up watching the television because he no longer cared what was in the news. He began to govern his life by his recollection of all those things that Anica had or had not liked, so that when he did such a simple thing as go for a paseo he would notice everything that she would have noticed until in the end it was as if he had assimilated her entire personality into his own and had found by that means a method of being perpetually in her company.

In his sleep the faces of his friends and relatives loomed and faded before his eyes offering conflicting advice and explanations. In his dreams he was catapulted back and forth between the confident expectation of success and the abyss of emptiness that was his daily life.

In his waking life he had periods of glacial calm followed by periods of dangerous rage, followed by periods of bottomless abjection, followed by exhaustion, followed by sleep that was strangled once more by nightmares from which he awoke in an ocean of perspiration and terror. When sleep evaded him he would run for kilometres in the night with his eyes closed and without crashing into anything, he would do press-ups until his bones cracked, he wrote hundreds of worthless poems, and he wrapped up presents to give to Anica which he stacked in boxes in Jerez' room.

He wrote her a letter saying that he must see her for one last time, that it was the last time that he would ever ask anything of her, that he felt as though he were dying and therefore needed to see her face and hear her voice. To his amazement she wrote back and accepted. She gave him a precise time to meet her, and gave him the address of a restaurant in the capital. She begged him to tell no one that he was coming.

If Anica had not spiralled downwards, it was because she knew and understood everything that had happened, and because she had faith that one day everything could be salvaged. Unlike Dionisio she had her devotion to her art, which, together with the child that was yet only a foetus, would at once absorb her attention and reduce her feelings of isolation. But she accepted Dionisio's invitation because she could not help herself.

In the interim Dionisio assaulted a pupil for laughing at the misfortune of another. He dragged the young man over his desk and threw him down the steps of the faculty. The students changed his nickname from 'The Knight of The Sorrowful Countenance' to 'Samson', and he was summoned by the principal, who had every intention of dismissing him. But he took one look at Dionisio and was vividly reminded of the story of Philoctetes abandoned forever on an island with his gangrenous foot and his eternal bitterness. In the face of such clearly epic sadness, the principal decided to write to the General begging him to take his son away on paid leave.

The General caused a sensation in the town by arriving in a Homeric helicopter gunship and landing it in the plaza in the middle of a concert by a Mexican mariachi band that was on an international tour. The General's intention was partly to scare the shit out of the local coca brigands, and partly to demonstrate once and for all to his son that his paternal love was without frontiers and limitations. Its more immediate effect was to disperse the comic-opera sombreros of the Mexicans to the four winds, along with their stick-on Zapata moustaches.

The General and two soldiers armed like guerrillas strode up the hill of the Calle de la Constitucion and walked in without knocking. They found Dionisio in a chaos of boxes, empty bottles, and cigarette ends, sitting in the middle of the floor on crossed legs, with a half-grown jaguar on either side of him in the sentinel's attitude of the cats of Bast.

The General threw some of his son's clothes into a suitcase, and then lifted him under the arms into a standing position and embraced him; but he stood without response with his arms dangling at his side and his fingers twitching. The General saw in his son's eyes that unblinking autistic look that suggested to him that his son was on a lengthy celestial voyage somewhere in between the stars.

When he and his cats were helped into the gunship it seemed to those who had gathered to gawp that the solicitous hands of the soldiers who were helping him were in fact the hands of kidnappers. It got about that Dionisio Vivo had been captured by US Marines and extradited to the USA for writing calumnious things about US foreign policy in his last coca letter. There was yet another predictable wave of anti-gringoism.

Mama Julia was horrified by his appearance. His hair had grown long, thin and lank, he had a strangled beard, and he had the look of interstellar voyage in his eyes that wept invisible tears more than the Bleeding Heart of Jesus wept blood. She shaved him and cut his hair because in her opinion it was a blasphemy to look so much like the Messiah.

After two days asleep in bed curled up with his cats in the absolute sleep of those who no longer live in this world, Dionisio woke up and got out of bed feeling detached. He went downstairs and found that his family were in full counsel around the kitchen table, and they greeted him as though he were a neighbour just calling in to borrow some coffee, because in a close family one never feels so apart that it is necessary to be exhilarated upon reunion.

He told them that soon he was going to see Anica. His sisters, who had arrived after two days of fervent and determined travel, informed him that according to their infallible intuition of a female Montes Sosa, Anica without one shadow of a hint of vacillation wanted him to ask her to marry him. Mama Julia, with the practicality of the females of her own line, told Dionisio that she was going to take him out to buy new trousers and shoes so that he could ask her to marry him in clothes that did not carry with them the atmosphere of past unhappiness, and told him that he should give Anica the King of Portugal's ring until such time as he could get a suitable replacement.

So it was that he returned to Ipasueño in the gunship to leave the cats with Juanito, and took the mailplane to the capital wearing new clothes and bearing in his hand a rose from which he had superstitiously removed all the thorns.

At first he could not see Anica in the restaurant, but then a tall man waved to him. He had to look at her twice before he realised that it was she. He thought that Anica must have let being a student go to her head, because she was wearing a man's greatcoat, a large floppy hat, and a black wig that on close inspection was revealed to be home-made. He laughed for the first time since he had last seen her, but said nothing because he was terrified of offending her upon such a crucial evening.

Beneath her amateur disguise Anica was looking at once pale and thin from her sadness, and fat-faced from chocolate and the natural mechanisms of pregnancy. They sat opposite each other across the table without knowing what to say, and then she told him that after Nocebueno she was going to go to study in Uruguay for four years.

Refusing to absorb or to contemplate this information, he took her hand across the table and felt it grow moist in his own as it always had. He told her quietly and with the air of one delivering a distillation of eternal truth that he loved her totally, that he desired to give to her his life and liberty. He said that he intended to find a better job in the capital, which would be easy now that he was well known, that he intended to support her through her studenthood and through the time when she was struggling to become known as an artist. He told her that he knew a great many influential people in the world of art because of his academic contacts, that she would love to be in his family, and that his family adored her already. He painted pictures in words of how they would spoil her, how he and everyone else would devote their lives to ensuring her happiness. At the end of this complex peroration he asked her in the simplest form of words to take his life and to marry him.

Anica was thrown into a maze from which there seemed to be no exit. She turned pale and her lips trembled, she averted her eyes and gazed out through the glass at the perpetual autumnal rain and the passing Cadillacs of the wealthy, and tried to think what she could say. With her eyes brimming she turned to him and said the only thing that seemed to her that it was possible to say: 'I want you to know that I could never marry anyone that I did not love.'

But Anica had left out the premiss antecedent to this declaration, a premiss that she took to be implicit, which was that she would never love anyone but him and would therefore marry no one else.

But Dionisio's mind, with its chronic literality of a linguistic philosopher and its masculine deafness to the unsaid, simply went numb and then computed the obvious implication that she was refusing him because she did not love him. He sat through the rest of the meal in the silence of one who knows that in the morning he will be stood before a firing squad without even the indulgence of a last request.

Out in the everlasting rain of the capital she embraced him tightly for the last time. Beneath her marquee of a greatcoat Anica was wearing her familiar faded lilac jumpsuit, and, wrapped inside that coat which enclosed them both, Dionisio pressed his body for what seemed to him to be the last time against the gentle puellic curves which had for so long been his new-found land that had constituted the entire compass of the world.

Anica was remembering the imprint of his body and the way that it seemed to tessellate with hers so that they fitted together like the fabled divided androgynes of the Platonic myth. He gave her the rose, saying, 'When that flower fades, remember that I never did.' She walked away into the dogged infinite rain and stopped in a doorway in order to weep with pity about the atrocious scars of the rope, and Dionisio walked away in his new clothes of a marital optimist and slept through the night in the café of the railway station with his head on the table because one place was as good as another for annihilation.

49 *Another Statistic*

'OK chicos, agreed,' said El Jerarca, drawing upon his cigar and obscuring himself behind the smoke, 'do a good job and have a good time, OK?'

Anica was walking home in the perpetual rain, carrying her portfolio of designs that seemed to be growing at the same pace as the infant inside her, when El Guacamayo and El Chiquitin drew alongside her in an old Ford Falcon, and El Chiquitin threw open the passenger door. He called to her, 'Hey, flaca,' and when she turned, she saw that he was pointing a submachine gun at her and was beckoning to her to get into the car. She momentarily considered flight, but it was if she felt that she was a prey to inevitability. She got into the car and El Chiquitin poked the gun into her neck: 'Fun time,' he said, and El Guacamayo laughed at the back of his throat and felt himself already growing tumescent.

They taunted Anica. 'Hey, flaca, guess what we are going to do. Hey, flaca, guess why. Maybe you don't know? Guess who saw Vivo and broke our little bargain? So guess who pays the forfeit, little flaca? Is it your Daddy, flaca? No, it isn't, because guess whose Daddy set it up all along, flaca, and we don't seriously intend to kill the man who sells us our toys, do we? Oh no. It would be cruel. It wouldn't make sense. But we'll tell you a little secret, flaca, OK? We think Daddy needs to learn a lesson, don't we? We think Daddy's been passing on information to Vivo now and then, don't we? And I'll tell you, flaca, we thought it over. We thought, "Why should precious papa suffer when it was you who broke the deal?" Would that be fair? No it would not. And we are very fair, aren't we, flaca? We act only with justice. And I'll tell you another thing, flaca, we like to enjoy ourselves a little now and then, and we thought, "Hey, isn't a young chica more fun than an old man?" And we thought, yes, all things considered, she is, so why not?'

Anica clutched her portfolio of designs that were to have made her famous, went numb inside, and could not think of anything at all. 'But I am pregnant,' she said.

El Guacamayo laughed so as to show off his gold canine teeth, and said, 'Ay, if we had known that, we would have brought along a white cockerel, eh compañero?' And El Chiquitin replied, 'Si, cabron, we would have brought a nice white cockerel."

There is a disease that affects carnations. It lies dormant in the soil for decades, and then suddenly erupts and destroys all the carnation crop over the area that it infests. When this happens, there is nothing to be done but burn the crops, abandon the greenhouses, and desert the land forever. Ambush is ever the way in which ugliness destroys beauty.

On the vast plain outside the capital were countless carnation greenhouses, where workers travailed in appalling humidity amidst clouds of carcinogenic chemical fertilisers and insecticides, producing perfect white flowers to adorn the lapels of wedding guests all over Europe, to grace the statues of saints in churches, to decorate the corpses of the freshly dead, and to fill out the bouquets of hopeful lovers.

The two assassins took Anica to a derelict greenhouse long abandoned because of the disease. El Chiquitin jabbed into her neck the submachine gun that her own father had sold to El Jerarca, and marched her into the building while El Guacamayo got out from the capacious trunk of the Ford Falcon his comprehensive bag of tools. Because it was growing dark he also brought in a lantern for them to work by.

El Guacamayo was wearing his magenta trousers, vermilion shirt, yellow shoes, and a magnum under his orange jacket. He looked at Anica while he ran his comb through his oiled hair and prepared himself mentally for the job at hand. She was still holding her portfolio, but then El Chiquitin unexpectedly tore it away from her and let its contents slip to the floor. El Guacamayo glanced down at the cheerful patterns of zigzags and commented, 'Very pretty, flaca. Like you.' He approached her and put his hand under her chin to lift her head. He inspected her with professional disinterest. 'Nice eyes.'

Anica found her voice at last, and said, 'Leave me alone. What do you want from me?'

El Guacamayo pulled out his magnum and cocked it. He pointed it at her forehead and said, 'Kneel.' Behind her, El Chiquitin reached up and tried to pull her down to her knees. She resisted until she saw the finger taking up first pressure on the magnum. She knelt, and felt again the submachine gun in the back of her neck. She was trembling, and her eyes were rolling to the side as if to seek an escape.

El Guacamayo reached down and undid his fly. 'I'll tell you what I want, guapacita. I want a good blowjob, and just for your information, the more fun we get from you the more minutes you get added to your life.'

From behind her El Chiquitin added in his squeaky voice, 'And our advice is to enjoy it, flaca, because this is your last chance to amuse a man or two.'

Anica looked at the erect penis before her face, with its purplish head and its fluid already glistening. She felt sick. El Guacamayo moved forward and tried to place it against her lips, but she wrenched her head sideways and began to heave. El Chiquitin took hold of her hair and pulled her head back up, forcing her face forward.

But Anica was bigger than El Chiquitin, and stronger. She struggled fiercely and managed to rise and pull away from him. Desperately she ran up the greenhouse, only to find herself in a corner. The men approached her like two predators upon a calf, and very deliberately El Guacamayo crippled her by shooting her through one knee while El Chiquitin knocked her unconscious with a blow to the side of the head with a timber that he had pulled from the decaying structure.

El Guacamayo went for his bag of tools, and from it he

took a butcher's knife. Deftly, in only a few strokes, he cut Anica's clothes away from her body, and then bent down to feel her breath against his face. 'I never fuck corpses,' he said, and El Chiquitin replied, 'Why not, if they are still warm?' so that El Guacamayo laughed and showed his teeth again.

El Guacamayo took some lard from his bag and smeared it between her legs. He took first turn and El Chiquitin went second. Both men came very quickly because absolute power is a piquant aphrodisiac, and because neither of them had had any need to learn to be a good lover. On the second occasion they took their time. In between hammering relentlessly against her body, they took breaks for cigarettes and a few doses of cane rum, and chatted about how she compared to all the others they had done this to over the years. They even had time to get nostalgic about the first time they had done it, to a twelve-year-old girl from the little pueblo, except that she had not been unconscious and had cried all the time. 'The younger the sweeter,' said El Guacamayo, and his partner said, 'All the same, this is a good one.'

When El Guacamayo had finally come a second time and El Chiquitin had pretended that he had, they looked down at her and thought about what to do next. They went to the bag and got out their aprons. El Guacamayo was very particular about not spoiling his clothes, and the other always copied him, out of solidarity and out of a sense of inferiority.

'Al reves?' inquired the latter, and El Guacamayo said, 'Yes, inside-out.'

They busied themselves about the task of cutting. 'You know the noise it makes when you take off the ears? Well it reminds me of the sound you get inside your head when there is sand in your food. It crunches.'

'I'm going to give her a big smile. Which knife is best for the lips?'

'I want the chisel for the top of the nose, OK? Can you pass it?'

'Shall I take out the eyes?'

'No, she has pretty eyes, and anyway, sometimes they

burst and you get that black stuff everywhere. Just give her a stare, OK?' So they cut off her eyelids and added them to the pile.

'Nice ring,' said El Chiquitin, who pulled it off the finger that he had just severed. 'It fits, look,' and he held up his little finger, upon which Anica's mother's engagement ring was now glistening in the lamplight. 'Pretty,' said El Guacamayo. 'There is something to be said for being small after all, eh cabron? Shall we keep the earring?'

'It's only plastic,' said El Chiquitin, adding the scalp to the pile. 'I am going to have a breast, so I can have a drawstring pouch like yours, the one you made from that daughter of the man we cut the hand from.'

'Take the right one, it's bigger.'

When they had in a neat but bloody heap Anica's fingers, toes, ears, eyelids, lips, nose, front teeth, vulva, scalp, and left breast, they stood up and wiped their hands on the shreds of her turquoise clothing so that they could take a cigarette break and admire the result of their transformation. Anica was still breathing, and the blood around the cavities of her face was frothing.

El Guacamayo took the knife that he had taken from the man they had butchered in Bucaramanga, and knelt down. He felt the blade for keenness and then sliced across her belly so that they could stuff into her all those parts of her body that this time took the place of the white cockerel that normally goes into the womb of a pregnant woman.

Then El Chiquitin took the knife and sliced expertly under her chin so that the tongue could be pulled out without severing a vital artery. They stood up again, and El Guacamayo said a little despondently, 'This is like going to whores. After a while the pleasure diminishes.'

The assassins urinated in turn over her wounds, and El Chiquitin said, as he always did, 'Urine is antibiotic, cabron,' so that El Guacamayo would give vent to his usual chuckle, deep in the throat.

'Shall we finish her off?'

'No need, friend, she will bleed well enough. And anyway, if she survived the doctors would kill her out of mercy, and if they did not, she would kill herself for the shame of looking like that. It's a pity, she was a good-looker.'

'She was too tall. I like them shorter than that.'

El Chiquitin wrapped the right breast in the remains of her shirt, and once again they wiped their hands on the shreds of her scattered clothing. They returned to their Ford Falcon with the sensation of a job well done, and drove to a bar so that they could take a break before going on to their next one.

50 *Leticia Aragon (3)*

Ignorant of what had happened to Anica and conscious only of his rejection, Dionisio Vivo collected memories and sorted them into chronological order. He collected stones two at a time. Two from an avalanche that had come down upon them when they were playing tejo, two from the road where they had gone running, two from beneath the tree of the bird that serenaded them at dawn, two from the park where he had recited a Gabriela Mistral poem about the beauties of nature, two from a place where he had almost been swept away by the current, two from the alley where they had defeated the thieves, two from the secret cave where they had found the shoe, two from outside the improbable Chinese restaurant, two from the place where they had met Aurelio, Misael, and the two black jaguars of Cochadebajo de los Gatos, two from outside the bar of the sicario's bungled assassination attempt, two from outside the clinic where he had received the elephant's dosage of antivenereal cocktail through the veterinary needle, two from his parents' house in Valledupar and two from the garden of the Naked Admiral and his researching wife.

He labelled all of these stones, and one of each pair he wrapped up in green paper and put in a box for Anica.

If Dionisio was condemned to misery on account of love, there is no doubt whatsoever that he was also saved by it. There is a kind of psychic telegraph that exists amongst those who live close to their emotions and are not afraid to express them, and so it was that without formal arrangement of any kind the members of his family would telephone him or write to him in rotation so that there was hardly a day when he did not receive direct evidence that he was not as vile and unadorable as he believed. His father wrote to him lengthily advising steadfastness, persistence, courage, and all the other underrated military virtues. His mother wrote to him epistles full of maternal compassion and informing him of the minute details of daily routine of which life is really composed, so that even in his utmost desolation he would know that today Mama Julia was going to make guava jam and then put a new bandage on the wounded puma. His sisters telephoned him and listened for hours to his ramblings before inviting him to come and stay so that he could be restored to life by his nieces and nephews, who, to the consternation of their mothers, would take rides on the glossy backs of his two giant black jaguars, and would force him to pretend to be a tree so that they could clamber amongst his branches. The Naked Admiral and his wife sent him books about the history of Caribbean Naval Warfare and a facsimile of the biography of Cristobal Colon written by his son Hernando who had accompanied him on his fourth voyage in 1502.

At the College his students miraculously transformed themselves into the bright-eyed darlings of a disillusioned professor's most unattainable dream. He had never taught so brilliantly in his life; he began to receive protests from other members of staff that their students of Chemistry, their students of Unknown and Impracticable Languages, their students of Recondite Botany with joint-honours Mediaeval Byzantine Hydraulics, were all abandoning the lectures that they had been reading from the same yellowed notes for thirty years, and were swelling the classes of Dionisio Vivo who always began his lectures with: 'I do not want you to believe any of this because it is all crap, but it is the crap in which the piles of our pseudo-European culture are embedded, so you had better understand it because no one who does not understand the history and taxonomy of crap will ever come to know the difference between crap and pseudo-crap and non-crap . . .'

His classes of smiling girls and callow boys applauded at the end of his orations and brought him presents of pineapples and panela, and souvenirs of holidays wrapped up in nasal tissue, and they stayed behind after school hours so that he could explain again the principle of the Identity of Indiscernibles, the Aristotelian Square of Non-Contradiction, the Empirically Real and Transcendentally Ideal Forms of Intuition, the Malicious Cartesian Daemon, the Hegelian Dialectic of the Inexorable March Towards the Absolute and its Marxist Dialectical-Materialist Inversion, the Argument for the Existence of God from the Nature of Necessary Truths, the Cultural Significance of the Rosicrucian Enlightenment, and whether or not there was a Possible World in which there was a town so like Macondo that in fact it actually was Macondo.

The girls in his classes fell in love with him in such a way as to be perpetually confused as to whether it was on account of his redeemer's sorrow or his remote atmosphere, and the boys wondered at the horrendous livid scar of the rope and the gash, and fell in love with his myth of indestructibility and his living legend of praeternatural machismo, so that there was not one of them who would not have wished to be him as he lectured upon the basis of pseudo-European culture in crap, with his two gigantic black jaguars sitting impassively on either side of him.

From the time when they were two very small comical gatitos with hoarse voices and destructive needle claws that had to be clipped twice a week in order not to leave the house in four-tracked shreds, to the time when they were so enormous that Dionisio had to improvise a sunroof in his car so that they could continue their kittenish preoccupation with back-seat driving and swiping at low-flying birds, the tigres were the mainstay of Dionisio's life. He took them everywhere even at the risk of summary arrest by INDERENA and the attempted kidnaps by the opportunist black-marketeers of the pelts of endangered species. They followed behind him at a thoughtful pace, and their indecipherable unblinking stare won unbelievable discounted bargains from the intimidated owners of shops and stalls who felt hypnotised into giving their master the best possible quality at wholesale prices. The cats pinned him to his bed at night with the weight of their resonant purring, their intoxicating odour of strawberries that was nowadays mingled with that of fresh hay, and their solidified dreams of the emerald paradise of the jungle in which there wandered unresisting tapirs whose succulent flesh tasted of the most expensive Swiss chocolate.

It was the tigres who, when he was watching from his window with the taste of volcanic ash in his mouth Anica's blank window on her twenty-first birthday, with one accord went up on their hindlegs and forced him to the floor so that he would roll around with them in a mock-battle laughing in between his fits of loss. And it was the cats who brought Leticia Aragon.

When Leticia arrived with a bag of her things claiming that the cats had dragged her by the sleeve all the way from the camp, Dionisio did not believe her because he had not let the cats out and had been playing with them minutes before by tickling their whiskers with the feather of a troupial. But Leticia was there at the door all the same, flanked by the cats.

Leticia was one of the ephemeridae of the human race. She had the fragility of a porcelain twig and the colours of a hummingbird. Her hair was as fine as cobweb and as black as onyx, and her eyes seemed to have no colour of their own but changed according to the refraction of the light. Her Venusian clothes hung upon her in such a way as to intimate that her natural state was nakedness in starlit forests, and when Dionisio formally shook her proferred hand it felt as though it was made not of flesh but out of coagulated light. 'I have come to stay,' she said, and then added, as if explaining some obscure point, 'I am a virgin.'

When Leticia left for Cochadebajo de los Gatos six months later with Dionisio's second child stirring in her womb, he was unable to remember anything about her that might have established who she was. But he knew that he had treated her appallingly and that she had never wept or even reproached him. She had always known that when he made love to her it was really to someone else, and she had agreed when he had said that if her child was a girl she should call it Anica. Only Leticia knew what it was that she had been doing for all those months.

She left leaving a note which said 'Now you should go to the other women. I have loved you without possessing nor being possessed, and that is the way it will always be.' She tied red cords with interwoven gold wire about the necks of the cats as a farewell present, at roughly the time that Anica would have given birth.

51 *The Firedance (6)*

It was not obvious to the people of Ipasueño what Lazaro was; his face, his hands and his legs were concealed in his monk's habit, and the special shoes hid his feet. It was true that he walked in spasmodic jerks and that his voice was like that of a vulture, but it was common to see things such as that, and who knew if there were not some good reason for his voice?

Everybody knew, however, that there was something out of the ordinary about Lazaro. Some said that he was an omen of death and that he had been seen carrying a scythe, and some said that he was a monk of a mendicant order. But others would say that no, a mendicant does not have an embroidered habit, and especially not a habit embroidered with jaguars and palms. He was a mystery, but perhaps not so much unlike all the other beggars who collected in the plaza or on the steps of the churches to gather alms.

Lazaro slept with some of the other beggars in the crypt of the church where Don Innocencio was cura. This priest had begun to lose the wealthy and respectable members of his congregation at exactly the time when he had started to preach the universal brotherhood of God's children, and had expounded the duty of the fortunate in the family to succour the less. He had lost them completely when he had begun himself to practise as he preached, and harbour the destitute in the crypt. Some of the scandalised respectable people even went so far as to attend El Jerarca's tasteless temple in the coca barrio rather than sit in the same church as the indigent.

In the company of beggars Lazaro learned something about humanity. There were some who were perfectly strong and healthy, but who hated work and responsibility, preferring poverty and carefree improvisation. Others were mad, and were clinging to reality only by the tips of their fingernails. Some were the victims of the most atrocious mistreatment by landlords or spouses, and some were fugitives of the law in some other department, who had arrived with nowhere to go and nothing to do. Others were those too sick or lame to work, who were begging just during the time that it would take them to die forgotten in a corner of the town. There were those who were alcoholic or in the terminal stages of coca dependency, who were easily confused with the insane, and who were more than likely to die suddenly of drinking rat-poison or gasoline. There were the mentally retarded, who lived permanently confused, and who were victimised and exploited the most by the other beggars, and it was for these that Lazaro felt the most pity, for they were the most likely to die from unnecessary accidents and self-neglect.

The company of the beggars called themselves 'Los Olvidados', not only because they were non-existent in the eyes of the world, but also because they themselves forgot who and what they were. For each one of them the memories of family and childhood seemed to pertain to another reality belonging to someone else. Those who had been strong and happy had been so, as it were, in a life before this one that had nothing any longer to do with it. For many of them, to be forgotten was all that they demanded of the world.

Lazaro learned from them about the great sorcerer Dionisio Vivo, who walked about the town with an empty look in his eyes and two giant black jaguars of Cochadebajo de los Gatos at his heels. Dionisio Vivo had the scars of a hanged man about his neck and the gash of a knife where his throat had been cut and he had not died. Dionisio Vivo knew how to conquer death and had worked miracles.

One day on a Saturday morning, in the plaza, Lazaro saw a man walk by who could be no other than the brujo himself, and he threw himself down at his feet. Dionisio stopped, and people who had been watching him anyway took a new interest in this sudden turn of events.

Lazaro threw back the hood of his garment, and some of the people screamed or gasped with horror. Dionisio Vivo looked down at Lazaro, who was extending his arms in supplication: 'Heal me, dueño,' he said.

52 *Las Locas (2)*

When Leticia left, writing him a note with all the ambience of a testamental deposition and a last request, Dionisio stood in the impermeable darkness of his renewed solitude and considered its proposition that he should go to the other women. He rolled up the piece of paper, and then unrolled it and read it again.

On the way down to the camp Dionisio entered the police station and left a note for Ramon:

Querido Cabron,

Understand me when I say that finally I have woken up and have come back to live in this world. I have been close to death; I have been reputed dead once, when the newspapers pre-empted the facts, and I have died once, for which I have the scars upon my neck. As one who has some familiarity with death and who therefore understands the full poignance of life, I wish you to know that I am your true friend loyal to death, and that I love you equally as you have shown that you love me, with the love of David and Jonathan. It is necessary to tell you this, old friend, because it is a debt demanded by life that I owe to you, and I pay it to you now because it is fresh in my heart. Dionisio.

Fulgencia Astiz, formidable Santandereana with a revolver in her belt instead of her superannuated Corpus-Christi anti-rape charm, with her bottles of aphrodisiacs and her campesina's muscles, matriarch of the camp, recognised Dionisio as soon as he entered the encampment. She took one glance at the man with the lope of an Indian, the scars of a hanged man, and the two hypnotic cats with yellow eyes and paws shod in black velvet, and she knew without doubt that this was the Dionisio Vivo of her maternal ambitions. She strode out and confronted him with her hands on her hips and her legs apart, and she addressed him with the impatient familiarity of an exasperated wife. 'Ay,' she exclaimed, 'now where the hell have you been all this time? We wait for months and nothing happens. We wait so long that we are so bored that when nothing happens even nothing seems exciting.'

'It was never the right time,' he replied. 'You have my apologies for the discourtesy. But now I am here.'

The young women of the camp emerged from their barracas, their plastic hovels, their shelters of corrugated iron and corrugated cardboard, and began to gather around Fulgencia and Dionisio with the self-confident courage of women who have fended for themselves, repelled armed rapists, thrown thieves and molesters over the cliffs, ignored ridicule, hunted vicuna in the sierras armed only with rocks and cunning, survived avalanches, and travelled hundreds of kilometres equipped only with an intuition of being a part of something momentous.

Looking at them standing with their arms at their sides, cooked by the sun of outdoor life, and battle-hardened by the enforced resignation of patient waiting, Dionisio had the impression of being surrounded by soldiers. He was confused by the feeling that here in one place were the representative types of all the women of all the diverse regions of the Nation; hardy, strong, inflamed with the very idealism absent in most of the men, practical as the men never were, incorruptibly themselves. One by one they stepped forward solemnly and kissed him formally on the cheek as comrades do.

Dionisio turned to Fulgencia Astiz, and said, 'I have a plan,' to which she replied, 'As do I.' Squatting before the flames of the campfire that night they discussed their plans, which turned out to have been almost the same.

*

In those months Dionisio achieved an anaesthetisation of his grief, which was transformed into a kind of awe. The women organised everything in their lives into strictly fair rotas that were never without a human touch; they suckled each other's children and did each other's washing in the streams, operated with no serious sense of hierarchy, embraced as old friends at the end of arguments in which they had been tearing out each other's hair and casting aspersions upon each other's legitimacy, and freely transcended all the incomprehensible restrictions of received morality in order to pursue the fireflies of their purpose.

In that musky jungle of women's bodies and the infinitely surprising varieties of love, Dionisio felt as though he was absent from himself. In the darkness of the improvised dwellings of cardboard and pieces of cars, out in the palpable starlight of the rocks and the momentary fireworks of meteors, he was puzzled by the sensation of being a man operating with the energies of someone else. He made love with the women with dead eyes and not a spark of passion in his heart.

It was the effortlessness of it that often struck him as he returned in the morning after no sleep in order to inform his classes that today he would tell them about more crap at the foundations seeping from the crevices of the culture which they had to understand in order to come to know intimately what they should under no circumstances believe or take seriously. It was the effortlessness of it that aroused in him the suspicion that he had been taken over, and yet he felt none of the knee-jerk rebelliousness of his nature that, if someone said, 'Eat, you are starving,' would cause him to lose his hunger. In his National Service, when the corporal had said, 'Clean your rifle, maricon, you pansy, or I will have you cleaning latrines,' Dionisio used to go and clean the latrines in order to bypass the obeying of an order, and the corporal would have to say, 'Clean your rifle, hijo de puta, or I will have you up before the Capitan,' and Dionisio would report himself immediately for having shit in his barrel, Sir, and several threads of pullthrough, Sir, which are dangerous, Sir, because if the Soviets invade tomorrow, Sir, as everyone around here thinks that they will, Sir, then the bullet might get stuck in the barrel and blow my own balls off, Sir, and then you have one more useless soldier, Sir, who is no more good against the barbarian Commies coming to destroy civilisation as we know it, Sir, and the Capitan would sigh and have him locked in the guardroom and go and listen outside the door and hear him scrounging cigarettes and telling jokes with the military police who were supposed to be giving him a hard time, and he would write another long letter to the then Brigadier Hernando Montes Sosa about the incorrigibility of his son, and would go and talk to the Corporal who would beg him to put that man in another platoon, Sir, I cannot take it any more and he is subverting the whole company and as far as I know, the whole battalion as well, Sir.

It often occurred to Dionisio that he was an honorary Colonel of a regiment in which he had prestige but no power; where the real Colonel was Fulgencia Astiz, and the General was as far behind the lines as generals always are. Alternatively, he thought, he was like the standard of a regiment that everyone salutes, and is stored up in the regimental chapel, and of which everyone scrambles for the honour of polishing the silver bands and the ebony staff.

And yet it neither amused him as it would have done in former days, nor did it cause him to doubt that he had lost control of his autonomy, and nor did it cause him a moment's guilt.

In the fullness of time, amongst those women who chose to stay in Ipasueño, amongst those who returned to the regions to take their own men, amongst those who chose to go with Dionisio and Aurelio to Cochadebajo de los Gatos to settle there, there were eventually born twenty-nine children. Of these, sixteen grew up to be women with the unusual name of Anica. Thirteen children grew up to be men with the stocky build of an Indian, and the startlingly blue eyes of the Conde Pompeyo Xavier de Estremadura. Every one of them bore upon their neck the henceforth hereditary scar of the rope and the six-centimetre gash.

53 *The Firedance* (7)

'What is your name?' asked Dionisio.

'Lazaro, dueño.'

Dionisio was puzzled and had to think about it before he realised. 'What is your real name?'

'Procopio, dueño.'

'Come with me, Procopio,' said Dionisio, and he reached down and took Lazaro's arm by the elbow in order to help him to rise to his feet.

Upon hearing Dionisio ask Lazaro for his real name, those in the crowd who heard knew immediately that magic was afoot; why else would one want to know a man's real name? They tried to follow Dionisio, but he turned round in irritation and said to them, 'Por el amor de Dios, just go away and leave us.' The people in the crowd suddenly thought that maybe the jaguars did look very fierce today, and maybe Dionisio Vivo would make their hair fall out if they did not obey him. They stood sullenly and watched the two men depart.

In the clinic the nurse took one look at Lazaro and knew what his disease was. Ugly and unhelpful she may have been, grim and hairy, but she was not ignorant, and she knew how to check Lazaro over in case her diagnosis was wrong. She checked through the *Paramedical Directory of Differential Diagnosis* and eliminated pachydermopteriostosis, peroneal muscular atrophy, Leishmaniosis, granuloma, erythema, Karposi's sarcoma, sarcoidosis, tertiary syphilis, myxoedema, and everything else she could think of. But all her tests and criteria came back to only one conclusion. 'You have lepromatous leprosy,' she announced.

She performed a skin biopsy, a nasal scraping, a nerve biopsy, a histamine test, and a sweating test, and discovered to her amazement that the bacilli that were present in large numbers were all dead. She looked down from her desk where she had been scrutinising a sample with the microscope, and said, 'You have already been cured, or had some kind of remission. There is no other explanation.'

Lazaro looked at her, sharing none of her surprise. 'I know,' he said, 'Aurelio the brujo did it. But I want to be restored. I wish to look like a man, and make love to a woman like a man.'

The nurse frowned and scratched her temple, compassion for once breaking its way into her soul and briefly illuminating it. She smiled resignedly, 'Vale, it is possible to correct the breasts and the face with plastic surgery, and nearly everything else too, and the other thing may be restored with injections of testosterone, but I have to tell you that no facilities exist for that in this country. We would have to send you to the Estados Unidos or to England, and that would cost an enormous amount of money. You could not possibly afford it.'

Lazaro bowed his head. He was disheartened, but, 'I cannot remain like this,' he said. He turned to Dionisio. 'What can I do? Can you not help me, as Aurelio did, and complete his work?'

It occurred to Dionisio that it might be possible to raise a public subscription, or hold a lottery in the Alcaldia, and he replied, 'I will see what can be done, but you will have to wait. It will take time.'

But Lazaro could not wait, and he resolved to throw himself upon the mercy of the richest man in the district that he could think of. He rose at dawn the next day and left the crypt, receiving before he left the blessing of Don Innocencio, who had been praying at the altar at the time of day that he loved the most, when there was nothing but peace in the world.

Naturally the nurse could not resist telling her husband about the leper who had turned up cured in the company of Dionisio Vivo, and naturally he could not resist telling everyone he knew, in the strictest confidence. Naturally, Dionisio was accredited with the miracle, and from now on he was pestered by the sick wherever he walked. When he told them to go to the clinic they were aggrieved, and attributed to him that worst of sins, which is spiritual idleness. This did not prevent some people from claiming that it was really he, and not the nurse, who had cured their chancres, their intimate weepings of varicoloured mucus, and the sprained tendons that they had imputed to the encroachment of terminal illness.

Hindered by the disobedience of his limbs and the limitations of his feet, Lazaro took two days to reach the Hacienda Ecobandoda, sustained solely by his hope. The way was long, and, in places, steep. He stopped frequently, taking advantage of the cedars to rest from the implacable assault of the sun. He would watch the vizcachas scurrying and think that one day he too would be able to run free. He would feel the play of mountain electricity in his hair, and watch as the alacrans, the mountain scorpions, negotiated their way through the play of the dust-devils. Once, in the distance, he heard yavari music, and knew that there were Indians nearby, creating their eerie sounds by playing the olla flute inside a pot. The music reminded him of beauty, and he thought that one day he too would be beautiful. Sometimes he would stop at the gaudy little shrines by the side of the road that commemorated the death by road accident of some unfortunate, and he would feel pity, because he himself was about to arise from the dead.

As he lurched onward he indulged in fantasies; when he was handsome again, would he seek out Raimunda and then spurn her? He smiled with vengeful satisfaction. Would he throw himself into her arms and forgive her, and make love with her in the hut on stilts? That was romantic, and he smiled with the thought of the rediscovery of that bliss. Would Raimunda be old and fat and ugly by now? He might find a young bride. Would Raimunda be married to someone else by now? He would win her away; they could elope together into the forest. How old were the little ones? He realised that he had no idea how much time had passed; he did not even know his own age any more. Was he thirty or sixty? He had lived outside life, and therefore outside time. His history was about to begin again after a long darkness. He liked the idea of being in the world again. Farewell to the dusk of the all-but-dead.

He slept the night amid the ichu grass of the pajonale, wrapped in the embroidered habit, and dreaming that one day soon when he passed an ariero driving his train of mules he would look the ariero in the eye, without his cowl obscuring his face, and say, 'Buena' dia',' and the ariero would nod in a friendly fashion and reply, 'Buena' dia', que tal?' and they would talk about the weather in a companionable way like ordinary people. He awoke with the cold once or twice, and thought wryly that there was an advantage to having no sensation in his feet and hands, but he slept again because there was a warmth like forgiveness and absolution, or smouldering palo santo wood, in his lust for the new world of the future where people would nod and say, 'Buena' dia'.' How excellent that would be. And Raimunda would love him again. That was for sure.

He reached the Hacienda Ecobandoda in the middle of the afternoon. He was covered in dust, and was hungry and thirsty, despite having drunk only recently at an arroyo and having breakfasted on a jackfruit that he had brought all the way from Ipasueño. At the gate was a surly-looking man with a rifle and a bottle of chacta in the pocket of his shirt. He was unshaven and squint-eyed, and he looked at the mysterious cowled figure with automatic contempt. He did not speak, but raised his eyebrows and shoved his head forward to indicate to Lazaro that he should state what he wanted.

'I have come to see El Jerarca,' croaked Lazaro. 'I have come to plead for his mercy. I am a leper, and I need money for the cure.'

The guard laughed ironically and feigned extreme courtesy. 'Certainly, Don Leproso, the boss always likes to help lepers. Now turn around and get out of here or I will put you out of your misery myself.' He lowered the rifle and pointed it at Lazaro's stomach.

Lazaro saw all his dreams collapsing as though they were a bridge with severed ropes. 'In the name of God, I beg you,' he said. But the guard prodded him in the chest with the barrel and pushed him over. He laughed.

At this point El Chiquitin arrived in a cloud of dust in a pick-up truck, with El Guacamayo sitting beside him in the passenger seat. They had just returned from an all-night session of violating two young girls in a choza and cutting them up, but were not too tired for a little fun. They listened to what the guard told them, and told Lazaro to climb into the back of the truck, which he did with great difficulty but with renewed optimism.

They left him in a corral and told him to wait, and then went to see El Jerarca and relayed the story to him. It so happened that El Jerarca was bored, and was receptive to the idea of a little spectacle, so he called everyone together, and the whole party trouped off to the corral in a chattering, happy gaggle, while El Chiquitin went to get the necessaries. El Jerarca took his seat in the shade of a ceiba tree, just as he did at corridas, and waited for the return of El Chiquitin, who shortly arrived with a large jerrycan. He pushed the can through the rails and climbed in after it, and then he carried it to where Lazaro was waiting patiently, feeling most important, in the middle of the corral. El Chiquitin was speaking very loudly to Lazaro, so that the others would hear and be amused by his drollery.

'We have a certain cure here in our hands,' he was saying. 'We call it "La danza del fuego" and it is very cheap, cabron, very cheap. It begins with a little wash in our curative water, so sit down and I will pour it over you.'

Lazaro started to make a speech of special thanks that he had been preparing for two days in his head, but El Jerarca waved his hand to signify that his modesty forbade, and Lazaro sat down.

Because of his disease he suffered from anosmia, and could not smell that the liquid was not water. He sat drenched in gasoline awaiting further instructions, and was still sitting patiently when El Chiquitin threw the match.

His first reaction was confusion and surprise because it was like being in the midst of a sudden whirlwind. His second reaction was that he could not breathe, and he started up upon his feet with his hands to his throat. He could see nothing in the rush of flame, and at first could feel nothing, partly because of his affliction, partly because of his incomprehension, and partly because the flame at first burned the superfluity of vapour rather than his flesh.

But that was only at first. When the searing bit him like a thousand piranhas his consciousness transformed itself into a single unrelenting scream. Demented with agony and asphyxia he whirled and ran in his column of flame while, unheard and unseen, El Jerarca and his company of lackeys cheered and clapped, wiped their eyes in merriment, and made the kind of remarks that passed with them for wit.

El Chiquitin was following Lazaro with the can, getting as near as he dared, and renewing the inferno before dashing backwards.

Even if his eyes had not melted in their unlidded sockets, Lazaro would still not have been able to see anything through the miasmas of his incendiarisation. He ran without direction, twisting and flailing, whirling and falling. He was shrieking and ululating in his agonies until finally the flames closed his throat. When he had fallen to the ground, had ceased convulsing, and had in the reverie of his death become whole and handsome once more, blissful in Raimunda's embrace, a hawkhead parrot circled the corral once, and flew east.

When they had gathered around the charred and seeping corpse El Jerarca said, 'Look boys, it was a woman. She had tits.'

But El Chiquitin pointed and said, 'And a polla. It was someone who was a man as well, boss.'

El Guacamayo pondered the remains and flashed his gold-toothed smile. 'Perfect cure, boss, not a trace of leprosy now.'

But El Jerarca took the fact that it was an hermaphrodite to be a bad omen, and he said curtly, 'It stinks. Take the meat away.'

'Where to, boss?'

'Vivo's garden, where else?'

'What was it he was shouting when he was dancing?' inquired El Guacamayo, 'I didn't quite catch it.'

El Chiquitin replied 'It sounded something like "Raimunda", but it couldn't have been. A freak like that couldn't have had a woman.'

54 *The Ring*

Ramon came into the house without knocking and went into Dionisio's room. Dionisio was sitting in his rocking-chair in a dream, and as Ramon entered he turned his head and smiled. Ramon bent down and fondled the jaguars' ears, and then straightened up.

'Hola, Anaximenes,' exclaimed the visitor, waving a bottle, 'look, I have some Chilean Cabernet Sauvignon.'

Dionisio stood up and embraced his friend, saying, 'Ramon, you must stop spending money that you don't have.'

'It is worth it, my friend, just to see you smile for once, and in any case, I bought it with the money that I get from the mad women for the rent of the goatfield, so it is money I owe to you.'

Dionisio went to fetch a corkscrew and came back with it. Ramon said, 'I see that you have shaved for once. Does this mean that I no longer have to come round here and do it for you? Does this mean that I no longer have to tie you down and cut your hair? You know I was enjoying pretending to be your mother, but it was wearing thin.'

'Tell me, cabron,' said Dionisio, 'how is it that you always have two days' stubble? Don't you have to shave in order to do that? And yet I never see you clean shaved.'

'A mystery, Heraclitus,' he replied, winking and tapping the side of his nose. Then he became serious and said, 'Listen, I have very bad news. About Anica. I am not supposed to tell you this because only relatives should be informed, but I have received a police report from the capital, and I have seen Señor Moreno before coming here.'

Dionisio went pale, and the glass in his hand shook a little. 'I don't want to talk about her any more, Ramon.'

'Well, don't talk then. Just listen. There is no way to be gentle about this, my friend, and I know that you have never stopped loving her, and so let us forget all the crap, OK?' Ramon looked at the floor, and then glanced up. 'The fact is that she is dead, and that it was plainly a coca killing. I am very sorry. I loved her as well in my own way, as everyone did. She was the best woman in this town.'

Dionisio could only repeat, 'A coca killing? How is that?'

'I am telling you no details, friend, because they would make you sick. But the body was in a bad state and it took a long time to fit it to a description of a missing person. Apparently Anica was registered missing by the warden of her residence, but nothing was done until this body turned up.'

Ramon and Dionisio looked at one another in silence, and then Dionisio gazed blankly out of the window. 'I got into the habit of thinking that she was dead,' he said.

'Do you remember her green earring in the shape of a triangle?' asked Ramon, and Dionisio nodded. 'Well, they found it inside her body, and that was about all that was identifiable. I am very sorry.'

Dionisio passed his hand over his eyes, and then said, 'Why?'

Ramon sighed. 'I saw Señor Moreno just now, and he was so upset that he told me things that were unwise to tell me. You know, Dio', he was supplying all the weapons to El Jerarca, and the most surprising thing is that it all seems to have been legal. Anyway, so Señor Moreno knew that they were wanting to assassinate you, and he was scared that she would get caught in the crossfire, so he did a deal, which was that El Jerarca would scare Anica away from you by pretending that if she didn't leave you, her father and all the family would be killed. And in return, Señor Moreno would give him a discount on a shipment. And so they threatened Anica and she left you to save her family. You know, Dio', she still loved you and everything she told you was bullshit, but she

253

only did it because she had to. Something else, Dio', she got herself pregnant on purpose so that she could have your child, and she refused when her father told her to get rid of it. Do you want me to carry on?'

Dionisio nodded, saying, 'I shall feel all this later, when I have thought about it, but carry on.'

'This is the hard bit, Dio'. It appears that she saw you one more time after her time was up, and El Jerarca didn't like it. Obviously he wasn't going to kill off his arms supplier, and so he let his men take Anica, and I am afraid that the child inside her died at the same time. You were going to have a little daughter, Dio', just as you wanted.'

'And so it was me that killed her. In fact it was because of me.'

Ramon shook his head. 'The big irony, Dio', is that if she had stayed with you she would have been completely safe because El Jerarca is terrified of you. You know, he thinks you are a brujo. If anyone killed her, it was her own father, and he thought that he was protecting her, so it was all done out of love. I think you should understand that. But I also think that El Jerarca knew that the only way he could destroy you was by destroying what mattered to you the most.'

'He was right, Ramon, that is what he did.' Dionisio drank some wine, and then after a long time he said, 'But I will tell you one thing, and that is that you have given me back all the faith that I had in her, and you have turned all the hate back into the love that it was before. Thank you for telling me, Ramon, because it was hard to live with all that hate.'

Ramon smiled and said, 'Well, that at least is something,' and Dionisio said, 'Anica went to a wise woman once, the one that lives near Madame Rosa's. I told her it was all rubbish, but you know that woman told her that the last year of her life would be the happiest.'

'I think it was,' replied the policeman, 'and it was because of you.' Then he stood up saying, 'I nearly forgot, I have something else.'

He undid the flap of his holster and pulled out his automatic. He held it barrel downwards and shook it. Out came a long slim cigar, and he handed it to Dionisio saying, 'It's for you, I find they get less damaged if I carry them like this. Listen, you had better enjoy it, because it is a real Havana, OK?'

Dionisio's eyes were watering, and his lip was quivering, but he managed to say, 'You know that proverb that this country is a beggar sitting on a pile of gold?'

'Yes.'

'If everyone in this country was as good as you, Ramon, it would be a paradise.'

Ramon smiled self-deprecatingly. 'You're not so bad yourself, Parmenides,' he said. 'You know, I keep thinking about these cats. I don't think they are real jaguars. They look to me like very overgrown black domestic cats, you know, the stocky short-haired ones.'

Dionisio looked at them and thought about it. 'But Ramon, that is what black jaguars look like anyway.'

It was many weeks later, and Dionisio was driving up into the sierra because he wanted to take the cats for a long walk along the andenes that the Indians had once built for agriculture. He had accelerated through under the bridge where all the addicts congregate, and was rounding a bend when he saw that a jeep had broken down, and two men were looking under the bonnet.

El Chiquitin and El Guacamayo had been returning to base when their fanbelt had broken, and they were in the process of trying to change it when Dionisio stopped his car, got out with his two cats, and offered to help. The two assassins straightened up when he addressed them, and terror instantly struck them to the heart.

Dionisio noticed immediately that El Chiquitin was wearing Anica's mother's engagement ring on his little finger.

Police Statement

Ipasueño Police: statement of Officer, Ramon Dario.
Copy to the Alcaldia.

Today the bodies of Eduardo Carriego (a.k.a. 'El Guacamayo') aged 27, and Evaristo Mallea aged 34, (a.k.a. 'El
Chiquitin') were discovered on the road to Santa Maria
Virgen. The full statements of those who found the bodies
are appended. We await the coroner's report, but preliminary
investigations suggest that the wounds on the bodies were
caused by wild beasts. The throats were torn out and there
were tracks of claws in fours, like those of a cat.

Nonetheless, the case is not in this way completely
explained. Attacks by wild jaguars upon humans are almost
unknown, there are no known wild jaguars in this area, and
the dimensions of the wounds suggest animals larger than
jaguars. It is impossible that the wounds could have been
caused by any smaller animal, such as a puma.

These two men were widely known to be assassins in the
employ of Pablo Ecobandodo, and it is suggested that this is
a 'coca killing' simulated to appear as the attack of wild
beasts. This is further suggested by the curious fact that the
tongues of the two victims appear to have been pulled through
the apertures in their necks.

Signed: Ramon Dario, Ipasueño Police.

Ramon put a copy of this report under Dionisio's door,
and scrawled across the bottom, 'Congratulations. You will
notice that I say nothing about tame jaguars.'

55 Ramon

Dionisio arose from his bed, went to the window to see what kind of day it was, and went to the telephone to ring the police.

He got no wrong numbers for a change, and a voice on the other end of the line said, 'Police.'

'Agustin, is that you? This is Dionisio from the Calle de la Constitucion. Listen, the bastards have got Ramon. Yes, I am sure that it is Ramon. Yes, it is a Colombian cravate. Okay, Agustin, me too. I will keep away the vultures. No, I will not shoot them. Okay.'

Dionisio put on only a shirt with a tail so long that it came down to his knees, and ran downstairs hoping that it was not Ramon. He emerged from the door and the first thing that he noticed was that the pajaro that had always sung at dawn was not singing. He approached the body of his dearest friend who had broken open so many bottles in the spirit of consolation and reassurance, and felt that once again he had been disembowelled.

Ramon was wearing no shoes, and his feet had been burned. Blood still seeped from the roasted flesh spotted with charcoal, and he saw from the dirt amongst the blistered pulp that Ramon had been made to walk before he had had his throat cut and his tongue pulled through. He had been killed with such contempt that his automatic had been replaced in his holster to signify a policeman's lack of power. Dionisio took the automatic and left it inside the door.

He bent down and brushed away some of the ants that were crawling over Ramon's face and going in and out of his mouth. He looked at his watch and wondered how long it would be before Agustin arrived. He bent forward and kissed Ramon on the cheek as comrades do. He ran his finger over the lips that had spoken so many kindly words of comfort and so many learned jests. 'Old friend,' he said.

He saw a piece of paper folded in Ramon's shirt pocket, and took it out and unfolded it. 'A birthday present,' it read. Dionisio reflected for a moment before remembering that today it was the birthday of El Jerarca who was holding in the Barrio Jerarca a seven-day carnival complete with the blessings of the tame priests, three brass bands, and a Morenado dance group from the region of the mines.

'So he closed your path, too, old friend.' He realised that he had not written a coca letter for months, and wondered at the cacique's malice that he should after all this time still be finding ways of spiting the one man who in all his fruitless life had made him see himself as he truly was.

When Agustin arrived, looking older and filling out his uniform with more virility than when he had first come here to take away a cravate, Dionisio saw that despite his professional pulling on of the yellow kitchen gloves, his eyes were already full of tears.

The young policeman looked down upon the body of the one man who at all times had guaranteed the morale of the station and filled it with the wit of his ironic cynicism. He gestured at the broken corpse with its atrocious signs of torture, and with his lips struggling for the words he said to Dionisio, as if explaining something, 'He taught me everything.'

Dionisio stroked Ramon's hair into place, and stood up. He and Agustin looked down again in silence, and then Dionisio said 'Are you the duty officer this week?' Agustin wiped his eyes with his sleeve and nodded. 'Then you must do me a favour.'

Agustin nodded again because his throat was too swollen with the unshed tears for him to be able to speak.

'Make sure that there are no policemen at the carnival, and if anyone comes to give any eye-witness accounts, take their statements and then use them to light cigarettes. If you have to make any investigations, ensure that you only interview people who saw nothing.'

Agustin nodded for the last time and pointed at Ramon's body. 'The bastards tortured him. He knew all the details of what they were doing.' He paused 'And he was a friend of yours.'

'This is another death of mine,' Dionisio said. He saw that Agustin could hold his tears no longer, and put one hand on his shoulder. As he began to shake with sobs, Dionisio put his arm about his neck and hugged him like a child. They stood together wrapped in each other's embrace, and Dionisio discovered that he still had no tears. He could not cry for his friend. 'Soon,' he said, rocking the young colleague of Ramon who was still weeping, 'I will do something that Ramon would have given his life to see. I have sworn it, and it is as good as already done.'

After Agustin and Dionisio had tenderly lifted the body into the back of the van that had collected so many corpses in differing states of decomposition that it reeked permanently of vultures and detergent, Dionisio watched it drive away and then went back inside, picking up Ramon's automatic on the way. He sat down and fell into a state of perfect stillness, and then he got up and went to his pile of paper ruled with staves. It was then that he composed in the space of one hour and without revisions his *Requiem Angelico*. He originally scored the Angelic Requiem for keyboard, quenas, and mandolas, and even in that form its effect upon the mourners at the funeral of Ramon Dario was unprecedented. Even the guard of honour of policemen outside the church in full-dress uniform felt tears spring to their eyes, not because the piece was sad, but because of its saudade preceding its triumphant serenity. All who have heard it since have pointed out that the place where one feels the breeze of the wings of angels in one's face and the numinous chill of the praeternatural running up and down the spine and making the hairs of the body shiver at the roots, is the very place where the nostalgic and loving melody of the first half suddenly rises up into the hymn of glory of the second half that in truth does sound like the choirs of heaven greeting the dawn of a new creation. The piece became known across the whole of Hispano-America, and was eventually brought to Europe by an anthropological musicologist who innocently assumed that it was traditional, and who himself later settled in Cochadebajo de los Gatos.

Having composed this love-song to true friendship, Dionisio took Ramon's automatic and felt how heavy it was in the hand. He summoned the cats and set off with them down the hill to the camp of Las Locas.

On the way a harassed man in spectacles with a notebook and pockets full of pens that did not work spotted him from afar with his unmistakable jaguars, and tagged after him for a week plaguing him with questions that he did not even hear because his mind was filled with only one purpose.

This gentleman was Narciso Almeida, a famously intrepid reporter of *La Prensa*, who for four years at the risk of his own life had been covering the country's internal cocaine war and recounting its horrors to the intelligent and the powerful of the nation. He had been sent on the fairly routine assignment of finding out why it was that one of the most celebrated campaigners against the coca caudillos had for so long lapsed into silence, but he became instead the man who, more than any other, became responsible, because of a single sensational article, for disseminating the fantastical myth of Dionisio Vivo.

Part Three

56 *Extraordinary Events In Ipasueño*

Your reporter arrived in Ipasueño with the brief that he should interview the widely-known Dionisio Vivo in order to ascertain from him the reasons for his having ceased to write what have now become known as 'The Coca Letters', the editor of *La Prensa* having become suspicious that Señor Vivo may have been silenced.

However, I have in the past few days been witness to such extraordinary events that it has been almost impossible for even a reporter of my experience to set them down coherently, or indeed to explain them. I shall simply relate what has occurred here and allow readers to make of them what they will.

When I arrived here I discovered almost immediately that either nobody knew where Señor Vivo lived, or else they were protecting him from enquiring strangers. Each of my questions was answered with the reply proverbial in these parts of 'pregunta a las mariposas'. Having been invited to go and ask the butterflies a great many times, I was content to sit in bars where I heard open talk of nobody else.

From the conversations that I overheard, it appeared that Señor Vivo was a man more of legend than of flesh and blood, for the information that I gleaned was of the kind that one finds in classical encyclopaedias. It appeared that he had thirty sacks of unopened mail awaiting him at the town hall, which of all the information that I collected was by far the least remarkable. The people here believe that he is entirely invulnerable to injury, and that any man who attempts to wound him suffers in his own flesh the wounds intended for Señor Vivo. They believe that he has magical powers to confound all attempts against his life, and that he has already died twice and subsequently arisen from the dead. They say that he has an enormous quantity of children by the women of the camp on the outskirts of the town, all the sons of which bear the same scars about the neck as he himself. I have verified this latter for myself. I should add that the women of the camp did not invite me to go and ask the butterflies, but threatened to throw me down a ravine. Señor Vivo apparently addresses them as 'sister', although I found their attitude most unsisterly. Señor Vivo apparently drives an automobile so old that the locals claim that it runs not upon gasoline but upon sorcery. They say that he can become a goat or a lion, cause vines to grow, and has a chariot drawn by tigers. They also believe that when bound his bonds merely drop off. Having managed to talk briefly with some of the students at Ipasueño College I established that he was regarded as an inspirational lecturer who likes to pour scorn upon the very subject that he imparts. I found that Señor Vivo is reputed to be absolutely incorruptible, and that when enraged he is capable of enlarging himself suddenly to a formidable size and ferocious aspect. Furthermore I heard that he is constantly in the company of two extremely large black jaguars that like him are invulnerable to harm, but which eat only for pleasure rather than sustenance. I heard that any man may befriend them who offers them chocolate. I heard that these unusual creatures are a distinct species of cat that derives from a place known as Cochadebajo de los Gatos. At the local police station I asked to be shown the whereabouts of this city, and I was shown in all seriousness a location upon the map which is entirely under water. The word I heard everywhere, in connection with Señor Vivo, was 'brujo' and I understood that he was held in very considerable superstitious awe, as well, apparently, as in great affection.

I decided that the most simple method of making Señor Vivo's acquaintance was to attend his lectures at Ipasueño College; it is apparently the policy of this college that Señor Vivo's lectures should be open to the general public, this being a means of enhancing that college's reputation.

In the following few days I sedulously attended each of Señor Vivo's philosophical lectures, at first out of curiosity, but subsequently out of interest. I may impart to our readers a general impression of them all by describing the first.

The classroom was grossly overcrowded owing to the presence of pupils who were officially enrolled in other classes, and people such as myself who had no official business at the college. Señor Vivo lectured (flanked by his imperturbable cats, of whom more anon) upon the monadology of Leibniz. He expounded this philosopher with such clarity and distinctness, such force and vivacity, such rationality and persuasiveness, that all of us present were rapidly convinced of the indubitable reality of Pre-established Harmony, the Principle of Sufficient Reason, Dominant and Subordinate Entelechies, the Principle of the Identity of Indiscernibles, and the Best of All Possible Worlds. Señor Vivo then announced that he was going to prove that it was all m****a (the colloquial vulgarism for excrement), and did so with equal clarity, rationality, and forcefulness. At the conclusion of the lecture those present applauded with manifest enthusiasm, and many stayed behind, thereby preventing Señor Vivo from taking siesta.

From the college I was able to follow Señor Vivo to his home, but I confess that there was a dignified air about him which absolutely inhibited me from approaching him, and so I contented myself with waiting patiently in the street outside until he should re-emerge.

He shortly appeared, wearing a very ill-fitting suit of which the trousers were plainly far too long and the jacket too small, which prompted me to reflect that he was one of those people who will always fail to look respectable. He had with him the prodigious cats, a musical instrument that looked like an enormous ornate mandolin, and a sheaf of handwritten music manuscript.

I followed him to the funeral of one Ramon Dario, a policeman, and, as I discovered, a close personal friend of Señor Vivo. Señor Dario had been gruesomely tortured and

265

then assassinated by the murderous rabble in the employ of Señor Ecobandodo, on the day before my narrative begins. In the middle of the service Señor Vivo, accompanied by four other musicians whom I later determined to have been musical students at Ipasueño College, played a piece of music composed by Señor Vivo himself in honour of his dead friend, entitled *Requiem Angelico*. This piece of music had a most profound effect upon us all (myself included, who had not even been acquainted with the deceased). It is a piece of the most strikingly singular beauty, consisting of two melodies. The first of these creates in one the sensation of heart-wrenching nostalgia and melancholy, and then very unexpectedly surges into the second, which is victorious and of inexplicable grandeur. From the point when the first melody transformed itself into the second, I can attest that there was not a single face in the whole congregation that did not have tears coursing liberally down its cheeks. Your correspondent confesses without shame that he was not an exception. I enclose herewith a photostat of this piece of music, which was made at my request by an official at the alcaldia, who also made a copy of it for herself.

The service was unable to proceed for some minutes, owing to the lachrymose condition of the priest, but when the service was concluded and the congregation had proceeded to the interment, Señor Vivo delivered an oration more magnificent even than that delivered by his renowned father over the cortège of General Carlo Maria Fuerte in Valledupar, which your correspondent covered for this organ some eight years ago.

I passed the night in a somewhat raucous establishment known as 'Madame Rosa's', misleadingly described hereabouts as an 'hotel', and in the morning I was sitting in the plaza when I beheld Señor Vivo walking past with the two cats. He was dressed only in a shirt with a belt, which actually had an automatic pistol in it. He had an appearance which I can only describe as messianic, since his hair was quite long, and he had eyes that were not only permanently fixed upon the distance, but which were most astonishingly blue. In considerable trepidation owing to the presence of the cats, which were, I would say, at the very least half a metre longer that the root species, and about four handspans higher, I approached Señor Vivo in order to interview him, but in all the time that I was with him, I failed utterly to induce him to say one word to me. For the first time in my life I felt invisible.

This did not prevent me, however, from being always in his company, during the dramatic, and, I have to say, incomprehensible events which transpired.

I followed him to the camp of 'Las Locas', where he was greeted by a woman of Amazonian aspect with a revolver in her belt, who had been one of the original 'sisters' who had offered me a brief but impressive trajectory down a ravine. They kissed upon the cheek, and I overheard Señor Vivo saying, 'Tomorrow, at first light.'

I then continued to follow him, noting that he walked very like an Indian and had a similar build, until we reached the area known as the 'Barrio Jerarca' which was built by the infamous Pablo Ecobandodo in order to house his workers. This area has the best facilities of the whole town, but it has to be said that the taste of almost everything in it is uniformly and grotesquely execrable, being designed to display wealth rather than to perform utilitarian functions. The church is possibly the most gaudy of all in this nation of gaudy churches, and inside it one has the deeply disturbing sensation of being incarcerated in a kind of desperate solitude caused by the voluntary absence of God.

On that day there was a carnival in progress to mark the anniversary of the birth of Pablo Ecobandodo, who claimed to be in his thirties but was generally thought to be in his late fifties or his early sixties. There was very considerable drunkenness and rowdiness, and this was exacerbated by the fact that there were three brass bands playing simultaneously in apparent competition with each other. I would estimate the number of revellers at about three thousand, of whom a great many were the variety of person that one takes great care to avoid even in daylight in this pernicious nation of brigands.

As Señor Vivo passed through the mêlée, everything about him fell into silence, and I remarked upon numerous people of no apparent natural sanctity crossing themselves and falling to their knees. Remarkably, Señor Vivo passed through unmolested, and it was clear to me that everyone without exception knew who he was, for which the most evident explanation was the fame of his two cats, which were following behind him, one on either side, glaring at the members of the crowd with such anthropophagous stares that a number of people were injured in the small stampedes that were engendered as a result.

Señor Ecobandodo was sitting upon a dais, surrounded by priests in voluptuous raiments swinging censers and blessing the crowds of sycophants. But as Señor Vivo approached, a look of concern passed over his face which I would describe as the look of a man at once astonished and terrified. He stood up, revealing himself to be a man of grossly distended girth, and made as if to go to his horse, a grey stallion that was tethered to a nearby lemon tree. But Señor Vivo had interposed himself by a manoeuvre that still I cannot explain, because it seemed to me that he arrived over a distance of seventy-five metres in a few seconds, without varying his steady pace.

Señor Ecobandodo appeared to be rooted to the spot, and I was able to see the vain attempts that he made to move. At this point one of the many armed bodyguards of the caudillo raised a submachine gun in order to fire at Señor Vivo, but then evidently thought better of it and turned the weapon against the cats. The burst of fire left the cats unharmed, and indeed they jumped at the spurts of dust in the road as if to play with them, but one of the ricochets wounded a woman in the crowd in the thigh. She set up a wailing that added to the tension of the drama that was then enacted before my eyes.

The two cats sat like guardians upon either side of Señor Ecobandodo, as if to confine him further to the space in which he was trapped. I saw that he had begun to urinate with fear, since a wet patch was spreading across the front of his trousers, and that his face wore a look of panic that was betrayed by his wildly rolling eyes and his contorting lips. I deduced from this that he was unable to move his head.

Señor Vivo then, before the eyes of the crowd who were by now uniformly kneeling, removed the automatic pistol from his belt and placed it very slowly between the eyes of Señor Ecobandodo. I then witnessed a phenomenon that again is inexplicable to me, which was that Señor Vivo appeared abruptly to become extremely large. I estimated that his height had increased by a factor of roughly one quarter. I sighted along the top of his head to the lemon tree, only to discover that by such an objective measurement he was exactly the same height as he was before. And yet I have to say that the impression of aggrandisation was quite unmistakable.

Señor Vivo implacably held the gun against the head of the caudillo, who by now had tears coursing freely down his cheeks, and then did something quite unexpected and quite remarkable. He very slowly put the gun back into his belt.

Señor Ecobandodo appeared to be considerably relieved, and seemed to be trying to force to his face a smile of ingratiation. He remained, however, incapable of speech. Señor Vivo then raised his hand, and, as if aiming a gun, placed three fingers of his right hand above the heart of his victim. A look first of astonishment and then of agony passed over Señor Ecobandodo's countenance, and then with a cry of supplication he threw his arms up in the air, whirled about once, and fell prostrate upon the ground. At this point a sigh went up from the crowd whose meaning I found hard to discern, and numerous people threw themselves headlong as if to avoid having to witness any more of these events.

Señor Vivo went to the lemon tree and untethered the horse. He turned to walk back the way that he had come, and several priests ran to the body in order to administer last rites, but it was plain to all that Señor Ecobandodo was irretrievably dead.

Señor Vivo progressed slowly through the crowd, who were still silenced except for the keening of the wounded woman, and the grey stallion wandered over to the body of its erstwhile master. It sniffed it briefly, and then turned away and followed Señor Vivo and the two perpetually menacing jaguars, walking behind them with the jewels of its accoutrements sparkling in the light, and the tether of its bridle trailing in the dust. At that point I noticed for the first time that Señor Vivo was wearing what appeared to be a woman's ring upon the little finger of his left hand.

A post-mortem conducted upon the same day by the doctors of Señor Ecobandodo revealed an infarction of the heart. But furthermore, the internal collapse of the muscles of the heart rendered even the identification of the working parts of the organ difficult to perform, and one of the doctors compared it to the effects of an exploding bullet.

I followed Señor Vivo back to the centre of Ipasueño, and then lost him suddenly in the vicinity of the police station. I passed the night in my 'hotel', but was woken very early in the morning just before daybreak by the sound of subdued voices in the street and the light of passing lanterns upon the walls of my room.

I aroused myself and looked out of the shutters, whereupon I saw a small company of the women of the camp passing purposefully by. I dressed hurriedly and followed them at a distance, once again fearing for my life at their hands. The band of women turned up the Calle de la Constitucion, which is the widest residential street of Ipasueño, containing many fine houses. Near the top the women stopped outside one of the houses. By this time the light was breaking, and I was able to see that the Amazonian leader of the women who had threatened me with death was consulting with Señor Vivo, who was accompanied by the two cats and the grey stallion that had been formerly the property of Señor Ecobandodo.

Señor Vivo looked suddenly in the direction of my concealment behind a tree, and gestured to me to come to him. Filled with embarrassment and consternation I walked as confidently as I could towards him, expecting to be at the very least reprimanded for snooping, but he said nothing to me at all, and I was to draw the conclusion that he merely wanted me to be there to witness the day's events.

Señor Vivo went over to a house opposite accompanied by the leader of the women and the two tigres and knocked upon the door. A servant answered it, to whom Señor Vivo spoke. She disappeared and shortly afterwards the occupant of the house appeared wearing his nightclothes. There ensued the following conversation:

> Señor Vivo: Now is the opportunity. Do you have weapons?
> The occupant: I still have a consignment. Do you want them now?
> Señor Vivo: Yes, I do.

At this point the occupant of the house appeared to be in some distress, and he put his hand to his forehead and said, 'So you will pay them for both of us?'

Señor Vivo replied, 'You have been living by selling death. You helped to cause her death, but I will do this for us both.' Señor Vivo indicated the large number of women, many of them armed, who were standing by the gates. The leader of the women gestured to the women to approach, and several of them followed the occupant into the house. They reappeared with two large crates and several smaller boxes that plainly held ammunition. The crates were broken open and Kalashnikov rifles were distributed amongst the women, together with shares of the ammunition.

Señor Vivo demanded of the occupant to be shown exactly how the weapons were operated, and the former demonstrated it with hands that were visibly trembling and a voice that was hesitant and wavering. Those who had watched the demonstration then passed on the information to groups of the women of the camp.

The whole band then set off through the town in full public view, for it was now one and a half hours past dawn and many people were about the streets. They stopped outside the police station, and Señor Vivo went in and then came out again with a young policeman who was not wearing his jacket, undoubtedly with the intention that in this way nobody would be able to record the number on his epaulettes. He became the only other male member of the band, myself excepted.

From this point the riderless horse of Señor Ecobandodo, still fully caparisoned in its ornamented trappings, was at the front of the procession, and I assume in retrospect that this was because the two leaders were following it to its former home at the Hacienda Ecobandoda, although at the time I had the uncomfortable feeling that the horse was actively leading us there.

We did not arrive at the hacienda until it was already noon, as it is a very long way out of town along a difficult track which for much of the way follows arduous inclines. Having arrived within one kilometre of the hacienda, the exhausted party then left the road and entered a valley which sloped upward and around in a curve, and here they took siesta until the early hours of the evening. I passed this time attempting to interview Señor Vivo, the woman whose name I learned to be Señora Fulgencia Astiz, and some of the other women. The former two declined even to notice my presence, and the remainder of the women either told me to go away and 'pregunta a las mariposas' or taunted me by adopting such antisocial tactics as showering me with orange peel and offcuts of pineapple.

Despairing of interviews I went to sleep amongst the rocks, only to be awakened by the two enormous cats, which had taken it into their heads to treat me as a cushion. I lay beneath their frightful weight for no less than two hours, until Señor Vivo himself called them away without taking it upon himself to apologise to me for allowing them to put me through such an horrendous ordeal.

I most unfortunately missed most of the details of the formidable battle that ensued, because the women spread out in order to ring the estate, and it was impossible for me to be in enough places at the same time to grasp the full mechanism of the struggle. Señor Vivo, however, near whom I stayed, entered the gates of the hacienda in full view of the defenders, who retreated to the house itself as soon as they saw him with the cats and their former master's grey stallion. He mounted the horse and remained upon it in the driveway in the full firing line of those within, but my guess is that no one dared to fire upon him on account of the myths that have widely spread, to the effect that anyone attempting to harm him would receive his own bullets in return.

In the meantime it seems that while Señor Vivo was perturbing the occupants of the hacienda by his mere presence, and thereby occupying their entire attention, the company of women that had encircled this very large estate clambered over the walls and advanced upon the network of buildings from all sides, announcing their arrival with blood-curdling yells and fusillades of bullets that struck so much of the rendering off the walls of the building that very soon the air was filled not merely with the stench of cordite, but with white cement dust.

The former lackeys of the caudillo, sensing inevitable defeat, emerged from the building with white cloths tied to the ends of their carbines, and made as if to surrender to Señor Vivo, who curtly commanded them to surrender instead to Señora Fulgencia Astiz, who ordered them to strip naked before leaving the grounds of the hacienda. This they did, and they left by the front gates under a hail of stones from the women, with their hands clutched over their nether parts of shame.

Half of the women then commandeered the building, and when I left with Señor Vivo and the other half, they were performing an inventory of its tasteless contents with the intention of selling most of them off for charitable causes, and speculating with each other as to the best way of dividing the building so that they could live there amicably together.

Returning to Ipasueño after nightfall, the reduced band of women then entered the Barrio Jerarca, meeting no resistance. They entered the repulsively opulent church where the deceased Señor Ecobandodo was lying in public view upon a catafalque laden with carnations whose purpose was not merely to honour him in his death but to conquer the already pervasive stench of purulence and putrefaction emanating from the corpse, which was clearly in the early stages of deliquescence and decay.

Señora Astiz pushed aside the attendant priests who were engaged in reciting the Litany for the Dead, and the catafalque was dragged out into the plaza in front of the church. Here Señor Vivo did something of which I have never seen the like since I entered the Army School of Electrical and Mechanical Engineers to document the casualties of the illegal torture chambers of those times. Señor Vivo took out a knife and slit the upper throat of the deceased. He pushed his hand up into the gullet, and pulled the already blackened and swollen tongue out through the cut that he had made. I confess that I could not help but retch at the barbarity of the sight, but I have learned since then that this was the standard form of barbarity employed by the deceased himself in the days of his hegemony in these parts. Señor Vivo performed this act with the utmost coolness, washed his hands in the public fountain, and then left upon the grey horse, accompanied as always by the jaguars.

Feeling too ill to follow him, I stayed and was a witness to the sight of the body of Pablo Ecobandodo being hauled over a lamp-post, where it hung upside down for two days, adorned with buzzards and dropping maggots onto the pavements, until the stench became so appalling that the police were called to take it away. I was informed by the young policeman who was with the band of women that the body was buried by the police beneath the refuse of the municipal rubbish tip. In this extraordinary fashion was the serpent strangled by the latter-day equivalent of the infant Heracles, and the hawk vanquished by the hummingbird.

I continued to attend Señor Vivo's lectures for another two days, and then one evening I called at his house, and was met at the door by a young man of strikingly good looks, who introduced himself as 'Juanito'. This gentleman was accompanied by a young woman named 'Rosalita', who I recognised as a resident at my 'hotel', and with whom he had plainly been disporting himself antecedent to my arrival. He declined to answer questions about his housemate, but was kind enough to show me around the house and to offer me a tinto, which I gratefully accepted. Señor Vivo was in his room with his two intimidating feline companions, and when I entered the room I perceived that he lived in considerable disorder. There was upon the wall a line drawing of the Egyptian goddess Isis, and very numerous photographs of a young mulatta woman who was plainly very tall, of almost Nordic appearance, and of outlandish taste in dress. The rest of the room was largely filled with musical instruments and books. Señor Vivo ignored me, and so I entered another room which was stacked with boxes, apparently containing presents, for they were full of parcels wrapped in green or lilac paper. One of the boxes contained numerous labelled stones, also wrapped in green paper, from which I concluded that Señor Vivo had an interest in geological formations.

Señor Juanito invited me to stay for the night, an opportunity I siezed upon, even though I had eaten nothing that evening, for the reason that I hoped to be able to discover more about Señor Vivo during the night. I was, however, unable to do this, because as soon as I was in my bed I was leapt upon once more by the monstrous and execrable cats, who slept soundly upon my immobilised body, pinning me to the bed in an invariable position. I was unable even to leave the bed to perform the functions of nature, and was rendered sleepless for most of the night by the infernal volume of their relentless purring and the alarming vibration which accompanied it.

I awoke in the morning to find that I was freed of feline encumbrance, and quickly dressed. I cautiously opened the door to the room of Señor Vivo, and perceived that he had already left it. But hearing voices outside, I hurried down the stairs and went out into the garden.

In the garden conversing with Señor Vivo was a small and fairly old Aymara Indian in full traditional dress, wearing trenzas, and accompanied by two cats the equal in size and colour to those of Señor Vivo, whose cats were also present, and engaging in a mock battle with those of the Indian. The two men ignored me, and talked to each other in riddles, enacting at the same time a pantomime that I took to be at my expense.

Señor Vivo said, 'And here is the beautiful young woman of whom I have heard,' looking to one side where there was plainly no one at all. The Indian replied, 'This is my daughter, Parlanchina.' He then addressed the vacant space, saying, 'Gwubba, this is Dionisio.'

Señor Vivo went through the motions of shaking the non-existent woman's hand, and then kissed her upon what would have been her cheek, had she existed. He bent down and patted upon the head an invisible animal, exclaiming, 'This is indeed a very pretty ocelot. Hola, el gatito, como estas?'

The Aymara then asked, 'Is all the dross burned away?' in response to which Señor Vivo replied, 'It is.' The Aymara then said, 'You will come to Cochadebajo de los Gatos. We will have need of you.'

Señor Vivo entered the house, and came back a few minutes later with an envelope which he handed to me without even looking at me. Upon the envelope it said, 'The Final Coca Letter', and I put it in my shirt pocket in order to read it later.

The two men, with the grey stallion and the preposterous company of cats, then proceeded to the women's camp, and Señor Vivo consulted briefly with the women there, saying that he would in a month be prepared to lead those who wished to come to the city of Cochadebajo de los Gatos.

After this Señor Vivo and the Aymara began to walk across country which included the most intimidatingly precipitous terrain, frequently addressing the invisible woman and her purported ocelot, and I felt further humiliation at being the victim of such a seriously executed thespian pleasantry. After about three kilometres of this unpleasant walk, I found that I was completely incapable of keeping pace with them, even though it appeared to me that they were walking in an extremely leisurely fashion. When they were so far ahead that I reluctantly was obliged to yield up the chase, I was left with no alternative but to return to the town of Ipasueno.

I remained in Ipasueno for a further week in order to contemplate these untoward events and to enjoy its amenities, at the end of which time I encountered in the street a young man whom I knew to be a member of Señor Vivo's philosophical class. He said to me, 'I have not seen you in class this week. You have missed all the lectures upon Spinoza. You would have enjoyed them.'

Astonished at this information, and believing that Señor Vivo had been all this time in Cochadebajo de los Gatos, I proceeded to the camps, where Señora Astiz informed me that she had seen him every day, and that I clearly was still nursing the ambition to be hurled down a precipice. Furthermore, I then encountered a group of travellers from Cochadebajo de los Gatos, one of whom, a white man of quite outrageous vulgarity with a protuberant stomach and a large ginger beard, told me that he had indeed seen the grey stallion, the objectionable cats, and Señor Vivo in (to use his words) 'our magnificent submarine city of unmitigated fornication'.

It is very clear that in all this Señor Vivo must have been perpetrating an elaborate joke at my expense. However I recommend to our readers the serious perusal of Señor Vivo's final Coca Letter, which seems to me to encapsulate the philosophy of this enigmatic and unfathomable man who has almost singlehandedly swung informed public opinion against the noxious traders in coca, proving once again the truth of

Dr Fabio Lozano Simonelli's famous observation that 'Journalism is to a large extent responsible for the formation of our National Being.' Readers will be aware that this is the last word of the man who has singlehandedly extinguished that trade in this region, in which it is fervently to be hoped that henceforth our citizens may live in peace.

Dear Sirs,

Irrespective of the ideology or the social structure under which one lives, it is a fact of common experience that the single force capable of both welding us together and imparting meaning and purpose to our lives, is that bond of natural affection which renders us most truly human, and which forges with its excellently gentle flame the essential conditions of mutual trust.

It is from this that there follows the absolute necessity of exterminating the compadres of the late Pablo Ecobandodo, who, incapable of love themselves, commit sacrileges upon it wherever and in whatever form it may be found.

> Dionisio Vivo,
> Professor of Secular Philosophy,
> Ipasueño.